RED SKY OVER DARTMOOR

RED SKY OVER DARTMOOR

TONY REA

Matador
9 Priory Business Park,
Wistow Road, Kibworth Beauchamp,
Leicestershire. LE8 0RX
Tel: 0116 279 2299
Email: books@troubador.co.uk
Web: www.troubador.co.uk/matador
Twitter: @matadorbooks

ISBN 9781788035552

British Library Cataloguing in Publication Data.
A catalogue record for this book is available from the British Library.

Printed and bound in the UK by TJ International, Padstow, Cornwall
Typeset in 11pt Aldine401 BT by Troubador Publishing Ltd, Leicester, UK

Matador is an imprint of Troubador Publishing Ltd

To all the soldiers, sailors and airmen from the
South Hams who died in the Great War, 1914–1918.

Martin Damerell
The Devonshire Regiment

Contents

Prologue, Early Summer 1920

Eber Trant was up and about early checking his rabbit traps and was rewarded with two does and a stunning red sky. Looking towards Dartmoor from the village he saw clouds tinted deep red by the light of the morning's hesitant awakening, accompanied by the sounds of a melodious dawn chorus of wood pigeons and collared doves.

Malaby Cross was ready for his morning stroll. His wife thought it was the obsessive in him that caused Cross to observe this daily ritual. Since the war, however, Cross himself considered every new day a privilege and he liked to witness the changing seasons this way. Then there was a more practical motivation: Cross liked to keep an eye on his livestock, his financial insurance.

Every day, come rain or shine, he set out on the same walk. Each morning he would leave the house and walk along the drive to the main entrance, turning left and using the road for a short while. Then he would take to the footpath which passed in a westerly direction through a few fields laid down for grazing. In all there were five fields to walk through, each bounded by strong Devon hedges, and in each hedge was a stile. Eventually this path led back to the road, which he would then follow as far as Lady's Wood. Through the woods was the Carew Arms inn, from which it was a short distance back through the middle of the village and over Lydia Bridge to home.

At a brisk pace, his morning walk took an hour.

Today Octavia, his black Labrador, was reluctant. She didn't seem as though she wanted the exercise. Octavia was old and had been off her food recently and now she looked at him listlessly from her blanket by the Rayburn. So Cross set out alone.

★

The Reverend Ansty was awoken by the birdsong. He dressed and drank the morning cup of tea prepared for him by Mrs Horswill, his housekeeper.

As he limped across to his church to say his morning prayers and ensure that everything was in order, Ansty considered Bessie Horswill's future. Mrs Horswill was elderly and he thought that she was no longer up to the job. She was getting forgetful, often running out of ingredients she had forgotten to order or omitting to change his bed sheets.

Mrs Horswill had been his father's employee and Ansty was reluctant to terminate her services. Last week, however, he thought the situation was becoming dangerous as she had left a frying pan on the hob and he had smelled the burnt fat all through the house.

He would just have to pluck up the courage to tell her, he thought, as he made his way slowly back to the vicarage for breakfast.

Ansty sat down alone to a plate of bacon and eggs, brown toast and delicious, thick-cut marmalade. There was a pot of coffee, not that disgusting syrup with added chicory, but real, freshly ground coffee. Mrs Horswill had done him proud today, he thought. Perhaps he should keep her on, after all.

★

Cross was enjoying his morning walk. Pity about the old dog, he thought. It wouldn't be long now until Octavia was all in, still, she had lived a full life and been active until very recently. As the crimson sun rose it cast a red glow across the morning sky.

Red sky in the morning, thought Cross, *something about a warning,* but he couldn't quite remember the rest of the rhyme.

Major Cross was making his way through the pasture and approached the third of the stiles. He raised his right leg, placing his boot on the step. Gaining height to clear the stile, he had all his weight on his right leg as he swung its partner over, when suddenly somebody stepped out from behind the hedge.

His path blocked, Cross stopped dead in his tracks and stared at the young man with a revolver standing in his way.

"Captain Bergeron! Well, what a nice surprise!"

"You know why I'm here, Cross."

"Could be a thousand reasons – it was war, man!"

"Could be a thousand, but isn't. Tell me about CSM Tozer," said Bergeron.

"Nothing at all to say. What do you want? It was war, Bergeron! Be reasonable!"

"Be reasonable? Is that what you were? Would you care to remind me at what point in that whole bloody mess you were reasonable? Start wherever you like, Major Cross."

PART ONE

WAR TO END WARS, 1918

GEE-GEE'S BATTALION

Lieutenant Colonel George Greatorex inspected himself in a mirror before joining his senior officers in the mess. The silver of his hair reminded him that he was almost an elderly man. Following a successful career as a regular army officer, and having served in both Boer Wars, Gee-Gee (as the whole regiment affectionately called him) had retired in 1910 as a major. During his retirement, to keep himself busy and continue serving his country, Gee-Gee commanded the South Hams Rifles – a volunteer regiment with a long history which had become part of the Territorial Force under the Haldane Reforms. Gee-Gee was its honorary colonel.

Upon the outbreak of war in August 1914 the South Hams Rifles had been placed on active service as 3rd Battalion, the South Devon Light Infantry, and Gee-Gee had been called out of retirement to take command with an immediate promotion to lieutenant colonel. Since then, Gee-Gee and his men had fought with kilted Highlanders on their right flank at Neuve Chapelle, alongside the ANZACS at Gallipoli and with Indian troops in Mesopotamia.

Gee-Gee put on his forage cap and left his room. He considered himself to be of the school of military paternalism – and was proud of it. Throughout the war, he had led and loved his men as would a father his sons – all of them. Though much of his role now necessitated him working with Staff, he shared a mess with his company commanders, making a point of inviting junior officers to dine with him whenever it was feasible. He inspected their platoons, visited the men whether they were in barracks, in reserve or at the front; he briefed his senior NCOs himself when he could. *Yes, he thought, old Gee-Gee is a thoroughly professional soldier.*

Now the battalion was back in France and Gee-Gee had some rather bad news to deliver to his company commanders. The South Hams Rifles would soon be back in action.

Gee-Gee descended the stairs in the large, comfortable, but partly demolished house in which he had made his HQ. It was three miles behind the front line; not too far for the company commanders to travel, the roads being in good order – considering.

Gee-Gee removed his cap as he entered the mess. "Good evening, gentlemen," he said to the officers who were awaiting him.

"Come, come, no ceremony. I'm sure you are hungry. Sit, sit," he urged.

They started with baked trout in a mustard sauce and two bottles of Sancerre. The main course of steak, roast potatoes and green beans was washed down with a few bottles of 1910 Margaux – which was the best claret Gee-Gee's quartermaster had been able to procure. They had finished with a delightful rhubarb sponge and custard and had now turned to the port. Gee-Gee produced cigars and with those, brought the assembly to order.

"Gentlemen, I'm afraid I bear bad news. As you know we have been attacked by the Germans, but you can't possibly imagine the scale of this attack. Let me inform you. Twenty-three German divisions of the 1st and 3rd Armies, under Mudra and Einem, attacked the French 4th Army to the east of Reims. A further seventeen divisions of the German 7th Army, under Boehm, assisted by the new 9th Army under Eben, attacked the French in the west.

"Two days ago, the attack to the east was halted by the French. Since then there has been nothing. The Boche have dug in. Well, that's comparatively good news for us.

"However, the bad news is that the offensive to the west of Reims is going in the Boche's favour. The Germans have crossed the Marne at Dormans. In attacking Reims in this way, Ludendorff is clearly aiming to split the French forces. Any questions so far?"

Major Cross fidgeted and looked at McGregor who sat facing him. McGregor looked down at his port. Neither men spoke. There were no questions.

"Our orders, gentlemen, are to counter attack the day after tomorrow at 0900. We will be assisting the French 9th Army, and as usual in this sort of thing, will be under French overall command."

Major Glenn grumbled somewhat at that and took a long draw on his cigar.

"General De Mitry's orders will come down to us from Division. Alongside ourselves – you will no doubt be pleased to know this, Major Glenn – there are 85,000 United States troops and some Eyeties. No preliminary bombardment, but we have French 75s in close tactical support – so communications with them will be crucial. You need to emphasise that point to your platoon commanders."

Gee-Gee paused and considered the throng. He knew that he was short of the best officers to command his four companies. He considered Majors Glenn and McGregor to be good, solid soldiers who had seen plenty of action between them. McGregor was attached from the Machine Gun Corps and commanded the company's heavy machine guns. Gee-Gee didn't think it made the best use of his experience, but following the formation of the MGC there was nothing he could do about it. Glenn had been commissioned into the battalion as a 2nd lieutenant in 1915 and had risen quickly from platoon commander – but that wasn't unusual these days.

Though they were jaded by constant marching and fighting, Gee-Gee knew he could rely on these two men to make sound decisions and do the right thing at the correct time.

Captain Ansty, on the other hand, was very young and had no experience of commanding a company. Ansty had been with the battalion since 1916 and was considered a safe pair of hands when commanding a platoon, but he had only just been made up to captain and taken on B Company. Gee-Gee knew it was a big step up, but there had simply been no alternative.

It was D Company which presented him with his biggest problem by far. Amongst its riflemen were some of the battalion's finest soldiers; unfortunately, this was not replicated in its officers. Major Cross, a former Territorial like himself, was in command simply because he was the longest-serving officer in the battalion and had to be given a company. Gee-Gee thought that Cross was the worst kind of officer; he was inept, lazy and had a nasty streak. Of greater concern still, he was likely to be led astray by the bad advice of others. To top all of this, Cross was preoccupied by concerns at home; his mother had recently passed away and his elderly father was ill.

Gee-Gee took a long draw on his cigar. Below the level of company commander, the situation did not improve. There were simply not enough experienced junior officers.

And now there was an additional, personal concern for him. His godson, Peter Roebuck, had arrived at the battalion last month and hadn't yet been in action. Peter was in Cross's company. There was nothing Gee-Gee could have done to avoid it. When Roebuck arrived D Company were short of a platoon commander – it was as straightforward as that. *Anyway*, thought Gee-Gee, *he will feel at home there*; Peter came from South Brent as did Cross, and most of the men in the company were drawn from the villages around Totnes. Peter now commanded 13 Platoon, which contained many of the South Hams boys. He would be fine, hoped Gee-Gee.

"Gentlemen," concluded Gee-Gee after thirty minutes of talk, "that provides you with both the outline and detail of the plan of attack. Remember, this show is about stopping the Boche advance and to do that, we must push General Boehm back to his own side of the River Marne. To remind you, essentially Majors Glenn and Cross's companies will go in under cover of McGregor's machine guns. B Company led by Captain Ansty is in reserve. Ansty, you go in only on order of Major Glenn, understand?"

"Yes, Colonel," replied Ansty, somewhat sullenly.

Clearly, thought Gee-Gee, *he thinks I'm molly-coddling him.* He chose to ignore Ansty's tone and moved on. "Any further questions? No! Good. Right-oh, gentlemen, off to brief your companies."

They finished the port and smoked the last of the cigars, then the four company commanders left.

Gee-Gee turned to his adjutant. "Let's hope it works, Branson. Let's just hope it works."

★

Cross trudged back to his company HQ. How on earth, he wondered, could the army know so much detail about the troops they faced? He was tired of this. Always the same boring things. Complex orders from the French came to division, then to battalion, and then he had to make some kind of sense of them and say something intelligible to his platoon commanders. Well, he could only try. By the time Cross reached his HQ it was approaching eight thirty and so he decided to leave the briefing until the following morning.

★

"Stand to, men," called the NCOs just before dawn the following morning. Private Eber Trant began to rouse himself from sleep, kicking the sluggish soldier at his side now and again to hurry him along. He paraded on the firing step with the rest of the battalion, awaiting a raid from Germans positioned opposite them.

They did this every morning, but the raid never came. If one were to come, however, then it would be at this time of day.

After a while Private Trant was pleased to hear "stand down" called as this allowed him and his pals some time to themselves.

"Got the tea made, Tranny?" demanded Corporal Will Trevelyan.

"Get your own bleedin' tea made, you lazy sod," replied Trant in jest as he poured for the three of them.

He looked at the other two men sat down together crowded into a small dugout in the rear of the trench.

Eber Trant had known Will Trevelyan most of his life. The two had played together in the streets of Ugborough and the fields surrounding it. They started school together and both received the cane from Mr Jordan when Eber dared Will to ring the fire bell. They played together through those endless hot summers, picked blackberries from the hedgerows and fished for brown trout in the River Erme where it passed under the Ivy Bridge. In 1916 they joined up together, choosing the SDLI over conscription.

Eber Trant and Will Trevelyan were, in a way, more like brothers than mates. The third soldier, young Colin Wilson – a northerner recently posted to the company – they had known only a few weeks.

"Drink up," said Wilson. "Nice drop of tea this morning."

"Proper job!" replied Eber Trant.

Trant had kept back some of the water from the tea making and began what had become a regular morning ritual. Into the warm liquid in the base of the tin he dipped a cloth and wiped his face. With what was left he proceeded to shave.

"Never have got the hang of this," he muttered. "With all the shit around here the army has us shave every day. Never got the hang of it. What's the point? Eh? Tell me that."

"Orders, boy," said Trevelyan. "That's what. An order is an order. Like when we joined up. Spent months we did polishing brass, polishing the boots. And as soon as we get out here, what happens?"

"We have to black the buttons and badges," answered Trant.

"Orders. That's what." Trevelyan opened the box of biscuits as he spoke. He cut the Canadian cheddar into thick slices, placed it onto the biscuits and handed it to the other men.

"Eber! The jam! Where's it to, boy?" he asked.

Trant produced a tin of jam and threw it to his friend. Trevelyan carefully opened the tin and spread its contents liberally onto his cheese before passing the tin on.

"No bacon for King George's Army, eh, my boys?" he joked.

Wilson broke into tuneless song: *"What do we want with eggs and ham when we've got pots of Tickler's jam?"*

"Shut up, Wills!" somebody shouted. "You can't hold a tune to save your bloody life."

"Tranny can, though," said another. "Go on, Eber, sing us a song."

They all joined in the familiar plea, "Tranny, Tranny give us a song, give us a song…"

"All right, all right, settle down. Now let me think." He sat with a mug of tea in his right hand.

"Now that would be dangerous," quipped Wilson, "Eber Trant thinking."

Feigning outrage, Trant jumped up and cuffed Wilson. Then he smiled and sat down again.

"How about this?" asked Trant as he broke out into song with a deep and rich baritone voice.

"*Tom Pearce, Tom Pearce, lend me your grey mare. All along, down along, out along lea. For I's a going to Widecombe Fair…*"

"Hardly original, Eber, is it?" said Trevelyan.

"B'ain't South Hams neither," said another. "Widecombe? I ask 'ee. That song's different all over damn' place! Can't you change t' name?"

"*Tom Pearce, Tom Pearce, lend me your grey mare. All along, down along, out along lea. For I's a going to Ivybridge Fair…*"

"There ain't no fair in Ivybridge, Eber Trant. Not since I been living there, there ain't. Cornwood maybe."

"Well, Cornwood don't fit the tune."

"Ugborough then! Proper job!"

"Start it again, Eber, then we can all join in," someone shouted.

"I don't know the words," said Wilson.

"Neither does Tranny!"

"Oh, don't you worry, boy. You'll soon learn they words," said Trevelyan.

"*Tom Pearce, Tom Pearce, lend me your grey mare,*" sang Eber Trant, and the others joined in…

"*All along, down along, out along lea. For I is a going to the Old Country Fair. With Bill Brewer, Jan Stewer, Peter Gurney, Peter Davy, Dan'l Whiddon, Harry Hawke…*"

"No! Not Harry Hawke, he's from down Widecombe way. Put in Reggie Hawker."

"Who's Reggie Hawker?" asked Wilson.

"Captain Reginald Surlow Hawker to you, my son. Once of the Royal 1st Devon Yeomanry. Killed in Mesopotamia."

"*With Reggie Hawker, Jan Stewer, Peter Gurney, Peter Davy,*"

Dan'l Whiddon, Harry Hawke, old Uncle Tom Cobley and all. Old Uncle Tom Cobley and all."

"Tranny, Tranny, change all the names, change all the names," chanted the men.

"With Jan Stewer, Billy Barter…"

"William Barter, Army Service Corps, still alive as far as I know," said Trevelyan.

"That's no surprise, serving with that dodging lot! The ASC… Away boys, somebody's coming," shouted a soldier. The others laughed.

"Peter Gurney, Harold Folley…"

"Private Harold Edwin Folley, 12th Trench Mortar Battery. They were all our mates, you see. My dad's friendly with Folley's parents, Henry and Dora Folley. Poor Harold died of wounds last year. Up near Calais. Nearly got home, he did. He was just twenty-three."

"Peter Davy, Major Bayly…"

"Major John Bayly. None of us actually knew him of course, him being a toff and all. He was master of the hunt and a soldier before the war. Royal North Devon Hussars – these days they're the 16th Devons. Major Bayly was taken ill at Gallipoli, he was."

"Dan'l Whiddon, Arthur Horton…"

"Arthur Horton, 2nd Battalion the Devonshire Regiment, died of wounds in a hospital near Boulogne, 1915."

"Harry Hawke, Bertie Walke… Dick Blight…
Dick Blight, Dick Blight lend me your grey mare,
All along, down along, round along lea,
For I's a going to the Old Country Fair,
With Reggie Hawker, Billy Barter, Harold Folley, Major Bayly, Arthur Horton, Bertie Walke, old Uncle Tom Cobley and all. Old Uncle Tom Cobley and all."

More tea followed. The problem with the tea, Trant thought, was the water, and the problem with the water was that it always tasted of petrol. Water was brought up from base at night by the supply patrols. It was carried in cans. But there were no specially made cans; or if there were then he had not seen them. So, cans previously containing petrol were re-used. Of course, they had been rinsed out, but the taste of petrol was never removed. The sugar did hide this taste, but never completely.

"And when shall I see again my grey mare? All along, down along, out along lea. By Friday soon, or Saturday noon…"

"Officer present," called Sergeant Hannaford and the men quickly tried to stand as Lieutenant Roebuck arrived.

"Sit down, men, enjoy your breakfast," he said. "Any problems last night?"

"Nothing, Mr Roebuck."

"No Hun patrols out? Anything moving out there?"

"Not a thing, sir. All quiet," said Hannaford.

Roebuck walked on repeating the questions as he passed other men along the line.

"On his mornin' rounds," observed Trant.

"He's a good sort, young Lieutenant Roebuck," pointed out Hannaford. "Proper job! Since he joined the company he's done well."

"Happen he is, too," said Trant and he turned away, singing.

"So they harnessed and bridled that old grey mare. All along, down along, out along lea. And off they drove to the Old Country Fair, with Dick Blight, Reggie Hawker, Billy Barter, Harold Folley, Major Bayly, Arthur Horton, Bertie Walke, old Uncle Tom Cobley and all. Old Uncle Tom Cobley and all."

★

At company HQ, Major Cross outlined the plan for the forthcoming attack to all four of his platoon commanders. Like the other companies in 3rd Battalion, Cross's was divided into four platoons, numbered consecutively starting with 1 Platoon in A Company. Cross's platoons were numbers 13 to 16, but the tradition in the South Hams Rifles had been to give the platoons names and they had stuck to this practice throughout the war. 13 Platoon, led by Peter Roebuck, was called Night-time. Captain Wadham commanded 14 Platoon or Twilight. Wadham had been an NCO in the Territorials, served in India and was commissioned into the SDLI in 1916. 15 – the light mortar platoon – commanded by Captain Speed, was known simply as TM – Toc Emma. Lieutenant Jeffries had been with the battalion only since March. His 16 Platoon was known as Full Sun.

The creases around Major Cross's eyes and flecks of grey around the temples of his closely cropped hair revealed his years. He was moustached – it was the fashion – and had a pipe in his mouth. The pipe wasn't lit. Cross's uniform was immaculate. The khaki-coloured serge jacket bore the crowns of his rank and was worn over a woollen shirt, with silk tie. His riding boots were gleaming black and he wore spurs.

"Questions, gentlemen?"

Speed was first; "Yes, Major, at what point do I pick up the mortars and close in with the rest?"

"Well… you'll simply need to play that by ear, Wizzo. Your decision."

"Company's down an FOO, sir." It was Lieutenant Jeffries. "Captain Richards was badly injured three days ago, and the gunners have not sent out a replacement yet."

"Bugger!" said Cross. "We can't go in without a gunner observer. Colonel Greatorex insists that close artillery support will be crucial. Billy," he turned towards the young subaltern sat to his left, "why didn't I know about this?"

Lieutenant Wainwright lifted his head and looked towards Cross. Wainwright hated his unofficial job as Cross's *aide-de-camp* and he knew the other officers called him the *chitty wallah*. As a major, Cross wasn't entitled to an adjutant, but he was lazy and used Wainwright to do most of his paperwork. Still, Wainwright knew Cross made mistakes.

"On your desk, Major," replied Wainwright. "Could I suggest Captain Bergeron, sir?"

"Remind me, please, Billy."

"Captain Bergeron is from Staff, attached as intelligence officer. He's a Canadian, and apparently speaks excellent French – could be useful in the circumstances. Been with us for a week or two, but there isn't a great deal for him to do. More importantly, Bergeron was formerly a gunner officer, Royal Canadian Horse Artillery. Troop commander at Vimy, followed by a stint as forward observation officer. He's got an MC – must be pucker."

"A bloody hero on horseback! That's the last thing we need," said Wadham.

"Might be exactly what we need," blurted out the lieutenant.

"Don't be so bloody outspoken, Wainwright," said Wadham.

"And he's got the Croix de Guerre," added Wainwright.

"What?" asked Major Cross.

Oh, my God, thought Speed, *how can he manage to appear both rhetorical and dumbfounded in uttering a single word?*

Cross had recovered. "Mmm," he said. "He might be all right, and we need somebody. Call him in then, Billy," he ordered. "Wizzo, I'll leave it to you to check him out and if you think he'll be up to scratch, brief him. That's everything, gentlemen. Dismissed."

★

That evening Bergeron arrived at Captain Speed's dugout, which doubled as Toc Emma's platoon HQ. He let Poilu, a small, wire-haired mongrel, follow him in.

"Hello Bergeron, sit down, sit down. I've wanted to have a chat with you for some time. Your dog, is it?"

"No. He's his own boss. He hangs around the trenches and kind of follows me around, that's all. Guess they can tell somebody who likes dogs. He's good to have around, though. Good ratter."

Speed poured whisky for each of them.

"So, you're down here from Staff, are you? Intelligence?"

"That's it."

"Mmm. I've been doing a bit of intelligence gathering on you – as it happens. You had something to do with finding out that von Hutier was planning the spring attack south of St Quentin, that right?"

"Surprised you know about that, Speed."

"Ah, well, I have an old school chum at Montreuil-sur-Mer, you see. We try to get together when we can. When the battalion is on relief and he's free – you know. Edward Jack, Royal Engineers. Met him?"

"Yes. I was working for Jimmy Marshall-Cornwall at the time. Eddie was in the same team."

"Well, I telephoned him this morning to *enquire* as it were. So von Hutier. Down to you, wasn't it?" asked Speed.

"I wouldn't say so. I was translator, that's all."

"Not what Eddie thinks. Tell me all about it."

"An RFC squadron intercepted some Boche flyers and shot down one of them. Pilot died of wounds a few days later. Buried with full military honours. You know the usual form in that sort of case, Speed. Army goes through the International Red Cross to get the bad news back to Germany. But those RFC cowboys can't wait, so one of them risks his neck – and a Sopwith Camel – to fly over enemy lines and drop Fritz's belongings together with a note.

"Well, a few weeks later a copy of the letter from the dead boy's CO to his mother pops up in a German newspaper. Local paper. Baden if I remember correctly. The mother had been so pleased to receive the bad news from an officer of such high rank – a full general and army commander. Letter was signed by General von Hutier himself – for some reason. An on-the-ball Frog spy in Geneva picked it up and it came through to us."

"And that's where you come in?"

"Von Hutier was well known – famous for his work at Caporetto and against the Russians at Riga. We were surprised the general was now on the Western Front, so I did a bit of background work. Wasn't too hard to locate the dead German pilot. The RFC knew approximately where those Boche flyers had taken off from, and exactly where they had made the drop. That placed von Hutier opposite the British 5th Army."

"Good work, though not much help to General Gough. Now tell me about your decorations."

"What is this, Speed?" he snapped. "A bloody interrogation?"

"I'll put this simply. Basically, we're an FOO down for the attack tomorrow and the old man's been told you might just fit the bill."

"And I thought I'd left behind all that crawling around in the mud and grime."

"Look, we all know it's not ideal, but we can't go in without an FOO. I'll come clean. It's like this: we're reluctant to put our lads' fortunes in the hands of somebody we don't know much about – if you get my drift. Some officers get moved on because they're not up to the mark. So, are you?"

Bergeron looked at John Speed, wondering whether he wanted an answer.

"Those gongs suggest you're pretty good – assuming

they're genuine. Jack knew about the MC, thought you got it near Vendeuil, with the Buffs. He didn't know about the French gong though. Said that must have been handed out directly after you left HQ. You could start with that, it's a bit unusual."

"The Croix de Guerre – French gong, as you put it – hardly counts. It was presented to all of us at the Bois des Buttes back in May."

"You were with the 2nd Devons?"

"Attached, just as I am here. I was asked to take command of some gunners. As it happens they ended up fighting with rifle and bayonet beside the 'Bloody 11th' and somebody decided I should get the medal too," said Bergeron. "I didn't do much to be honest with you, Speed. Probably saved the life of a soldier who couldn't swim – but nobody gets the Croix for that."

Speed looked puzzled. Bergeron paused to search for something in his jacket pocket.

"My MC's genuine – enough," he said, handing over a cutting from the *London Gazette*. "Here, read for yourself."

Speed silently read the citation:

Captain M. P. Bergeron RCHA. Military Cross. Led a section of men over enemy-held ground to deliver important messages to rear. Entered a fortified position under fire in order to range artillery fire. Notwithstanding the danger to himself, he then led the section of soldiers back to their unit, encountering the enemy on two separate occasions.

Probably doesn't tell half of it, he thought.

STEADY THE BUFFS!

Tobacco smoke swirled around the room like miniature tornadoes, rotating in slow-motion whirlwinds and carrying with them the pungent aroma of cheap French cigarettes. Alone in not smoking amongst the men present in the makeshift company HQ was a captain of the Royal Canadian Horse Artillery.

The absence of a cigarette was not the only feature that marked Bergeron out as different. He was by far the tallest soldier there, and he looked too young to be a captain.

"What are you up to, Toynbee?" he asked.

"Trying to finish a bloody poem, actually, Bergeron," replied the lieutenant sitting at a desk. Toynbee was chain-smoking cigarettes and writing. "I can't get any decent pipe tobacco, and that doesn't help. Reduced to these bloody Frog things." He took up a packet and looked closely at it. "*Gauloises*, they're called. Strong as hell and rotten smell!"

Bergeron sat down next to him. He examined the ticket sales counter and the posters which were still advertising the possibilities for relaxing excursions to the seaside – Le Touquet, or the spa in Vichy. The railway station in Vendeuil was an ideal place to set up an HQ, but there would be no trains. All the lines had been broken long ago by fighting that had devastated the countryside across northern France.

"I didn't know you were one of those types."

Toynbee looked up. "Oh, just dabbling. What do you think of this?"

Toynbee pushed a notebook at Bergeron. "You're attached as an intelligence officer, so you ought to be bright enough to tell me if it's any bloody good so far," he smiled. "Here, have a read." Bergeron gazed at Toynbee's scrawling handwriting. The poem was entitled *Genesis*. He read it out loud:

"In the beginning was creation –
Eden at the start.
Now in the garden, devastation,
Mass destruction at the heart.

Genesis to Revelations
In four short years transformed
As a mighty clash of nations
This Armageddon spawned.

They said it would be over by Christmas Day,
But Epiphany came and went.
On meagre rations in every way
We starved our course through Lent.

And as we approach our Pentecost
The Generals begin to count the cost."

He gazed at the notebook. *What utter bloody drivel*, thought Bergeron. Toynbee was eagerly awaiting his comments.

"I'm no expert," said Bergeron.

"Come on, I'm not thin-skinned. I know it wouldn't make *The Muse*, but I'm keen to improve it."

"Well, I can see that you're trying to link it to the Bible and to the Church year, and that works – up to a point. But, well… why that bit about rations?"

"I'm not happy about that line either," said Toynbee. "Maybe I could flip it."

"Flip it?"

"Well, the rations weren't meagre, were they? In fact, the food is pretty good. If we think about the human cost, well, there was a positive glut of flesh out there. So how about..." He beckoned Bergeron to return the notebook and began scribbling.

"Here, how about this: *With surfeit of flesh in every way, we made our way through Lent.* That any better?"

"Perhaps – but why not use *fodder*? I mean, well, the men are cannon fodder, in a way, and fodder is food, isn't it?"

"I knew you were bloody intelligent, Bergeron. Listen: *They said it would be over by Christmas Day, But Epiphany came and went. More cannon fodder every day, yet we starved our way through Lent.* No sonnet is the work of one man alone! It's getting better. Not ready yet, but improved. Thanks, old man."

"Do you blame the generals then, Alan?"

"Not at all. Haig is a bloody good general, look at all the changes he's made: the tanks, the way we use those Lewis guns. No, I blame those bloody politicians. Lloyd George and Churchill. Who else to blame? But once this bloody war is over, that'll be the way to sell poetry."

"Explain?"

"Well, nobody is going to want to read about soldiers having a good time on their rest and recuperation, are they? I can't write about living it up on red wine in Amiens, shagging every French whore that moves. No. The folk back home will want to read about how grim it was for us, about how the generals mucked up. I know it's not true, but it'll sell poems – mark my words!"

"The folk back home may want to read about how the politicians betrayed us," said Bergeron.

"Mmm. Maybe, but the politicians will have already shifted the blame onto French, Haig and the Frog generals."

"I've looked at some of Sassoon's work. It's pretty good, I'd say," offered Bergeron.

"Oh yes, his work is bloody good. Technically close to perfection, I'd say. But look what he writes about – what most of the poets published in *The Muse* write about. Death, dirty trenches, botch-ups created by the top brass. That's what sells, but it's not all been like that, has it?"

"No. I suppose not."

"As a matter of fact, most of my war has been spent hanging around waiting for something to happen," said Toynbee.

"Different for the men, though."

"Yes, but unless one were particularly unlucky – which I admit does happen – it's still not all bad. Nobody is in the front line for long. Two days at the front and four days back, where the showers are hot and the food plentiful and not at all bad tasting. I'm not suggesting it's been a picnic, Bergeron, but it has its highs as well as lows."

Bergeron considered all of this as he handed the book back to Toynbee.

"The ninth line is too long," he said.

"Yes, I agree. I'll have to work on it. Anyway, enough of this chat, I'll have to get on." With that, Toynbee put his head down and carried on scribbling.

★

Reinhold Schetter had been sitting in the same trench for over twelve hours. It was comfortable enough, and food and drink came forward regularly. For the last five hours, however, it had been intolerable. Schetter's own artillery had begun shelling the British at 0440 hours Berlin time. This barrage had been so heavy and intense that it was impossible for Schetter to think, let alone have a conversation with his comrades. The ground was constantly shaking. He could tell that some of the shells contained gas because the faint whiff and smell of it had worked its way back to the German trenches.

For days before, wave after wave of assault troops had been making their way forward into the Hindenburg line. It seemed to Schetter that the entire German army was on the move. He knew that many of these soldiers had travelled across Europe from the Russian front now that the Reds had called a halt to fighting.

Schetter had been a school teacher in Munich before being conscripted into the 1st Bavarian Infantry Regiment in 1916. He was officer material, he had been told, but he had refused all offers of promotion, preferring to stay in the ranks.

He liked to read: books, newspapers, whatever he could get hold of. For an intelligent and interested soldier such as Reinhold Schetter it was easy to work out the strategy of the generals. Last year Russia had been shaken by revolution after revolution, but still fought on. Now it looked like the Bolsheviks were settled in power. Lenin was in charge of Russia and Trotsky oversaw foreign policy and the war. Or was it the peace? The Russians were out of it now – *lucky bastards*, he thought.

Here in the west, things were different. Although the French and the Tommies had problems last year – mutinies, indiscipline, that sort of thing – it seemed to Schetter that they had overcome their problems. Worse than that, from his point of view, fresh and well-equipped American soldiers were beginning to appear. He had come across them himself and had listened to many stories about these 'Doughboys' from others. They were raw; they made mistakes, but they were brave and well equipped. And there were many thousands of them; all Germans knew that.

So, Schetter thought, German strategy was obvious. Move troops as quickly as possible from the Russian front to France and launch an all-out attack before the USA was fully involved. Simple, and it looked like he was to be part of it.

Tactics? Now tactics were more complex, thought Schetter. General von Hutier, fresh from the east, was now in command of the German 18th Army. This army had been re-formed, trained and drilled in von Hutier's tactics. The boys from the eastern front knew this way of fighting already, but to Schetter and his comrades it was all new. Many of the best soldiers (and Reinhold Schetter was proud to have been included as one of the best) had recently formed concentrated stormtrooper units. Each major formation 'creamed off' its best and fittest soldiers into stormtroopers. Now, several complete divisions were formed around these elite units.

A stormtrooper's job was to go over the top first, but not on a wide front as before. Rather, they were to probe and find weak points, infiltrate and bypass Tommy's front line, leaving any strong points to be 'mopped-up' by follow-up troops. Schetter and his fellow stormtroopers were to attack and disrupt enemy headquarters, artillery units and supply depots in the rear areas, as well as to occupy territory rapidly.

★

Captain Fine of the 7th Battalion the Royal East Kent Regiment – known throughout the British Army as the Buffs – looked at his watch. Fine had been placed in command of a scratch force inside Vendeuil fort. The area around this fort was defended by the 7th Buffs and he was at the centre. Fifteen hundred yards behind him was Colonel Ransome's battalion HQ.

The ancient fort had been built by Vauban, Louis XIV's military engineer, and Fine considered it virtually impregnable. It was large and strong, surrounded by a dry moat and with high ramparts built of solid French stone. Directly in front of the fort was B Company and on their right, to the south as Fine looked towards them, was A Company. C and D Companies were held in reserve.

Captain Fine's biggest worry concerned his men. He was in command of a makeshift force, comprised of a fighting platoon of Buffs, some Royal Engineers and two platoons of men with bad feet and other problems who had been weeded out to work alongside the Engineers as labourers. They probably could hold the fort, but Fine didn't think they would be able to fight their way out of it.

★

Just before dawn Bergeron looked towards the east. He wanted to see, once again, a red sky as the sun rose over France, over ground he had got to know well. This morning, however, he could see nothing.

★

It was dawn and Captain Fine continued his inspection of the parapet on the east-facing wall of Vendeuil fort. A thick morning mist prevented him from seeing as far as the village, itself. Damn!

★

With five minutes to go, Lieutenant Hofmann ordered Schetter's platoon to stand up. Somebody started singing the national anthem, and soon they all were joining in.

   "Deutschland, Deutschland über alles, Über alles in die Welt..."

★

The pretty face smiled at him from the poster. Her lips were glossed and sensually red. Her dress was of a brightly coloured floral pattern and it was cut to emphasise her slim waist and ample bosom. She was on her way to Le Touquet and Bergeron decided there and then that once this bloody war was over he would visit the resort himself, just to see if she was still there.

He glanced at Sweeney, the commander of B Company, and whispered to Toynbee, "Toddy looks worried."

Major Benjamin Sweeney had every reason to be worried. A German attack was expected imminently, his men were the front line and he believed they were spread far too thinly. He would need artillery fire support, but the weather over much of northern France this morning was misty. "Blasted fog!" muttered Sweeney; he was worried that it would severely hamper communications.

★

The officers looked at their watches. As the hands on his watch moved round to zero hour exactly, Lieutenant Hofmann ordered his stormtroopers up and out of the trenches. The same happened on Schetter's left and his right. Bugles sounded the attack along the line. This was it, he thought.

Reinhold Schetter's unit stood opposite the British lines, south of St Quentin. Their first objective was Vendeuil, bypassing any strong points, and then to proceed as far as possible in the direction of Ham. Grey skies, limited visibility. There were no targets visible to Stormtrooper Schetter or his officers. So they went forward in light deployment – rifles slung, relying on stick bombs to deal with any resistance. The stormtroopers held their stick bombs high at the ready as they moved quickly forward. Reinhold Schetter could not see twenty metres in front of himself.

★

The German soldiers came in great swathes. As soon as they came into view the Buffs opened up with rifle and machine gun fire. But the attackers simply moved aside, avoiding the more intense fire and moving ahead, pressing home their attack on any weakness detected in the British line. Soon Sweeney had Germans in front of him and to his left. He desperately needed covering fire. "Foo-Foo," he called to Bergeron. "I need a word with you urgently!"

About bloody time, thought Bergeron. "Yes, Major."

"Where are your guns, Foo-Foo?" asked Sweeney.

"The supporting artillery batteries are sandwiched between Vendeuil fort and battalion HQ. Here." He pointed at the map.

"I need supporting fire over the ground to my front and left flank. Without it we're done," said the major.

"I can't get through, sir – wires must be cut again."

"What else have you got as back-up?"

"Well, I can try to use flags or a signal lamp. But with this mist…"

"Well, you'll have to try, man!"

Bergeron could see it would be useless. The flags simply could not be seen. A signal lamp? Well, it might work, he supposed, but the odds were stacked against it.

"Could we send a runner?" asked Bergeron.

"A lone man won't stand a bloody chance," said Toynbee. "We've reports of Boche in small parties behind us as well as in front. They're all over the bloody show!" Sweeney nodded his agreement.

"Can you spare a section?" Again, it was Bergeron speaking and he addressed Toynbee.

"No. I need all the fire I can muster," interjected Sweeney. "If I thought they'd get through, I'd risk it, but…"

"Give me a good NCO and a couple of men and I'll get a message back to the battery," said Bergeron.

Sweeney looked at him.

"It's worth a shot," said Bergeron. "There's no other way to get detailed instructions through."

"Could you send a flaggy, Foo-Foo?" asked Sweeney.

"No. I'll go. It's my responsibility. The flaggies can try signalling. You never know. If I make it, I'll try to bring some men back with me to mend the wire."

"No, Bergeron. We need you here. If the wire is mended or if this bloody mist clears, then we'll need you to get that fire support in." It was Toynbee speaking.

Sweeney made the decision. "Lieutenant Toynbee, get me the best NCO from your platoon and two good soldiers."

"Sergeant Gough is my best man, sir. He's the Lewis Gun SL," said Toynbee.

"Keep him. Just give me a decent corporal and a couple of men," said Bergeron. "Get them to report here in five minutes."

"Do as he says, Alan," said Sweeney. "Order them to leave packs behind, just take their rifles, ammunition and some Mills bombs."

"Well done, Foo-Foo," said the major. "Find him a rifle, Alan."

"No point me taking a rifle. I can't shoot straight to save my life!"

"You're missing the point, Bergeron. If you don't carry a rifle, then every Hun that sees you will be aiming for you! Try to look as much like the men as you can."

"Oh. Thanks," said Bergeron.

Minutes later Bergeron, helmeted and with a Lee Enfield slung over his shoulder, pocketed the map he'd been given by Sweeney and checked his revolver. "What's your name, Corporal?"

"Bates, sir."

"Well, I'm happy to make your acquaintance, Bates. Any tips for me?"

Corporal Bates looked quizzically at his new officer. "Keep low and move fast, sir," he offered.

"That sounds good to me. Let's go, Bates!"

Keep low, move fast, he repeated to himself. *Keep low, move fast.*

Bergeron led Corporal Bates and the two other East Kent soldiers out of the Vendeuil railway station building. He could hear screeching mortar shells and whizzing bullets that seemed to be everywhere, but the four men got to the crossroads easily enough. From the crossroads, Bergeron observed that less than 500 yards away was a sunken road. That would provide them with good cover, he thought, but they would have to make a dash for it over open ground. He also saw German soldiers on each side of them. To his left, there was a force of Germans engaged with C Company. They seemed pretty well occupied and so shouldn't be a problem, thought Bergeron.

More worryingly, on his right and working their way towards him and his section was a strong force of Boche. The Germans were between Vendeuil woods and the rear of Sweeney's company.

"Corporal Bates, we'll have to send one of the lads back to company HQ with a message for Major Sweeney. He's got a platoon of Germans behind him, and would he please be so good as to open fire on them immediately to give us cover; and order the man to stay there – if he tries to get back to us, he's dead. Got it?"

"Got it, sir."

Two minutes into the bloody mission and we're down twenty-five per cent, thought Bergeron. It couldn't be helped. The soldier ran back and obviously delivered his message as a few minutes later a hail of bullets from Lewis guns and rifles showered onto the unfortunate Germans.

"Come on, boys, now's the time! Keep low and move fast – fast as we bloody well can!"

With that, the three of them jumped up and sprinted towards the sunken lane. Bates stumbled, recovered, got back into his stride and dived into the lane first, followed by Bergeron and the private.

"Bloody hell, but you're quick, Bates!"

"Four hundred yards champion back at Aldershot, sir – but I think I just beat my best time!" They both laughed.

Bergeron looked at the other soldier, who was panting heavily. "You all right, Private?"

"Wally's just fine, sir. Hasn't had enough gaspers today, that's all."

"Gaspers?"

"Woodbines, sir."

The sunken lane provided them with good cover for about thirty yards, which they walked slowly to catch their breath. From the end of it, and whilst Sweeney's covering fire kept the Germans occupied, they rushed for the cover of the woods. From the far side of the woods, Bergeron had a clear view of the fort. It had suffered shellfire and was now under attack from a group of Boche soldiers who had come around the west side of the woods. They were no threat to his section, thought Bergeron. His problem was that he could not see the battery of British guns through the heavy mist, which was showing no signs of lifting.

"Corporal, can you see our guns? Behind the fort?"

"No, sir. Can't see a bastard thing in this fog. Sorry, sir."

A flash of light, followed by the report of eighteen-pounder field guns, solved their problem.

"C'mon, lads. Let's make a dash for it!"

This was a longer distance, but the soldiers knew they had the cover of thick mist. They could afford to take the run a little more easily. Once again, Bates was the first of them to reach the *piquets*, where he was immediately challenged by shots over his head.

"Hold your fire, put your bloody guns down," bawled Bates.

The surprised artillerymen pulled aside the ammunition boxes which had been set out to provide a barrier. A sergeant looked at Bergeron. "Sorry, sir," he said.

"Take me to the officer commanding, quickly, soldier. Who is he?"

"Major Black, sir. This way."

"Captain Bergeron, RCHA, attached to 7th East Kents. Message from Major Sweeney. They're in trouble, Major. Can you first lay down a barrage of HE here?" Bergeron pointed to the area behind Sweeney's company, between them and the woods. "There are Germans attacking their rear. Follow up with shrapnel just here, Major." He pointed this time to the area east of Vendeuil which was also under attack.

"I can do that, Captain. But we won't know if we're on target, will we? Wires are down everywhere."

"No problem, Major. I'll take the boys over to the fort. The mist is lifting a little so I should get a good enough view from the top. We'll signal you from there."

"Think you'll make it? Well, if you can there's a signaller in the fort. Been flashing to battalion HQ on and off all morning. Captain Fine insists on keep sending the same message, *Counter-attack urgently required*. If you get in, tell him there's no bloody chance, there's a good fellow. As soon as we see you on the ramparts, Bergeron, we'll open fire with the HE. Off you trot then, Captain."

Bergeron and the two soldiers pushed out between the ammo boxes and began to retrace their steps towards Vendeuil fort. Suddenly, Bergeron stopped. "Down, lads," he called. In front of them, working their way along the lane that eventually led to Ham, he had spotted four German soldiers.

"Keep low to the ground, boys," ordered Bergeron. He pointed to the Germans. "Corporal Bates, see them?"

"Sir."

"I know you can run, Bates. Now it's time for me to find out if you can shoot."

"No problem, sir. Wally," he said to the other soldier, "you take the two on the left – start with the bastard on the outside. I'll work in from the right. On the captain's order."

The two soldiers took aim in lying positions. Bergeron heard the comforting sound of cartridges being loaded into chambers.

"Whenever you're ready, sir," said Bates.

The fort was, by definition, a strong point and Reinhold Schetter together with his fellow stormtroopers had bypassed it. They were making their way towards battalion HQ when they spotted the three Tommies out in the open. The Germans were at an immediate disadvantage as they had their rifles slung. They saw the British soldiers when it was too late to do very much about it.

"Fire!" ordered Bergeron.

Two shots rang out, quickly followed by two more rifle shots that were lost in the noise of battle. Reinhold Schetter and three other German stormtroopers lay dead on the road to Ham.

"Good work, you two," congratulated Bergeron. "Now, up we get and into that blasted fort."

It was now 1230 hours. The Buffs had been fighting from the fort all morning and the mist had not lifted very much. With Bergeron's directions, Major Black's battery of eighteen-pounders managed to delay and frustrate the Germans attacking B Company and Vendeuil fort. The outcome, however, was inevitable, thought Bergeron. The Buffs – together with the rest of the division – would have to retreat or be killed or captured. It was only a matter of time.

Bergeron bid farewell to Captain Fine and wished him luck. In return, Fine promised covering fire to enable this gunner officer and his two riflemen to make their way out of the fort and back to Vendeuil.

"Ready, boys? Back to company HQ. We'll retrace our steps. Keep low and move as fast as you can to that sunken lane. Go!"

They reached the lane, recovered and began walking along it. Then Bergeron encountered something he was not expecting. A group of about a dozen British soldiers were running along the lane towards them. The soldiers were carrying their weapons, but looked like an undisciplined mob. There was not an officer to be seen. *Bugger*, thought Bergeron. *This is all I need.*

"Recognise them, Bates?"

"No. I'm not sure. They're East Kents. Possibly A Company, sir. Looks like they've lost their nerve, sir."

Bergeron spoke quietly to Corporal Bates. "Cover me, Bates. I hope you won't need to drop one of these buggers, but if you do it'll be on my order and you'd better be quick. Let's see how it goes."

Bergeron stepped out in front of the fleeing men. He stood with his rifle held in both hands and raised above his head. "Stop!" he shouted. Corporal Bates, with Wally Parish behind him, levelled his rifle at the hip and pointed it in the general direction of the gang. The soldiers came to a halt.

"Who's in charge?" demanded Bergeron. No answer. "Have you been given orders to withdraw?" Again, no answer.

One soldier yelled out, his voice revealing panic, "Out of the bloody way. There's hundreds of Germans coming, we've got to get away. The other boys are withdrawing!"

Bergeron looked down the lane. Sure enough, it looked as though German troops were moving in behind the fleeing East Kent soldiers. He didn't have long. He looked these renegades over, quickly but carefully. There were no NCOs amongst them. They were young, and most of them looked very frightened.

"Listen to me, men. Your job in this war is simple," he said. "It's to follow orders. Now, nobody gave you the order to retreat, did they? So, you're going to stand. From now on you are all under my command, so you follow my orders. Understood? And just in case you don't, Corporal Bates here has my order to shoot the first man to disobey."

As if on cue, Bates pulled back the bolt on his rifle, loading a cartridge into its chamber. Wally Parish followed suit.

"No, you're not going to run away, you're soldiers – men! You men belong to one of the oldest regiments in the British Army. Yours is a regiment with a great tradition, and you're going to uphold that tradition today. You're going to fight like men today."

Bergeron looked at them; he wasn't sure they would obey one officer – an unknown artillery officer at that – backed up by two riflemen.

"Steady, the Buffs!" he shouted. "Corporal Bates."

"Yes, sir."

"Get these men deployed on each side of the sunken road. We'll give the Hun a run for his money! Grenades first, then independent rifle fire. And be quick, Bates. No time to waste."

"You." Bergeron addressed the man who had spoken. "Name?"

"Private Benson, sir."

"I'm watching you, Benson. If you don't put up a particularly good fight, Private Benson, you'll be on a charge of desertion when we get back to HQ. You'll be shot! Understand?"

"Sir!"

Bates quickly deployed the men and did what he could to calm them. Soon the road was flanked on each side by six or seven riflemen, with the corporal in charge on the north side. Bergeron was on the south side with Wally Parish. After just a few minutes Bergeron saw a platoon-sized group of German stormtroopers edging their way along the lane from Vendeuil.

Bergeron noticed that the Germans were very professional and well trained. They worked their way along in two rows, one on each side of the lane. Ahead of the main column were scouts, who communicated to the rest with hand signals. He waited until the lead scout was almost clear of the sunken part of the road and in the open. He watched the scouting soldier stop and look at the terrain ahead, then he saw him beckon to the rest to follow. At precisely this moment Bergeron gave the order for the grenades to be thrown. Bates, on the other side of the road, did likewise. The sunken road exploded in a hail storm of shrapnel and grenade casing.

As the sound of the grenade blast was replaced by the moans of wounded men, Bergeron bawled out his orders. "Shoot the bastards, kill them!" The Buffs opened fire on the surviving Germans. Four or five Germans at the rear of the platoon turned and ran. "Bayonets, after them!" shouted Bates. "Kill the buggers!"

It wasn't necessary. As the Germans retreated so they encountered Major Sweeney and what was left of B Company. Like rats in a trap, thought Bergeron, the Boche were caught in a deadly cross fire.

★

"Captain Bergeron told you to be ready to shoot one of them?"

Toynbee was debriefing Corporal Bates at the makeshift HQ. The battalion had withdrawn as everyone had expected. But, following Bergeron's intervention, they had done so in good order, performing a classic fighting retreat which had slowed down the German attack and provided the British top brass with vital time to deploy their limited reserves.

"Yes, sir," answered Bates.

"Would you have done so?"

"Sir!"

"And he really shouted out 'Steady the Buffs'?" This from Major Sweeney.

"Yes, sir."

"Well, I'll be. Quick thinker and cool as a bloody cucumber!" said Sweeney.

"Dismissed, Corporal, and well done, man!" Toynbee turned to Sweeney. "If there were witnesses other than a corporal's say so, I expect Bergeron would at least be mentioned in dispatches, Major."

"Oh, there were witnesses, Alan. Oh yes. Fine had a reasonable view from the fort and signalled HQ. Bergeron and Bates had been seen to make it to the battery and then back again to the fort. Bloody marvellous! In war, Toynbee, small-scale actions such as ours yesterday really matter. Foo-Foo will get a medal for getting the message through to the battery and for ranging in the fire, I'll see to that. No mention of desertion though, eh? The men were understandably confused and then were rallied by an officer. That's all need be said."

"Any news of Fine and the men in the fort, sir?"

"Nothing. Must have surrendered. One way or another, Fine's fighting days are over. By the way, Alan…"

Toynbee turned to face him.

"Well done yourself yesterday, and get that man Bates made up to sergeant."

"Yes, Major."

★

Toynbee marched his platoon west towards Amiens. They were overdue a rest. He found them billets in a village midway between the front line and the ancient textile city.

From the room he was occupying, Toynbee could just see the towers of Amiens Cathedral in the west.

There came a knock at his door. "Come in," he called.

It was Bergeron, his uniform slightly tattered, a rifle slung over his shoulder and a small package in his hand. He offered the package to Toynbee. "Open it," he said.

Toynbee opened the package and inside found what looked like two folded pastries.

"*Les ficelles Picardes*," announced Bergeron. "Tuck in!"

Toynbee took a bite, handing the second back to Bergeron. "Delicious," he said. "What are they, exactly?"

"Sort of oven-baked, cheese-topped crêpe. Pancake to you, Alan."

Toynbee took his notebook from the desk. "Found time between writing up reports to do this," he said.

Bergeron took the notebook and read aloud from it:

"In Eden the creation.
Eve absent from the start
Her tended garden, devastation
Mass destruction in its heart.

Genesis to Revelations,
In four short years transformed.
As misguided warring nations
An Armageddon spawned.

We hoped it might end by Yuletide.
Epiphany came and went
Yet casualties did not subside
And we prayed our way through Lent.

New armies join the fight with us – we approach the Pentecost.
As generals plot their strategy, do they ever count the cost?"

He handed the notebook back to Toynbee. "Better, Alan. Better."

BERGERON'S NEW ACK

Speed handed the cutting back. "You'll do for me, Bergeron. Are you up for it? We can't exactly order you, you see."

"What's the team like?"

"Bit of a scratch outfit as it happens, but they seem to be functioning. Bombardier Ryan is in charge at present. He'll be your ack with two gunners. They're both newly posted, but they seem to be doing well, according to Ryan."

"They're called flaggies."

"Sorry?"

"Private soldiers in the artillery are known as gunners, as you say, but in forward observation teams they're always referred to as the flaggies. Pretty obvious when you think about it – they wave those flags like Billy-oh."

"Of course."

"I didn't mean to sound superior, sorry. What's this Ryan like?"

"Irish. A good soldier, bit of a reputation for fighting. Some of the better soldiers have, I'm afraid."

"Well, I'll give it my best, but the sooner the RA get cover sent up here the better."

"Good man – good to have you on board. Marc, isn't it?"

"That's right, and you?"

"John. John Speed, but call me Wizzo, everyone else does." He brought out a map and pointed Bergeron towards it.

"The battalion is to attack in two companies. We'll be on

the left, here. 'A' is the company on the right. We have another company and the Emma Gees in support. Major Cross wants the three attack platoons – that's Night-time, Twilight and Full Sun – spread across our front, with my mortar platoon in support. You'll need to call us in as well as the artillery – if that's all right with you?"

"Yes. That's all in order, Wizzo, and I'm sure we'll do a good job."

"Oh, and the supporting artillery is French. Present any problems for you? I'm told you speak the lingo rather well."

"Well enough, I expect. That's good, by the way. Having French guns in support."

"Why, pray?"

"Those French 75s have a much faster rate of fire than anything we have. Fifteen rounds per minute, if the crews have been well drilled."

"I'll sort out the deployment. I'll put Peter Roebuck's platoon on the right, linking up with A Company, Howard Wadham in the centre – you'd best go in with him so that you've got a good view of overall progress – and young Jeffries can take the left."

"Why hasn't the company commander done that planning already?"

"Let's just say he delegated."

"Sounds bad – if I might be so bold?"

"You might – be so bold, that is – with me, Marc. Not so sure it should get up to HQ or Staff, though. Cross's… how can I put it? A tad lazy. He doesn't get windy, though, and he's done nothing wrong. Gee-Gee, the CO, really has no choice. We're not exactly over-run with officers – as you can tell. But the boys are good. This company has some of the best soldiers in the battalion, based on the territorials – South Hams Rifles. We still refer to our private soldiers as riflemen."

Bergeron felt uncomfortable. Something was wrong. He didn't like the feel of this situation at all: a lazy OC who delegated far too much; an ack with a reputation for fisticuffs; a senior captain who bragged about his men.

He got to his feet and shrugged. "Where will I find Bombardier Ryan?" he asked.

★

At that precise moment Ryan was fighting to save his skin. He'd been having a reasonably pleasant time smoking, drinking rum and playing cards with three NCOs from the South Devons in a snug, warm and fairly well-presented dugout. The Devonshire men had been teaching him a card game called Euchre that he hadn't come across before. They claimed it was local to South Devon and not known much outside that area. Ryan was good at cards and caught onto the rules quickly. Later they had switched to Pontoon and had been playing for money. By eight thirty Ryan had won a sizeable purse and much rum had been drunk. Unsurprisingly perhaps, an argument broke out when Corporal Davis, one of the West Country men, had accused Ryan of cheating.

Ryan couldn't believe what he was hearing. He took up his winnings, placed them in a pack which he slung over his head and shoulder, then got up from the table to leave. As he did so, and with a pained, affronted expression, he said, "On my mother's life, sure I've never cheated in my whole life."

Ryan slowly made for the dugout's exit, but the burly Corporal Davis stood up and blocked the door. "Now, now, Paddy," he said. "No need to be angry, just leave the money and the Woodbines on the table and go."

"I've won this fair and square, Davis, and I'm keeping it. Now out of my way!"

Ryan attempted to push past the bigger man when a blow struck him hard on the back of his neck. He stumbled at the shock, turned around and saw a lance corporal behind him launch a punch aimed at his stomach.

Though he had been drinking, the Irishman was quick. Very quick. He jumped back just as the punch would have struck him, causing his assailant to stumble forward. Ryan caught him on the back of the head with both hands, pushing down and bringing up his knee sharply at the same time. The lance corporal's head crunched between Ryan's knee and hands, breaking his nose. As the NCO raised himself, Ryan punched him under the chin with a left-hand upper cut and swung at his bloodied face with his right fist. The man slumped to the ground.

Taken by surprise at how quickly their ally had been dealt with, the two other soldiers took fright. Lance Corporal Guard decided to sit out this particular fight. Corporal Davis was more belligerent. He decided to launch a rapid, all-out attack of his own. Davis waded in with fists flying, which was a mistake.

Ryan dodged and ducked the attempted blows dealt by Davis, who hardly touched him. Then, using well-aimed, short, swift left jabs Ryan forced Davis to move around clockwise so that the large Devonshire man was no longer blocking his exit. Glancing around to make sure his escape route was open, Ryan ripped into Davis with a succession of blows. One, two, three jabs to the face followed by a right-hand body blow so powerful and severe that it bent Davis in two. As he slumped forward Ryan landed an upper cut that caught him full in the face and knocked him over.

The Irishman quickly made his escape and hurried back to his own dugout which was occupied by himself and two young gunners. With Captain Richards gone, Ryan was now effectively in command. He set himself down, his chest heaving and blood on the back of each hand. The two soldiers looked at him; Jones was first to speak.

"What you been up to, Bom?"

"Nothing. Tad of bother, you might say. Get me a drink, would you?"

Sainsbury poured some tea. "Been fighting, Bom?"

"None of your business, sonny," said Ryan, though he was only two years older than Gunner Sainsbury. Ryan took a long sip of the strong, sweet tea. "But here's a tip my da' gave me. Rule number one, keep out of trouble and keep your nose clean. Do all you can to avoid a fight."

The three soldiers hadn't noticed as Bergeron poked his head into the dugout. "And rule number two, Bombardier, is?"

Ryan almost gagged. Hot tea splurged from his mouth and dribbled down his tunic. "'ttention!" he said.

"Don't move, boys, just sit there and listen. My name is Captain Bergeron and you're lucky because I'm your new commander. As you know – or should know – we're in action tomorrow and you'd better be ready. I need a word with you, Bombardier," he glared at Ryan. "Outside. Now."

Ryan rose slowly, put his mug on the table and picked up his hat. He put the hat on his head – deliberately placing it at a rather jaunty angle – and moved out into the trench. Bergeron took Ryan out of earshot from the dugout and stood him to attention.

The two soldiers made a fuss of Poilu.

"Stand at ease, Bombardier."

Ryan stood as ordered, hands behind his back. He was a small man, probably less than five feet six inches tall, which brought his eye level just above Bergeron's left shoulder.

Bergeron looked at this new colleague. He had to work closely with his ack and needed to trust him. He gazed at the NCO, who hadn't made a good impression. He'd obviously been fighting. His uniform was well worn and dirty; what's more, the soldier was incorrectly dressed.

"Ryan, isn't it?"

"Yes, sir."

"Irish?"

"Sir."

"Catholic?"

"Yes, sir."

Bergeron gazed at him, trying to make sense of Ryan. His eyes went over and over from head to foot and back again as if in inspection. Ryan was short, but muscular – strong looking. "And just what did your daddy tell you was rule number two, Ryan?"

Ryan hesitated. "Well, sir, he said to me that I was to do all I could to keep out of a fight, sir. But, if I saw that a fight was bound to happen and there was no way to avoid it, then I was to get in first and do it fast. And hard as I could, sir. 'Get your retaliation in first, son. Fast and hard, lad. Hard as you bloody well can, then run like hell.' That's what my da' used to say to me, sir."

"Bombardier Ryan, you will not engage in fighting anyone, other than the Germans, whilst under my command. Understood?"

"Sir."

"Have you been drinking, Ryan?"

"No, sir." Ryan looked affronted.

"And Ryan, are you sure you're Irish?"

Ryan looked puzzled. "Yes, sir."

"Not Australian then?"

"No, sir."

"Then why the fancy head-gear, Bombardier? Not been issued with a forage cap?"

"Oh this. Sorry, sir." Ryan took off the offending hat. "Aye, sir, I'll get my cap right away, Captain. It was a gift from a mate, sir. New Zealander as it happens. We'd been defending this trench and he copped it, like. Well, he…"

"All right, all right. Put it back on. Suppose I need new gear myself, can't go on wearing these blasted red tabs, can I?"

"Be a bit of a target for the Hun, sir, if you did."

Bergeron didn't smile at the attempted joke. "I'm in charge now, Bombardier. I don't particularly want to be but that's how it is. I'll keep this short, Ryan, then you can get back to your tea. How's the D2 cable back to the field gun batteries?"

"In good nick, sir. Some breaks occasionally, but the Frog crews go out regularly enough and mend them quickly."

"D3 and Fullerphone both working?"

"Sir!"

From his experience at Vimy, Bergeron knew that the most secure means of communication to a supporting battery of guns was a landline – called a D2. This was easy to lay and maintain when run through a system of support trenches. At each end was an instrument like a telephone, about the size of a large box of chocolates. This was called a D3 – but the Germans had managed to intercept conversations so the D3 was not to be used. Instead, the Fullerphone had been introduced three years ago for communication in Morse and so far, Bergeron had been informed, the Germans were not able to pick up its signals.

However, once an attack was underway he knew it would be near impossible to keep the connecting wires intact and so lamp and flag signals would have to be used for simple and prearranged commands. The most effective way to get a more detailed order or request around a moving battlefield was still the runner. If all else failed there was the SOS flare. The guns would be zeroed on a point in no man's land, and if no alternative signals got to them, on sighting the SOS flare they would open up on this fixed point.

"We'll use the D3. Won't matter if Fritz picks us up. Ryan, can you speak French?"

"No, sir."

"So how does it work?"

"Frog lieutenant speaks English. Well, he tries to."

Bloody hell! he thought. *I've got an Irish leprechaun trying to be understood by a French officer, both of them speaking broken English in accents neither can comprehend. Recipe for disaster.*

"I might take the D3 from you if needs be then, Ryan. No offense. You can concentrate on keeping the wire intact. What about those two?"

"The flaggies, sir? Gunners Jones and Sainsbury. Good as they come!"

As if you'd bloody know, Ryan, he thought. *Oh, for a decent ack who knows what he's about!*

"How do you usually manage from the advance points?"

"Lights, flares and flags, sir."

"Your semaphore up to scratch, Bombardier?"

"Sure enough, Captain. And if all else fails, well, young Dick Sainsbury there, well he's just about the best runner in the battalion, sir."

"Ryan, look, I'm Canadian not British. Most of my people don't go in for that starchy stuff quite so much, so let's just cut out the 'Captain'. You can leave out the 'sirs' for that matter – got it?"

"Yes, erm, yes, boss."

Poilu came out of the dugout and Bergeron stooped to stroke him.

"Bombardier Ryan, I have a theory about soldiers. Most of them are simply doing their job – and most don't do more than they need to. Well, that's fine with me – bit like that myself, I suppose. But there's one thing well worth remembering. That system works just so long as the job in hand gets done. Gets done quickly and gets done very, very well. Do you understand me, Bombardier?"

"Yes, boss."

"Then you're dismissed, report to me at 0700. You'll find me with 14 Platoon in the centre of the attack."

"Twilight Platoon. That would be Captain Wadham's unit, boss?"

"I believe it is, Ryan. Problem with that?"

"I hope not."

"Dismissed, Bombardier. Come on, Poilu." Bergeron returned Ryan's salute and walked back towards his own quarters; the dog followed, his tail wagging furiously.

Doncha Ryan returned to the dugout. He sat down and picked up his mug of tea. "Bastard thinks I'm a shirker! Now, where were we, boys?"

★

Peter Roebuck's uniform made him stand out from the others. It was still relatively clean and smartly pressed. The buttons and single pip on his jacket had been dulled prior to the attack, but there was still the semblance of sheen on the leather of his Sam Browne belt. He stared at the table.

Roebuck's mind just now was full of thoughts of the first time he had met Sarah Wainwright. It had been last summer, in the garden of Mr and Mrs Collingwood's house. He was visiting with his mother. Sarah had brought them a tray of lemonade and, as she poured him a glass of it, he had fumbled and caused her to spill the drink over her dress.

"Oh, I am so sorry," he blurted, blushing frightfully.

"Peter, you clumsy oaf," chided his mother.

"It's all right, Peter," said Sarah. "I'll just have to pop inside and change it."

When she returned, Sarah Wainwright was wearing a dress almost indecently short, thought Peter. He also thought she looked beautiful. That had been the beginning. Peter and Sarah saw each other scores of times through the summer and autumn of 1917. They would meet for lunch or tea at each other's houses. They went for long walks in the lanes and footpaths around South Brent and Diptford, holding hands and sometimes even kissing.

Then Peter volunteered and was commissioned into the South Devon Light Infantry. He had left Devon in December 1917, just before Christmas, and the last time he had seen Sarah was on the platform at South Brent railway station as he waited for a train to Exeter, where he would change for Aldershot. His parents and her mother were also present, so their parting was conducted in a most dispassionate fashion. Both Sarah and Mrs Wainwright asked that he remember them to Billy, Sarah's brother, who was serving in France with the 3rd Battalion.

As he looked out of the train's window, he saw that Sarah was still standing there on the platform, waving frantically, as the train moved off and picked up speed on its inevitable journey eastwards.

Peter Roebuck looked his age, which was eighteen. The current fashion amongst junior officers was to sport a moustache, but his was still downy and did nothing to make him look any older or more commanding.

Speed carefully removed small glasses from a cardboard box which sat on a shelf at the back of the officers' dugout. He poured tots of whisky into the glasses. One for himself, one for each of the other platoon commanders, and one for Bergeron.

"This one for the road, as it were," he said with a forced smile. "*Santé!*"

"Cheers," said Bergeron and he raised his glass to the other men, then downed the liquor.

Likewise, Speed, Wadham and Jeffries downed their shots. Roebuck reached for his glass, his hand shaking a little, then he paused. He first took a sniff, then a sip.

"Down it in one, boy! Come on," said Wadham.

"I don't feel like it," Roebuck said. "What will it be like out there?"

Speed replied, "It will be fine, just fine, Roebuck. Don't worry. Everyone has their job, we all know what to do. It will *happen*."

"Yes," Roebuck pulled the whisky glass to his lips again. "It's all very well for you," he said, taking in all of them with one sweep of his eyes. "You've seen it before, done it before."

"Bloody hell! What do you want us to say, Roebuck? It will be hell, bloody hell out there," said Wadham. "But we have absolute trust in you, Roebuck."

"I don't," offered Roebuck. "I'm not sure that I can do it."

"Yes you can," said Speed. "And you shall. We all shall. You, me, Wadham. We'll do it because we owe it to the men. We all get frightened, son."

"I… I'm not frightened," blurted Roebuck.

"Really!" It was Wadham again.

"No. It's not that I'm afraid to die, or even of getting badly wounded, you see. No, it's not that at all. I'm worried I might do something wrong. The men all know I'm new. They all expect me to mess up. I'm afraid that I'll freeze. That's what I'm worried about. That I'll freeze in front of the men and make a mistake, or just not do something. Most of all I'm afraid that I'll look frightened in front of the men."

"Don't be such a nancy boy, Roebuck," said Wadham.

"You blow the whistle and get up the ladder first," said Speed. "After that nobody will even look at you. Just move forward. The NCOs will deal with the men. They will get the lads through. We've some damn good NCOs in this company, and Warrant Officer Tozer is the best NCO in the battalion. He'll see them all through."

Wadham spat on the floor. Then Speed asked, "Have the men had their rum?"

"It's being doled out now," answered Jeffries. "It all came up the line intact last night. Tozer is organising it. And he ordered the men not to eat a thing. They have rations in their packs. They can eat when… if… they reach the Marne."

"Let's get the hell out of here," said Speed, as he put on his helmet and moved purposely towards the doorway. The others followed suit and soon all officers were on ladders in front of the men, poised to go out into no man's land.

★

Bergeron watched as Tozer and the other NCOs finished off supervising the rum ration. Each man was given a ladleful into a mess tin.

"Why no breakfast, sir?" asked Private Wilson.

"Do you want a straight answer to that one, boy?" enquired Tozer, the tone of his voice telling the soldier he was in no mood for frivolity.

"Yes, sir, please."

"Because if you get a wound in your guts, boy, you'll have a better chance of it not going septic on you if your stomach's empty. Now drink up your rum, pick up your rifle and get ready to shoot a few Hun."

"Get the men to their stations, Sergeant Major Tozer," ordered Speed, and there was a bustle as the men shuffled closer to the step ladders. Bergeron watched as Tozer and the other NCOs marshalled the men of D Company into position. He, Ryan and the team were close in behind Wadham.

Roebuck heard Speed say, "Order the men to fix bayonets, Sergeant Major."

"On command, company will fix bayonets," bawled Tozer. "Fix bayonets!"

Bergeron looked at his watch for what seemed to him to be

the hundredth time. It was 1057 hours. Then he saw Wadham had his whistle to his mouth. He looked again at his watch – 1058. This was it. One, two, three whistle blasts. He saw Wadham climb up the ladder, followed by his platoon sergeant. Now, Bergeron himself was climbing the ladder, and as he did, he could hear the rattle of McGregor's machine guns. Soon the French guns opened up, not ranged yet, but landing in the general area of the German front line. On Bergeron's left was Roebuck, revolver in his hand out of the trench first and bravely leading his men onwards.

Then, it seemed to Bergeron to be at the exact same moment, he saw and heard an explosion, the smoke from it obscuring Roebuck and a small group of his men. The smoke cleared – nothing.

Bergeron ran over and jumped into the crater-shaped shell hole that was left following the explosion. Roebuck was lying on his back. His body jerking and blood seeping from beneath him. A corporal was lying in a pool of blood, another soldier – also wounded – bent over him talking to him: "Will, Will, wake up. It's me, Eber. Wake up, Will!" he implored. A younger private just kept talking nonsense: "Who's Bertie Walke? Please tell me, who's Bertie Walke?" he kept asking.

Bergeron forced his eyes away and called for the medics. He clambered out of the shell hole and ran forwards a few steps. At his side a sergeant, hit before he had taken half a dozen paces, fell forward onto his face without putting even one hand in front of him to cushion his fall. Bergeron knew the sergeant was dead before he hit the ground. A German machine gun position, which he could see on a slight rise behind the German reserve trench, was doing the damage. A second position, further to the south east, was adding to the problem. Bergeron sensed that the assault was stalling.

Wadham, ahead of him, dived into a shallow crater and

Bergeron's small team were in sharply behind him. Bergeron followed.

"What do you think, Bergeron?" asked Wadham.

Bergeron stared at the infantry captain. Wadham was a large man, possibly fifteen stones or more. He managed to look smart enough in his uniform, even now as he crouched in the crater. But he also looked tired and unhealthy, thought Bergeron. He had deep grey bags under sullen eyes, and his skin was yellowish. Wadham's sallow appearance was not helped by his downwards-drooping moustache, for it seemed to give him a perpetually sad expression. He also had a scar running from his right cheekbone into his moustache. Bergeron struggled to know what to say to him.

"Hold on, Howard, I'm no infantry tactician. I'd say you're totally exposed to those Emma Gee posts." He gestured to the left. "I can range our guns and mortars onto them from here, but you and your boys must be up there to take the machine guns when fire is lifted. Major Glenn is in advance of you. I suggest you keep the lads going before any Boche mortar fire kicks in. Get them moving as quickly as possible, then you'll be fine. I'll catch up once I've called in the Frog 75s and got them on target."

"Get the fire in then, Bergeron," said Wadham. "I'll stay with you to make sure the message gets through."

"No need."

"Bugger off, Bergeron, I'm staying put! Tozer and the NCOs will take the boys on – I need to keep a strategic view of things."

"Roebuck went down early, and his sergeant. His platoon is without a commander."

"They're trained solders, Bergeron. They know what to do in such a situation. I'm sitting it out here – you get on with your job, man!"

Bergeron looked at Ryan. The small Irishman just shrugged.

"Where are we up to, Bombardier?"

"Jonesie and Sainsbury have been busily laying wires, boss. I've already got contact down the D3 with the French Command Post."

"Well done, Ryan."

Bergeron checked on his map. Then, in fluent French, snapped co-ordinates down the line. Thirty seconds later a shell exploded, slightly short of the first machine gun post. He altered the fire quickly and efficiently, and barked down the phone, "Two-minute barrage, high explosive, fire for effect!" He turned to the nearest flaggy: "Sainsbury, lamp signal to Captain Speed for mortar rounds. Quick as you can, gunner!"

The land around the German MG posts erupted with combined mortar and gunfire. The machine guns stopped. Soldiers of D Company started moving forwards, slowly and still vulnerable to rifle fire from the German trench – all but Roebuck's platoon who stayed still, providing a sitting target.

Bergeron leapt out of the crater and ran towards the South Devon men.

"Ryan, be ready to run the wires into that trench as soon as you see we've captured the Emma Gee posts. I'm taking Night-time Platoon forward."

"Aye, aye, boss."

Armed only with his service revolver and moving quickly, Bergeron shouted to the first NCO he saw.

"Name, Corporal?"

"May, sir."

"Get them moving, May! Come on. If we stay here any longer Fritz will zero in with his mortar fire. Up! Move! Get the boys to the trench. Take your section and get the first MG post, I'll take the rest of the boys and grab the second. And May…"

"Sir?"

"Keep low and move fast, Corporal."

Training and experience made the young corporal respond to orders. Likewise, the soldiers of Roebuck's platoon. Between the two of them, Bergeron and Corporal May soon had 13 Platoon moving away from the mortar rounds that just then started exploding behind them. McGregor's machine gunners had meanwhile assessed the situation and were providing covering fire with four Vickers guns.

Peter Roebuck's platoon of South Hams men poured into the German front line trench. Mills bombs and bayonets now played their part – more useful than rifle fire once inside the closed trench. One German died as he was speared by a young soldier who ran quickly for him and lunged his bayonet at the German's stomach. Others worked in teams, bombing and working their way along the trench. Two German soldiers ran towards them shouting and firing, but a cool-headed lance corporal killed one of them with a shot in the chest and winded the second.

Bergeron could see that May was quickly closing the ground between him and the first machine gun post, still silenced by the bombardment. It was Bergeron's job to take the second. He picked on the three soldiers nearest to him.

"Packs off, rifles slung. Grenades only. Keep low and follow me."

They sprinted the 300 yards as best they could and reached the second MG post just as the artillery fire subsided. The barrels of German guns were beginning to poke out of the firing loopholes. Bergeron dived for the ground in front of the machine guns and tossed a Mills grenade into the pillbox. Two of the South Devon riflemen went in through the back door, but Bergeron saw the third soldier in hand-to-hand fighting with one of the German machine gunners who had managed to get himself out.

Sod it, thought Bergeron. *Why did I tell them to sling their rifles?* He had his pistol in his hand, but could not risk a shot. Without thinking, Bergeron sprinted and leapt onto the German soldier's back, his size and momentum knocking the man off balance. His right knee was thrust into the unfortunate man's spine, whilst Bergeron's left arm was around his neck. With his right hand Bergeron was beating at the German's face with the butt of the revolver. Blood spurted. The German screamed and fell back, Bergeron fired into his belly.

"Thanks, Captain," said the soldier, who couldn't have been older than nineteen. "Thought I was a dead 'un then."

"Name?"

"Private Trant, sir."

"You're not out of the woods yet, Trant. Get down, and quick!"

Bergeron took a deep breath. He had spotted two Germans moving towards them. Now, the soldier in front, a big sergeant, raised his rifle and pointed it at him. Bergeron quickly raised his revolver and let off two shots. He missed.

Trant had his rifle to hand now, but before he had chance to fire, two shots rang out in quick succession and both Germans fell.

Bergeron looked to his right and saw his ack.

"What are you doing here, Ryan? I told you to bring the wire up."

"Flaggies are seeing to that, boss. Thought I'd stick with you to get a bit of, well, excitement."

"Bloody good job you did, Bom. Thanks. Where did you get that?" He pointed to the automatic pistol in Ryan's hand.

"Oh this?" Ryan waved the Mauser. "Ah, well, I suppose you might say I stole it, boss. Back in February. I was with a section of scouts and signallers in Noyelles. We happened onto a house that Fritz had been using as a store. Brim full it was! As well as a stash of these here broom handles," he waved the Mauser pistol, "there was also a dump of brass band instruments." He laughed. "Sure, kept the lads happy for days after. Anyway, boss, the gun's previous owner wasn't around at the time. And as he was a Hun to boot, then I'd say I was just giving the gun a good home."

"I'll let you off a charge then. Small bore though, doesn't have the stopping power of a Luger or a revolver."

"Well, suppose you could be right. Though it stopped those two, boss!"

Bergeron looked at the two dead Germans.

"You see, the Mauser is a very accurate weapon, boss, and I just happen to be a natural good shot. So, you might say, we're a useful partnership, me and this here pistol."

Corporal May arrived and looked at the German sergeant. "Killed by a single shot," he said.

Bergeron gazed on the corpse of the sergeant. Judging from the neat hole on the left breast pocket of his tunic, the bullet had hit him in the heart. The other German had died the exact same way.

"Looks like you are a good shot," he said to Ryan.

Bergeron pointed at the dead Germans. "They're *Gardekorps*. That's Prussian Guard to you, Private Trant. Fritz has got some heavies here."

Bergeron bent low to examine the dead sergeant. On his belt was a dark brown leather sheath. Bergeron took out a knife from the sheath. It was light and well balanced with a handle of hand-worked bone, its blade as well-honed and sharp as the German armourer could make it.

"I could have done with this a few minutes ago." He turned to Ryan. "If you can steal from the enemy, Bom, then so can I."

"Sure, you're allowed the odd souvenir, boss."

Bergeron gazed at Ryan and then at the dead German.

Unlike many he had known, he harboured no thoughts about spoils of war.

"It's no souvenir, Ryan."

Bergeron looked again at the weapon in his hand, opening and closing his fingers around the handle. He had taken that knife simply because he saw there and then that it was perfect, and he wanted it to use. "No. This is a knife that I think I might be able to use."

The four of them smiled. "Well done, all of you," said Bergeron.

The fight was drawing to its close. Most of the Germans were dead or had fled. Glenn called in Captain Ansty's company to mop up, and soon McGregor followed, his machine gunners quickly setting up positions at the rear of the German trench.

★

Bergeron found a bottle of red wine and some sausage in a German dugout. He now took it to Ryan and the team.

"Well done, boys. Very well done. Here, take this as a show of my appreciation. Ryan, a word, please, outside."

The two men sat on a firing step. Bergeron offered Ryan a sip from his flask; it was whisky.

"What's your name, Ryan?"

"Don, boss."

"Dan?"

"No. Don. Some call me Donny. It's short for Doncha, boss."

"Doncha, what kind of a name is that?"

"It's Irish, boss. Don't mock."

"Let's stick with Don. Tell me about Wadham. Has anything like that happened before? Off the record, Don. Promise. If I'm going to work with this outfit, then I need to know where the dangers lie."

"Captain Wadham's a disaster, boss. He's a bully, ordering junior officers to do things he wouldn't do himself, pushing the NCOs about – unreasonable demands with the threat of a charge. Just because he's second-in-command…"

"What? I thought Speed was 2IC."

"No. Speed runs much of the show, but Wadham's second-in-command. And, on top of all that, boss, as you saw for yourself today, he gets the wind up too easy, like. The men call him Howard the Coward."

"Well, he sure gets windy, I saw that. Howard the Coward, you say. Carry on."

"Well, to my mind, the worst thing about him is that he can't make a decision. He dillies and dallies, putting his men at risk, doesn't care about them, boss. Doesn't give a monkey's. Sod'em Wadham might be a better nickname."

Bergeron couldn't hold back a giggle at the humour injected by Ryan, even in these circumstances. He quickly pulled himself together.

"Why on earth is he in command of a platoon, let alone 2IC of a bloody company then? Couldn't they find him some cushy job as an adjutant for some fat colonel somewhere?"

"Beats me, boss. Just how it is. He's been around a bit and is next in line. Doesn't matter that he's a piece of shit! And another thing: he hates CSM Tozer."

"Why?"

"Don't rightly know, boss. Wadham was an NCO himself, earlier in the war. Did you know that? When he came into this outfit as subaltern, Rogers was his platoon sergeant. Rogers was soon promoted to CSM, but Wadham remained a run-of-the-mill second lieutenant – only promoted when all the other officers had got 'emselves wounded or worse. Don't know for sure. Maybe Tozer is everything that Wadham isn't, if you see my meaning."

"I've seen Tozer in action. He seems solid."

"Oh, he's more than that. CSM Sidney Tozer is the dog's bollocks, boss…"

"The dog's what?"

"Bollocks. He was a Territorial before the war. Soon became an NCO. Awarded the Military Medal out in Gallipoli. "Give you an example. Early this year, we went into a line that had been held by some Taffies. Trenches were a mess, real mess. Took the boys a long time to get them shipshape. Snipers were a big problem. The Taffies had let them intimidate. Low morale, boss. Low morale and poor leadership and even good men can let things slip. Tozer sorted it out."

"What did he do?" asked Bergeron.

"First he stopped the sniper. Got a good fix on his position at night when we could see a flash from his rifle. Two bits of string set thirty yards apart. Each pointing directly at the bastard. Next morning Tozer had two platoons on the fire step with guns trained on him. Lifted a helmet to make sure Sniper Fritz was awake. Yes, he was. Five minutes later we put up a helmet again. Bang! Direct hit. He was a good shot that sniper. Only this time, whilst he's reloading, Tozer let him have three rounds rapid from each man. That's 120 bullets, boss, and all on or damn near the target. Sure, we had little problem from snipers after that. Then he got the boys to sort out the trench, latrines, everything. Dirty work, but everyone felt a lot better once it had been done. Yes, boss, the CSM is a first-rate soldier, a leader."

"What about the others?"

"Other company commanders are good enough. Major Glenn is fine. A Regular, Sandhurst man, plenty of experience there, too. McGregor is a good officer, he's wasted on the Emma Gees in my opinion – for what it's not worth. Ansty – well, he's just moved up. He was a platoon commander here. A good one, too. The boys still think a lot of him."

Ryan looked around himself.

"Here, boss, in D Company. The major is a waste of space, if you don't mind me saying."

"Just carry on, Don."

"Wizzo – er, Captain Speed, and the major's assistant, young Lieutenant Wainwright, seem to run the show between them. Don't know where the company would be without them, really." He paused to take a sip of whisky.

"I know who Wizzo is, Ryan. And the *chitty wallah*."

Doncha Ryan smiled at the young Canadian officer.

"Full Sun Platoon? Well, Lieutenant Jeffries is keen enough, but no experience there at all, boss. NCOs doing most of the work. Wizzo is good, as I said. Night-time Platoon? Well, you saw what happened today when Lieutenant Roebuck and his platoon sergeant went down. Nothing below the veneer, so to speak."

"And you, Don? You seem a pretty handy soldier, if you don't mind me saying so."

"Volunteered in '16. Knew a bit about mechanics. Thought about the Engineers, but decided on the gunners. Volunteered for this particular job 'bout a year ago. Suits me, boss. Just doing an important job well, and otherwise keeping my head down."

"When it suits you, Don Ryan. When it suits you. Didn't keep your head down today, did you? Poked it well up above the parapet, I'd say. Well, thanks again for that."

"Boss, ask you a question?"

"Go ahead."

"You did pretty well yourself today, for a gunner officer that is! How come?"

"Well, you could say I just happen to be a natural good soldier."

NIGHT-TIME PLATOON

Because his left hand was shaking slightly, Bergeron placed it in his pocket. He could feel it twitching as if it retained an existence of its own, quite apart from him. Probably nobody would notice, but he took no chances.

Bergeron was in the company HQ alongside Wainwright. The HQ had been set up inside a deep German shelter. They were both sitting on a door – possibly a kitchen door, judging by its thickness – that served as a bench for junior officers. Being taller than most, Bergeron's head was brushing the roof of the shelter. There they sat and awaited the debrief on yesterday's action.

The attack, they discovered, had succeeded with only moderate casualties; four men had been killed, but there were double that number with injuries – some serious. Lieutenant Roebuck was badly wounded, said Major Cross, "… but he's likely to survive if the bloody medics can keep his wounds clean until he's safely in a rear base hospital".

"There's nothing clean here, sir," offered Wadham. There then followed a discussion of the merits of immediate evacuation of casualties to Amiens.

Bloody hell, thought Bergeron, *there's a war on*. He looked at Wainwright who raised his eyebrows. "Excuse me, Major," he interrupted as somebody raised the issue of the liberal use of Salvarsan.

"I was just wondering what you are planning to do about Night-time Platoon."

"Do?"

"Well, they're without an officer now."

"NCOs can lead them, Bergeron," interjected Wadham. "You know as well as I do that the British Army only has subalterns commanding platoons to give them experience for the next job. They don't lead, do they? The sergeants do that. That's what I did when I was an NCO."

"But Night-time's platoon sergeant went down too. The most senior NCO is Corporal May. I met him today and he seems a good soldier, but he can only be twenty years old."

"Twenty? Well, that's older than Roebuck was. Anyway, what's it got to do with you, Bergeron?" Again it was Wadham speaking, not Cross.

"Calm down, Howard," said Bergeron, as Wadham glared at him. "It's nothing to do with you, and that's for sure." He turned to face the company commander. "What do you say I take them on, Major? Just for the attack on the reserve trench? We're not using artillery, so I've nothing else to do. What do you say?"

"Let him do what he bloody likes," muttered Wadham.

"Captain Bergeron is not exactly under your command, sir." It was Wainwright speaking. "He's attached as intelligence officer and therefore – technically, that is – he can go more or less wherever he likes." Bergeron was surprised that the young officer was being so outspoken, but this was all new territory to him.

"You're not under my command, Bergeron," said Cross. "Listen, if you want to lead Night-time Platoon that's fine. However, and you'd better think hard about this, if it goes belly up, it was nothing to do with me, do you understand? You were acting on your own accord as an attached staff officer."

"Got that, Bergeron?" asked Wadham.

Bergeron ignored him and looked directly at Cross.

"Yes, Major. I completely understand."

"We've got a special job for Night-time anyway," said Wadham. Major Cross looked surprised.

"Gee-Gee wants one of our platoons to lead the attack with a raid, in darkness, directly before the main assault tomorrow. They're to capture and hold a central position, then provide enfilading support to the main thrust. You can take them in, can't he, Major?"

Cross hesitated. "Yes, yes, Howard. Study the maps then brief the men, Bergeron."

★

"So, it looks like you've talked yourself into a tight hole, boss. Chances are Wadham thought that one up after you volunteered, not before."

"Well, I've done it now. It may not be a bad plan, if I can get them across no man's land without being seen or heard. Once we're in the trench, I'll set off a flare. McGregor's MGs will start up and the main assault will begin. Will I have to brief the men? What's usual? Perhaps an NCO could do it, as Wadham says."

"No. The men will expect an officer to brief them."

"Any advice?"

"Any junior officer has to gain the respect of his men very quickly, boss. These lads are used to young officers coming in – and going out, like Roebuck. They're already jumpy. They've seen you in action, so that's good – but you'll have to let them know that you've a plan and that you're confident they can carry it out. The more confident you seem, the better chance they'll have of doing well."

"Anything else, Bom?"

"Yes, boss, just three things."

"Three? Go on."

"First, get May to find you the toughest, roughest fist fighters and scrappers in the platoon to be first in. Forget the rifles. No use at close quarters. The lads'll have to sling them. Forget the helmets and packs, too. Arm the boys with as many Mills bombs as they can carry, knives, clubs, knobkerries, pistols, knuckledusters… whatever you can find or scrounge that'll be useful in a hand-to-hand fight.

"Rifles are useless in a trench in the dark – but you'll need 'em as soon as the hand-to-hand fighting is over. Pull out every third man to carry spare ammunition and the other equipment, and have them lag behind a bit with the Lewis gun section.

"Second, if you can get him, take CSM Tozer with you. He's as good as three men and the boys would follow him anywhere."

"And the third thing, Don?"

"Take me too. After what I saw the other day I think you may need somebody to watch your back."

"Now listen on, Bombardier Ryan," laughed Bergeron, "my back's just fine!" He smiled at Ryan. "You're in, Bom, but I thought you believed in keeping your head down?"

"Oh, I will, boss. Sure, I will."

★

Bergeron made his way along the support and communication trenches to get up to company HQ; he had an appointment to see Major Cross. As he walked past them, the men would nod and give half salutes in his direction. Bergeron approached a soldier with a bandage around his head and he stopped.

"What's your name, soldier?" he asked.

"Rifleman Dart, sir."

"What have you done to your head, Dart?"

"It's nothing, sir. Grazed by a ricochet thinks the medic who patched me up."

"And he sent you back up the line?"

"Told me to get back to the clearing station with the walking wounded, sir. But I said to him I'd rather be with me mates. So he left it up to me, sir, and here I am."

"You sure you're fit?"

"'Sir! Bit of a headache, that's all."

"Well, make sure you drink, Dart."

"Beer or rum, sir?"

"Water, keep hydrated, you idiot!" Bergeron smiled to himself, he never failed to be uplifted by the fortitude and loyalty of these men.

Continuing his journey, Bergeron eventually sighted the company HQ. A duty soldier was posted outside. As he pushed aside the gas blanket, removed his forage cap and descended the steps into the dugout, Bergeron saw that Wadham was already there.

"Sit down, Captain Bergeron," said Cross pointing towards the makeshift bench.

Bergeron, being careful not to sit too far on one side and tip the door, sat down.

"Now, what do you want, Bergeron?" asked the major.

"This raid, sir. Please can I take the CSM with me?"

"Not a chance, Canada Joe," said Wadham.

"What's it to you, Wadham?"

"No, no and no! You are not to take Sergeant Major Tozer on this raid," insisted Cross. "That is an absolute order. He's needed at company level, understood, Captain Bergeron?"

"It's not a raid, as such. The rest of the company will be following us in – so Sergeant Major Tozer *will* be working for the company."

"No!" shouted Wadham. "We're promoting May. Here." Wadham handed over a set of stripes. "You can give him these. *He's* your platoon sergeant."

Bergeron could see it was pointless arguing. They had made up their minds and that was it – it was probably all Wadham's work as Ryan had suggested. He stood, put on his cap and saluted Major Cross. Being careful not to catch Wadham's eye, he turned and climbed the steps out into the trench. "Blast!" he blurted out, and the duty soldier gave a start.

Bergeron left company HQ and made his way back to his quarters. Everything was quiet. The decision to wait for over thirty-six hours to launch the attack on the reserve trenches served no good purpose, he thought. The Boche would simply have more time to dig in and prepare. *Bloody shambles*, thought Bergeron.

Once back with the platoon, he called for Ryan and May.

"Sergeant May." He handed over the extra stripes.

"Get these sewn on. Congratulations! I expect the extra pay will catch up with you eventually. What's the strength of the platoon?"

"Twenty plus me, boss," replied the newly promoted sergeant.

"That's twenty-three with Bombardier Ryan and myself. Lewis gun section intact?"

"Yes. Corporal Yeabsley is in charge."

"They're in support. Choose the best ten lads for a punch-up and divide them into two sections. Scrounge as many hand guns and Mills bombs as you can. And knives – bayonets if you can't find enough. You know the kind of stuff, May?"

"Yes, boss!"

"You'll lead one section. Take Bombardier Ryan with you. Your job is to peel off to the left while I take the other section right. We'll have fifty or sixty yards between us. We get as close as possible to the trench as we can without alerting Fritz. Tell the boys to keep low and we need absolute silence. As soon we are in the trench – or if we get rumbled before – then we rely on speed and surprise. Keep them low and move them fast, Sergeant May. Once in, we both turn to meet up. Got it?"

May, looking at the stripes in his hand, nodded agreement.

"The remaining lads and the Lewis gun section are to come in behind us once we've linked up. They'll bring the ammunition and packs. Signal is a green flare – make sure Yeabsley knows what to do. It's also the signal to our heavy Emma Gees to open up, so they'd better be quick to jump in. Off you go, May, and remember: keep low, move fast!"

★

Bergeron felt awkward in the unfamiliar dress. Before dawn, as the new day was just beginning to rouse itself, he had removed his tunic and put on an old Mackintosh in its stead. He pushed two grenades into each of the raincoat's large patch pockets and fastened his leather belt tightly around his waist. Into the belt, he pushed a Webley revolver and a hatchet, the latter of which he had purloined from a sergeant of pioneers the day previously, along with the knife he'd taken from the *Gardekorps* sergeant. Instead of a helmet, he wore a black woollen balaclava folded into a cap. Then Bergeron climbed slowly from his dugout and walked forward to find Peter Roebuck's old platoon. *No*, he thought, *they're my responsibility now, my platoon.*

"By Christ, boss!" exclaimed Ryan when he saw him. "Sure, you look more like a highway robber than an artillery officer!"

"Bugger off, Ryan. Let's just get this over with."

Together, Bergeron and Ryan walked to the jumping-off point. Night-time Platoon were kitted out for a trench raid.

Faces, badges and buttons were blackened, heads covered by woollen hats. The men were armed to the teeth as if members of a street gang, their rifles slung over their backs. Some were silent, others chatted. One or two men smoked, others just twitched or fiddled with equipment.

"Not carrying a weapon, Paddy?" asked May.

Ryan, wearing a leather jerkin and his ANZAC hat, was armed only with the Mauser and a bayonet, both of which were holstered, leaving his hands free. He looked at May and then looked down at his own fists. May, following Ryan's gaze, realised that the small Irishman had knuckledusters on each hand.

"Used to do a bit of boxing," said Ryan, smiling.

Bergeron approached them. He tried to appear confident as he outlined the plan to the men. Soon it was time. "Right, boys, as quietly as possible until the balloon goes up, then go in as hard as you bloody well can."

Bergeron went up the ladder first and swung to the right. He was followed by five of the soldiers selected by Sergeant May. "Keep low and move fast, lads," he whispered as he led them forwards.

May himself went next, followed by the other five. They struck out to the left, Ryan bringing up the rear. Corporal Yeabsley, his Lewis gun team and the soldiers that were being used as 'pack mules' waited two minutes and then followed, making for the centre of the target area of trench, but moving slowly and keeping very low.

Bergeron moved carefully and deliberately, trying to reduce any noise he made to an absolute minimum. The soldiers with him were good, quiet as proverbial mice. To his left, though he couldn't see or hear them, May and Ryan were also making good progress.

Then a voice whispered in the dark.

"Captain Bergeron, sir?"

"Quiet, shush."

"Sir," the voice whispered.

"Who is it?"

"It's me, sir, CSM Tozer."

"Tozer?"

"Sir. Found out from Major Cross's batman that you were asking for me. Well, I'm here."

"Tozer? Bloody hell! Well, good work, CSM. Come on then, take the lead. You've done this far more times than I have." He whispered to the men, "Silence boys. Follow the CSM."

Tozer led them up to the edge of the German trench. There was no move from the sentries – they hadn't been spotted. *So far so good*, thought Bergeron. Using hand signals, Tozer got the section to spread out along the parapet and prepare Mills bombs. Just then shots were heard on their left. This was it.

"Grenades, then in after the blast. Now!" shouted Tozer.

The grenades exploded, then Tozer jumped into the German trench. He charged at a wounded German staggering towards him, and caught the man in the face with a punch that knocked him over. Tozer followed this with a kick into the groin. The Germans on sentry duty were killed, wounded or stunned by the grenade attack, but Bergeron knew the noise would be stirring others from their sleep.

"Find the entrances to dugouts, Mills bombs again," he ordered.

Bergeron took two soldiers and began to work along the trench to the left to link up with the second section of men. They acted quickly and efficiently, tossing their grenades into the German dugouts and causing mayhem. Some Germans emerged from bombed dugouts, but they were taken completely by surprise and most were too shocked to fight. The few to show any resistance were immediately attacked with knives, cudgels and fists.

A large German armed with a spade ran at Bergeron, shouting and cursing him. As he came closer he raised the spade before him, pointing the blade at Bergeron's throat. Bergeron stood his ground, then moved to his left at the last moment, making it difficult for the German to re-aim the jabbing blows that would surely follow. Bergeron swung him a back-handed slash with his hatchet, bringing the axe blade across the man's face. The German screamed.

It was not pretty work, thought Bergeron, but Ryan had been correct. Rifles were next to useless in this fight.

May and Ryan were having a tougher time on the left flank of the platoon's attack. A German sentry had thought he heard a sound in no man's land. He shouted a challenge to which there was no response. Then fired two shots to rouse his colleagues.

Firing those shots was the last act of the soldier's life as Sergeant May jumped on him and thrust a bayonet into his gut. May's left hand was clamped over the sentry's mouth, but too late. The alarm had been raised. A squad of Germans appeared from a recess in the trench line, then quickly ducked back as they saw the British soldiers. Ryan heard the clicking of rifle bolts as they prepared their weapons for firing. The Irishman lobbed a grenade into the part of the trench where they were. He and a South Devon rifleman rushed the Germans after the blast. Ryan pounced on a stunned German and hit him about the face with three right jabs of his knuckle dustered fist, then floored him with a crunching left into the stomach. The young rifleman attacked the only other survivor with a heavy, homemade club with six-inch nails driven into it. Three more Germans appeared, but Ryan drove them back with Mauser fire. May soon had the section organised and their bombing work cleared the rest of the trench.

Bergeron was running along the trench in the lead of his section. A German NCO saw him, turned and fled, only to be gunned down by Sergeant May who had found himself a Luger. The linkup had been a success. Bergeron took out the Very pistol and fired a green flare skywards. "Come on, you boys!" he shouted. "Get yourselves in here and quick!"

The Lewis gun team and reserves piled into the trench just as heavy machine gun fire could be heard to their rear. It was McGregor's Vickers company opening up. Their fire was expertly directed over the heads of the other South Devon companies now taking forward the attack, and onto German support trenches.

CSM Tozer arrived by Bergeron's side. "Everything going well, sir. All we need to do now is to keep Fritz occupied on both flanks for a few minutes till the rest of the company arrives."

"Get it sorted then, CSM," ordered Bergeron.

Tozer sprang into action. "May, get that Lewis gun into action on the right flank, take half the other men. Only take the replacements, May. Captain Bergeron, sir, I suggest you accompany young May there. Bombardier, can you shoot straight?"

"Aye, I can that, Sar'nt Major."

"Well, let's see. Grab a rifle and come with me."

Ryan could hear the chatter of the Lewis gun accompanied by rifle shots. He and Tozer quickly set up a firing line as best they could, aiming at the side of the German trench on their flank.

"Just watch this, Ryan. Three clips, rapid," ordered CSM Tozer. "Fire!"

The fire line exploded in a frenzy of noise, fire and smoke. The riflemen took just two minutes to discharge three magazines of bullets, each of which contained ten rounds.

"Jesus!" said Ryan. "That was some shooting. Look, I've only just put in the second clip!"

"Well, it's a bit of a cheat really. They're not really aiming, you see. But yes, these boys are good. May's got the Lewis gun, but he's also got the conscripts. They can't fire anywhere near as fast as old-time soldiers. But these boys," he waved towards the five South Devon men, "they trained as riflemen in the Territorials, the old South Hams Rifles. They can let off twenty rounds a minute for a short period. Twelve to fifteen if we want aimed shots. And they're accurate, believe me."

"I do, sir, I do believe you," said Ryan.

Once the line had been secured and things had quietened down, Cross and Wadham arrived in the trench.

"Where's the CSM?" Wadham asked of nobody in particular.

"He's checking the wounded," said Bergeron.

"He's on a charge!" replied Wadham.

"A charge? Don't be bloody silly!"

"Sergeant Major Tozer is on a charge," said Cross, "and be respectful when addressing a superior officer, Bergeron, or you'll be on one yourself."

"Sergeant May, take two men and bring the CSM here immediately," ordered Wadham.

May hesitated.

"Do as you are ordered, Sergeant," said Cross, but still the young NCO did not move. He looked at Bergeron.

"Do as Captain Wadham orders," said Bergeron.

"Yes, boss," said May and walked off sullenly. Bergeron turned to Cross.

"You can't arrest Tozer," he blurted out. "He's a bloody hero. Do you know what he did back then?"

"Captain Bergeron," Cross sounded authoritative for once, "there is no cause to swear. The CSM is not a hero. As you well know, a CSM has specific responsibilities in any attack. It is his job, and his alone, to ensure supplies are brought up and that the wounded are taken back. As it was, Captain Wadham, as my second-in-command, had to take on those responsibilities, thus leaving his own platoon without an officer commanding."

"No, he didn't! We didn't need supplies sending up and there were hardly any wounded. Thank God and the CSM for that. No one needed to be taken back, and what's more, we didn't need the mortars, again because of the CSM."

"Shut up, Bergeron," said Wadham. "You weren't to know that and neither was Tozer. It was just lucky we didn't need them. You're bloody lucky not to be on a charge yourself. You should have sent Tozer back."

"Sent Tozer back? Like bloody hell I would! We needed good men out there – leaders, to take charge, to take the lead. Something you wouldn't know about, Wadham."

Wadham sneered and muttered something inaudible.

"Now, now. No need for talk like that, Bergeron," said the major. "You were in charge. That's what you wanted, that's what you got. You ought to have sent Tozer back. Now, I am handing over Night-time Platoon to Lieutenant Wainwright. You are relieved, Bergeron. Now disappear, there's a good man!"

Bergeron glared at Cross. He was speechless as he rose.

"Go back to what you came here for, Bergeron. *Intelligence!*" added Wadham as the big Canadian officer departed.

★

Bergeron headed straight back to his platoon quarters and began to pack his gear. He heard somebody coming down the steps and turned around to see who it was and Wainwright jumped down the last three steps.

"Wadham put him up to it, I'm bloody sure of it," shouted the young lieutenant as he sat down on a spare bunk, breathless.

"Yes," said Bergeron. "You're probably right. What's the situation like out there now, Billy?"

"The CSM is being held on two charges. The first charge is desertion, with a subsidiary charge…"

"Desertion!"

"Desertion. With a subsidiary charge of quitting his post without authority. That's what it's bloody well like out there. Nobody's happy about it, Bergeron. I'm sure none of the men are happy about it, and I know I'm not. But of course, there's nothing anybody can do now the charges have been made."

"No court martial is going to wear a charge of desertion on Tozer!" raged Bergeron.

"No, but the second charge might well hold. Quitting a post without authority is a serious enough charge on its own. Carries the death penalty. Though there's no saying a court would uphold it."

"You seem to know a lot about this, Billy."

"Been around a while. I've spent this war so far being Cross's bloody *chitty wallah*, doing his administration for him, clearing up after him and generally doing my level best to keep him out of trouble. I've picked up a lot of knowledge about what goes on back from the lines. It happens, Marc. Actually, they could also have had the CSM up for disobedience to a lawful command – he was supposed to be sending up supplies and…"

"It's all a load of bull shit, Billy! You and I both know that Tozer is a good soldier and there is no way on earth that he should be being held up on any charge. What can we do?"

"Me, I don't know. I'm sure Gee-Gee doesn't know a thing about this and he should. I've a good mind to write to him. I've been keeping notes about everything here." He pointed to a small, green bound diary on the table. "My mother always brought my sister and me up to speak out for what we considered to be right – to do things in our own way and with a passion. Yet…" he paused, looking sad. "Going over Cross's head – I don't know. Anyway, I'm in charge here now, so the only whistleblowing I shall be doing for a few days is leading these men." He forced a smile. "You, Bergeron? Well, you can appear as a defence witness, but they'll try to cast doubt on your character – try to say you couldn't cope, you didn't order Tozer back because you were too frightened. That sort of thing."

"What nonsense!"

"The main problem is this, Marc: I'm not sure that this will get to a proper court martial. It's more likely that the major and his side-kick Wadham will sort it out here and, if they do, it will be sooner rather than later."

"Then I'm going to Gee-Gee."

"You?"

"Yes. I've got less to lose than you have. You do your job here, Billy, and I'll see to Gee-Gee. Any front-line experience?"

"None, sadly."

"Look, it's important that the men respect you for making decisions – but it's even more important that you make the right ones. Sergeant May is a damned good NCO. My advice is you do whatever May suggests, just make it look as though you thought of it. Got it?"

"Yes. Thanks, Marc – and good luck with Gee-Gee." Wainwright stood and shook the Canadian warmly by the hand.

"Good luck to you too, Billy," said Bergeron as he picked up his bag ready to leave. He looked down at the dog. "And I don't know what Poilu will do – he lives life his own way too. He may follow me, but if he doesn't then keep an eye on him, will you?"

"You can count on me."

★

The bombardment began soon after Bergeron had left Night-time Platoon. The German gunners retaliated against the 3rd

Battalion's attack on their comrades' trenches with two hours of ferocious shelling. They used heavy artillery based a long way behind the line, and supported that barrage with field guns and trench mortars. Nothing could move in the British trenches.

Many of those soldiers had experienced an incoming artillery bombardment before – and this was one of the most devastating they had witnessed. Afterwards, none of them were able to convey in words the intense fear it generated.

Bergeron was on his way back towards HQ ready to speak to Gee-Gee when it started and luckily had found a dugout. He was sharing it with the brigade padre and a couple of sapper NCOs. Bergeron had often been at the firing end of such a bombardment, but now he was receiving. He was frightened. He and the others could do nothing but try to find cover and remain there. Waiting – hoping – for it to cease. Praying.

Cross, Speed and Wadham crouched in what they had made into a company HQ and drank whisky.

Bombardier Ryan was crouched alongside Gunners Jones and Sainsbury in a deep former German dugout shivering and shaking and hoping for the bombardment to stop.

CSM Tozer had been taken to the rear, and kept under guard in what earlier in the day had been their own front line trench and was now the reserve. At least he avoided the worst of it.

DREAM OF ANGELS

"Fire!" Lanyards are pulled and the three guns explode in noise and smoke almost simultaneously.

"Fire!" Men push fingers into their ears. The lanyards again. More smoke, more noise, the sharp, astringent smell of burnt cordite.

"Fire!" Well-drilled figures in khaki uniforms move swiftly to reload. Shells are passed from man to man – the soldiers in khaki curse and sweat as they reload. A shell goes into the gun, followed by the casing containing explosive. The breech is shut and locked.

"Fire!" Fingers in ears, lanyards pulled. Another explosion of fire, smoke, noise and smell. Then the figures slow. Their movements are now in slow motion as they work to reload the field guns.

"He's off again," said Gerry Finn, looking across at the new patient in the small hospital bed between them.

"*Oui*, always the same. Unrelenting!" said Soignon.

"Fire!" Men push fingers into their ears. The lanyards yet again. More smoke, more noise, the smell of cordite.

Now other figures appear in the distance – are they children? Yes, two children, a girl and a boy. What are they doing? A building is on fire and they try to escape, running away from it – but they can't run. They are moving in slow motion too. The building – a house, a farmhouse perhaps – is being shelled.

There, inside the house. Can he see two older people? "Ready to fire, sir," says a bombardier.

"Stop!" shouts the girl. "Ne le faites pas. S'il vous plaît, arrêtez. Our parents are inside. Please! Please stop it!" There is no sound coming from her lips, but Bergeron understands every word the girl mouths. She is running towards him, slowly, slowly. Now there are hundreds of girls running towards him, and they speed up. Then they metamorphose into German infantrymen. These soldiers are charging at him now. Bayonets on rifles, they curse and rage at him.

"Fire!" he orders. Men push fingers into their ears. The lanyards are pulled. Thunder, flash, smoke, smell. The Germans, the children and the house have disappeared.

"Fire, fire, fire!"

Now there are other figures around him. Figures in uniform. Women in white, stiff and starched dresses push along clattering trolleys. One of these women places a band around his left arm – then she makes it go tight, tight by pumping air into it. Too tight – he shouts out. He feels his arm will explode, but no. They try to make him eat, then a thermometer is thrust into his mouth. He spits it out. They all fuss around him. A mouth moves; faces nod in agreement. No sound. This time he doesn't know what they are saying.

Bergeron became aware that he was lying on his back. He could hear what may have been the sound of wheels squeaking along a wooden floor. He smelled the polish, and freshly laundered cotton, antiseptic and, in the background, another earthier and less pleasant smell. No, it was a stench.

He opened his eyes and looked to his left. A body swathed in bandages; a bearded face that smiled at him.

Bergeron turned his head to look the other way, to his right. Here a man dressed in pyjamas sat in the bed. The man was awkwardly holding a book; it was Hardy – *The Mayor of Casterbridge*. As if sensing he was being observed, this man turned towards Bergeron.

"Hello, hello! What have we here? Decided to join us in the land of the living, have you? That must have been some dream you were having, old boy," said the occupant of the bed.

Bergeron stared at him for a few seconds. "Sorry, it's just a dream? Oh God – is it? I don't know. If it is, then it's the same dream repeatedly. It's always the same. Can't stop it."

"Your doctor – what a handsome-looking thing – says it has something to do with the painkillers and sedatives they've kept you on. Should wear off, so the medics say."

"How do you know that?"

"Easy to know most things that are said in here, old chap. Thin curtains, no regard to privacy, eh? I'm sure it will. Wear off, I mean. Sure, sure. They're always right, 'cept when they're wrong of course. Name's Finn, by the way. Gerry Finn, 2nd Ox and Bucks."

"Bergeron, RCHA." He offered a hand in greeting.

"Sorry, old chap. Right arm's gone and the left is badly broken, I'm afraid. In a bit of a muddle, you might say. Funniest thing is I can still feel it – my right hand. Sometimes still think it's there. And on your left is Soignon."

Bergeron looked again to his left; the bearded face still smiled. "*Capitaine Philippe Soignon, le Deuxième Chasseurs à Pied*. At your service, though I am sorry, I can't be of so much assistance without those." He pointed down the bed.

"What happened?"

"A shell – a big one. They think my legs are gone. Perhaps, with lots of money and good doctors in Paris, they would be saved, but here? Well, you know what army surgeons are. And these are not much better."

Bergeron tried to make an appropriate face and turned away from the Frenchman. He felt more comfortable addressing Finn. "2nd Battalion, you said. Regular?"

"God, no!" answered Finn. "Answered the call in September 1915. Father knows the battalion CO. He got me gazetted into the Ox and Bucks Light Infantry – better serve with those you know, eh? What's more, I'll be out of uniform just as soon as this bloody show's over!"

Bergeron pointed towards Finn's arm. "Looks like you might be out sooner than that. What happened to you?"

"In charge of a night raid. All's going well and we make the enemy front line in search of a prisoner or two. Then Herman the Hun decides to have a go at us. Lights up the sky with his flares and opens up on us with his Emma Gees. Then it's silence, till one jolly German chappie tosses a potato masher into the bloody sap we're crouching in for cover. I shout at my lads, 'Incoming! Take cover!' and grab the sod of a thing. Well, it goes off before I can chuck it back from where it came. Bang! Took my right arm off. Just my bloody luck, hey?"

"And your left?"

"Don't know. The explosion knocked me for six and I ended up lying on my side at the back of the sap. That must have done it. But the lads were all still in fine fettle. Fought off Fritz, and got me back to a clearing station. In bloody agony I was. Agony! The fright and shock must have kept the pain away at first, because I can remember the journey back to our front line, being dragged along by those two soldiers of mine. But once I'd safely returned from the action," he looked at Bergeron and made a face, "Jesus it hurt! What about you, old man?"

"I was… I can't remember much. One minute I was in a dugout, taking shelter. I was drinking and talking and… Well, next thing I know I'm here talking to you. How long have I been here?"

"Couple of weeks. Unconscious when they brought you in. Thought you were a dead duck, old son. Me, that is, not that handsome doctor of yours. Always the optimist, that one. And what a place to be holed up in, eh? What a bloody place? A hospital staffed and run entirely by women, and us surrounded by all these lovely lassies attending to our every need – well, not exactly *every* need. I'll be so sad to leave!"

"What do you mean, entirely women?"

"Ha-ha! Thought that would grab your attention! Yes, this place is entirely sorted out by the fairer sex, old man."

"Nurses?"

"Yes."

"What about doctors?"

"All the lot of 'em. Not a bloody bloke in sight!"

At that moment, as if on cue, Gerry Finn saw two nurses approaching his and Bergeron's end of the room.

"Look! My God, an angel! It's the fair Nurse Harris come to treat us."

Bergeron lifted himself on the bed a little. "Which is Harris?"

"The tall, slender one. Auburn hair."

The woman he saw made an immediate impression on him. Her elegant face was defined by high cheekbones and a well-shaped nose. She wore her hair up, off the sides of her face, piled high on her head. She was dressed in white, an ankle-length dress gathered at the waist by a white belt. The dress was collared tight around her neck, in the popular style of a man's shirt. With it she wore a necktie. In front of her, she pushed a trolley, which contained a bowl of water and many bandages.

"Nurse!" shouted Gerry Finn. "Please could you help me up in the bed a little way?"

She walked over to Finn and helped him rearrange himself.

"Thanks a lot, Nurse. That's so much more comfortable."

"You are so welcome, Mr Finn. And what have we here? Why, Captain Bergeron has decided to wake himself from his slumbers. How are you feeling today, Captain?"

Bergeron noticed that she spoke slowly and with a drawling, north-American accent which he supposed meant that she originated from the southern mid-west. "I'm fine, thank you, Nurse. Well, I've got a thumping headache, actually."

"I can get you something for that."

"Nurse, is it true what Finn there has been telling me? That this place is totally run by women?"

"Yes. That's so. Is it a problem for you, Captain?"

"No. Of course not. But, well, the doctors? They are properly qualified?"

"I'll let Doctor Weston know you've come around. I'm sure *she'll* want to examine you. Then perhaps you can ask her yourself."

Isobel Harris left Finn and Bergeron to their romantic or worried thoughts. She clattered her trolley over to the bed at the end of the ward and once she had reached it, drew the curtains together. There she began, as gently as she possibly could, to change the bandages and dressings that covered the torso of the patient.

He screamed, and it seemed to be the most agonised screaming Bergeron had ever heard. He looked at Soignon and Finn.

"Poor devil's badly burned," said Finn. "Flyer, apparently. Came down in flames. Lucky to survive. Or unlucky, depends how you perceive the sort of life he faces now – if he makes it."

Nurse Harris called for help. A second nurse and an orderly ran over to the curtained bed to assist. It took them fifteen minutes to get through the work, throughout which the airman screamed.

Eventually, the man settled to just the occasional cry and the three women came away from his bed. Isobel Harris was the last to leave him, a look of anguish on her face; her apron dirtied by the slime that had oozed from the airman's wounds.

As she walked passed Bergeron, he looked up at her.

"Nurse," he said.

"Yes, what's wrong, Captain Bergeron?"

"Nothing, but... are you all right, Nurse Harris?"

Isobel Harris looked at him. Her thin lips moved to form the very slightest of smiles and her eyes were full of gratitude. "Yes. Yes, I'm all right. Thank you."

★

It was the following day that Doctor Weston came to the ward to see Bergeron. He was struggling to eat his lunch.

Finn, Bergeron and the others were used to army food, used to surviving on ration packs for days on end. But at least, thought Bergeron, rations tasted of something, and there was always some sort of booze to add sparkle to the most spartan of meals. Hospital food was something else entirely. He was sipping some sort of fish soup, served with two slices of grey-looking bread spread thinly with margarine, when he heard footsteps on the wooden floor.

"Captain Bergeron. Sorry I couldn't get over sooner to speak to you. I've been busy."

Australian. Early thirties perhaps. Good looking. *Oh, why do I think of women this way?* he thought.

"Oh, that's quite all right, Doctor," he said, rushing to swallow a mouthful of soup which induced a cough.

"Slow down, Captain. I'm not in a rush now. How's the soup?"

"Filthy and disgusting!" shouted Gerry Finn, and some of the other men laughed.

"I'm not asking you, Mr Finn." The laughter quietened.

"Well, it's perhaps not the best," offered Bergeron, "but I'm sure it will do me good."

"And you're hungry?"

"Yes."

"Well, that's a good sign. You certainly look much brighter than when I saw you last. Tell me, have you fallen in love with Nurse Harris yet? Or one of the others? That would be a good sign too!"

He didn't know what to say, so remained silent and felt the blood rushing to his cheeks.

"Oh, don't be bashful, Captain," she said. "Most men do, you see. When they come in here they're usually either unconscious or in pain. Once that's been sorted out, they fall in love with a nurse, or with one of the orderlies."

"Or with a doctor?" called out Finn.

Mary Weston ignored him and drew the curtains around Bergeron. "Let's have a look at you. Shirt off, please."

"Just do as you're told, Bergeron... and enjoy!"

"Mr Finn, do stop it," said the doctor.

Bergeron had never undressed in front of an English-speaking woman before. He moved slowly. Clearly in pain, but also embarrassed, he removed the shirt.

"Lean forward," she ordered confidently, which had the effect not of settling him, but of making him yet more nervous. Doctor Weston perched on the bed behind him and examined his back, gently tracing her finger along the length of it, occasionally pausing, prodding and asking him if such and such hurt.

"You're mending up well, Captain," she said. "But you'll not be going back to the fighting any time soon. Off to England to recuperate. You can get dressed now."

"Doctor?"

"Yes."

"Are you an army doctor?"

"No. I'm a volunteer."

"Volunteer?"

"With the Scottish Women's Hospitals. Does that matter to you?"

"If you're not in the army, you could call us by name. Mine's Gerry," shouted out Finn.

"Mmm. Perhaps I could."

"What's your name, Doctor?" asked Finn.

"Mary. Mary Weston, but you may call me…" she paused. "You may call me Doctor Weston," she said with a smile.

Bergeron was pulling his shirt back on, and Doctor Weston helped him with the sleeves. "I never knew places like this existed. I mean hospitals without male doctors," he said.

Mary Weston had a round face with jet black hair. Unlike Nurse Harris – who was always immaculately turned out – the doctor's hair was slightly dishevelled and came away from her head in curls. She had full lips, dark brown eyes and thick eyebrows, the latter giving her a somewhat stern, or perhaps studious, look. Bergeron thought her beautiful. Yes, he had fallen in love (it was a good sign).

"Doctor Weston, I need to know what happened," he said. "Can you please tell me exactly what happened to me?" He looked up at her.

"Medically, yes. You came here unconscious and with severe lacerations, some of them deep, caused by fragments of wood and other debris that had been driven into you. Mostly into your back. You were also badly concussed and had a broken left leg. Dr Greenwood set your leg and I dug out the bits and pieces from your back. You are a very lucky man, Captain Bergeron. None of your vital parts were badly injured. Very lucky indeed. But I don't know how you got these injuries, if that's what you want to know. Some kind of explosion, obviously."

Bergeron was staring blankly at the doctor. "You mean, you did the operation?" he found himself asking.

"Why not?"

"Well, I thought…"

"You thought surgery was a man's job?"

"No, no."

"Yes, yes. And no. No, it isn't a man's job. There's no such thing as men's jobs and women's jobs, Captain. Didn't they teach you that in your training? I carried out the surgery on your back. Me. A woman. And Doctor Greenwood, a woman too, set your leg. We're both surgeons and completely up to the task, Captain." She turned to go.

"I'm sorry," he offered, weakly.

Mary Weston stopped and looked back at him.

"No need, it's not your fault. I'm sorry too, I overreacted. I'm tired."

"Busy?"

"Far too busy! But I should be used to your reaction. It doesn't come only from men. It will take another generation to convince people of what we women are capable of."

"Tell me, please, you are working for the Scottish Hospitals, but you're Australian, aren't you? How did that come about?"

"Oh, where to begin?" she replied. "When the organisation was first set up they sent out teams to Serbia and Russia. That's where most of the British girls ended up. Later, when they set up here in France, and in Belgium, they needed more volunteers."

"That's where you come in?"

"Yes. There was no way I could do anything useful in Australia and the Australian Army wouldn't take women. So, I came over to Britain to offer my services."

"And I'm so pleased you did. Thank you, Doctor. You saved my life."

"Hardly. You'd have pulled through anyway in the hands of even a clumsy male surgeon. Though I will accept credit for my excellent neat stitching – better than any man could have managed."

Bergeron smiled. "Thanks anyway."

"Look, Captain Bergeron, I have to go. I will check on you again tomorrow. By the way, you had a visitor. A corporal – Irishman. He was sent away as you were unconscious, but he said he would try again. If he turns up, do you want me to let him in?"

"Yes. Yes please."

★

Two days later Ryan was sat at Bergeron's bedside. He had a black eye.

"Good to see you, boss."

"Good to see you too, Bom. Been fighting again?"

"Oh that, sorry."

"I'm sure you didn't mean to, and I'm sure the other chap has two black eyes."

"Four! There were two of them, you see. Two against one, not a fair fight, was it?"

Bergeron laughed, but the laughter gave him an intense paid in his side.

"I came a week ago, boss. Managed to get a short leave, travelled to Abbeville by train and on to here. A nurse told me that you were unconscious, but improving. She said it might be another week before you were conscious and up to receiving visitors."

"I keep having this dream – nightmare."

"Want to talk about it?" asked Ryan.

"No. Not now, anyway. Sometime maybe."

"Can't believe you've landed yourself in hospital with lady doctors. How come?"

"Long story. I found out bits and bobs from Captain Finn here." He pointed to Gerry.

Ryan stood up. "Pleased to meet you, sir," he said.

"Sit down, Bombardier. We don't stand on ceremony here. Good to meet you too. Captain Bergeron has been telling me about you, seems you're a rather good egg."

Ryan looked perplexed. Bergeron carried on talking. "The nurses and doctors are volunteers. Scheme seems to have been kicked off by a dear old thing called Elsie Inglis. Scottish I think. Suffragist type, it seems."

"Bit of a Florence Nightingale, boss? Lady with the lamp?"

"Doctor, trained in Edinburgh. Well, it seems she trotted over to the War Office with the idea of serving as a doctor in the army. 'What? Women in the army? No! Not having that. We can't have women treating the men. Outrageous!' says some red tab."

"Well, that don't surprise me."

"So she does it herself anyway. She sets up an outfit called the Scottish Women's Hospitals. Seems they're funded by the women's suffrage movement."

"Oh, that explains it. Good luck to 'em, I say."

"Yes. Probably they were out to prove that women can do what the establishment thinks of as 'men's work'. Good luck for us, too, though," said Bergeron. "Anyway, our dear Elsie and her crew set up a load of hospitals, all staffed by women, to help out the Allied war effort."

"You mean there's more than this one?" asked Ryan.

"Crikey yes! Our Elsie sent out teams to Serbia and Russia as well as here in France. I believe the old darling went out to Serbia herself. That's where most of the British girls ended up."

"And Elsie English is still in Serbia?"

"Inglis. No. I hear that the poor old thing died last year. Something internal, apparently."

Bergeron was silent for a full minute, then he looked at Ryan again.

"What the bloody hell happened to me?"

Ryan told him that the German Artillery had scored a direct hit on the dugout. It was three hours after the shelling stopped before Bergeron was dragged out unconscious. The others, said Ryan, had been killed outright.

"You were lucky," said Ryan.

"Very lucky."

"It was the non-stop barking of Poilu that convinced some medics to dig for you. Poilu probably saved your life."

Bergeron, Ryan informed him, had been in a field hospital not far behind the front line for three days, too ill to be moved. He recovered quickly, became stronger and had eventually been moved here.

"I don't remember a thing, Don. I must have been drifting in and out of consciousness – and dreaming – for days. I remember the CSM being placed on a bumped-up charge. I was talking to Billy Wainwright, then I stormed off to find Gee-Gee. Then it all goes blank. Tell me what happened, Don. From the beginning if you wouldn't mind."

"There's no good news, I'm afraid, boss. We all hoped that the Provost Marshall would get involved and order CSM Tozer be moved to a Military Police holding camp somewhere behind the lines. Now that would have been good news, would have got him away from Major Cross and Wadham's bad influence and facing a fair court martial."

"Would have?"

"Soon after the bombardment, after you had been pulled out and taken away, we found out that the case was being sorted out at company level."

"Oh no!"

"CSM Tozer was shot by firing squad, boss. Major Cross got the ugly thing done behind everyone else's back."

"Oh my God, no!" Bergeron placed his head in his hands, then looked up at Ryan.

"Have to say, Don, I'm surprised the men went through with it."

"Rumour is that Wadham assembled a squad of some new arrivals and a few villains. Lots of rum and promises of reprieves, boss."

"Rumour?"

"Well, lots of talk but nobody will admit to being in that squad. And no NCO seems to have been present."

"All sounds very strange to me, Doncha. Must have been

witnessed by somebody. Doesn't it have to be signed off by a medical officer? Isn't there supposed to be a padre present?"

"That's exactly what I was thinking, but I don't know about the rules. Anyway, I just happened to hang around where I shouldn't be when a youngish medical officer was being briefed by Major Cross about the firing squad. But that was two days later, boss. The MO was sounding to me to be very reluctant about signing any death certificate, because he wasn't there when it happened, but..."

"The MO turned up two days after Tozer was killed?"

"Yes, boss. Cross hushed up the MO's protests. He was pissed off at any suggestion it wasn't a properly run execution squad and seemed to be chivvying him into making a report as quickly as he could."

"That bastard Cross. And Wadham doing his dirty work for him!"

"Well, there's good news there. Wadham's down as missing in action."

"Go on."

"A few days after the firing squad, Cross was moved. Gee-Gee gave him a job at HQ and Wadham took over D Company. The company was defending the line and was overrun by the Germans. Battalion lost two of its company commanders that day, boss. Captain Ansty was badly injured and Wadham's not been seen since. He's either dead or been taken prisoner, and judging by the speed of their attack, I don't think they were taking prisoners."

"Good riddance, I'd say."

"Yes, but there's worse to come, boss."

"Worse? Can it get any worse? Go on."

"Young Lieutenant Wainwright's dead too."

"What? Billy Wainwright, how?"

"Hun raid on our position, night after the bad news of Tozer's death reached us."

Bergeron was stunned. He looked at Ryan; the Irishman was holding back something.

"What's on your mind, Don?"

"Well…"

"Anyone else cop it? Come on, out with it. Just tell me the worst."

"Well, that's the strange thing, boss. No one else was touched. In fact, no one else saw any Germans that night. I was in the support trench and didn't see a thing. Just the noise. I went up the next morning and asked around. Nobody saw any Germans."

"They might have scarpered once shots were fired, Don."

"Yes, they might have." Ryan remained silent for a full minute.

"But you don't think so, Don?"

The Irishman remained silent, a pained expression on his face.

"What on earth are we going to do?"

"Do, boss? Well, first of all you are going to get well then get out of this place. Back to Blighty, no doubt about that. Me? I must be back with the regiment by Saturday night. Talk is all this will be over before long, by Christmas at the latest."

"I think I may have heard that one before, Don," he said, and for the first time in weeks managed a smile. "I'm getting better – be out of here soon. We need to know more about what happened that night. Who knows anything, Doncha? Who could I ask?"

"There's a few you could talk to. You could try Lieutenant Jeffries. He was duty officer that night. Picked up a broken leg and flesh wounds a few days later and sent back home for a while. Should be easy to track him down."

"Yes, his father lives in Hampshire I seem to remember – Winchester."

"Perhaps have a word with May, too, he's still with the battalion. If you could find the MO he might have something to say."

"Did you catch his name, Don?"

"No idea who he was."

"Billy Wainwright kept a diary, he might have recorded it. What happens to officers' belongings after they're killed, Doncha? In Canada kit would be returned to the family."

"Same thing here, boss."

"When I'm back in England I'm going to find Jeffries and hear his version. May too – if I can find him. I'll try to find Wainwright's family – they might have his diary. If what you think is true, Doncha, then I swear that once this war is over I will not return to Canada until I find Cross. There'll be some reckoning to be done."

"Boss…"

"Yes, Don?"

"Find Eber, Eber Trant. He knows something about the rift between Major Cross and the CSM, I'm sure of it."

"What makes you think that, Don?"

"At first I thought it was Wadham's idea to see off Tozer. It was plain that Wadham hated the CSM, but after hearing Cross speak to the MO, I wasn't so sure. So I started quizzing some of the lads. Nobody said much, but there was something about what happened before the war. I've got a feeling Trant knows more than he was saying. I think he knows why Cross had Tozer done in."

"Done in? You think it was murder then?"

"Yes, boss. Yes, I do." He paused. "And, boss…"

"Go on."

"Count me in, boss. If… when you track Cross down, let me know."

How the Reverend Acquired
a Limp

Captain Richard Ansty could not rest. He was worried about his officers and his soldiers, though that wasn't so unusual. What was unusual was his concern that events surrounding CSM Tozer over in D Company were contributing to declining morale across the whole battalion. Major Cross had been sent up to battalion HQ for goodness knew what reason and so Captain Wadham now commanded D Company. Ansty didn't trust him. More than anything, he was worried about his own company's vulnerability to attack by the Germans.

It was October 1918; the battalion had suffered badly this year and its strength had been reduced to a fraction of what it had been even last year. The replacements were of poor quality. His men were simply too thinly spread. He would have liked to have deployed two platoons along his section of front with one available in support and another occupying a fall-back position – the reserve trench. But the section of front he had been ordered to defend was simply too long. Instead of his desired formation, he had three platoons, each stretched far too thinly, defending a front line of hastily dug trenches. There was no reserve trench, so Ansty had divided the fourth platoon – strengthened by his small HQ – into three fighting sections which were concealed as best they could be in natural ground hollows. Ansty just prayed that the Germans didn't have much in the way of artillery, or these soldiers were all dead men.

Yesterday Gee-Gee had informed him that a Boche attack seemed imminent, so today he had decided to inspect the three platoons deployed on the front line himself.

Accompanied by his CSM – Warrant Officer Jakes – Ansty began in the north west and worked his way along the weak front line positions.

"What do you think, Sergeant Major?" he asked. "Can we possibly hold this line?"

"Yes, sir. So long as the Germans come at us in line, then the lads can hold them off. Our lads can all shoot, sir. But if the Hun decide to concentrate their attack on where they think or find us to be weak, sir, then they may well be able to break through."

"Exactly what I think, Jakes." Which was why Ansty had decided on the deployment of his reserve.

If the Boche attacked him in line, his men could hold them off for a couple of hours – and that would be long enough. The casualties inflicted in that time would force a cessation. If, however, the Germans used the same stormtrooper tactics they had employed back in March, he could strengthen the point of their attack with the closest reserve section, bringing in the others as quickly as possible.

However, the reserve sections, not afforded the protection of trench cover, would be extremely vulnerable to German machine gun, mortar and artillery fire. It would be a close-run thing indeed.

"Sergeant Major Jakes."

"Sir."

"Gather the mortar section from each platoon. Take them 500 yards back from the front line and issue them with smoke shells. If the Hun decides to concentrate his attack, we'll need smoke to hide our reserves as we move them across that open ground." He pointed to the fields behind them. "If he does break through," added Ansty, "we might just catch him in a pincer, and that'll give him the bloody shock of his life."

★

The Germans attacked at 1530 hours that same day. As CSM Jakes and Captain Ansty had suspected, their attack was not a frontal assault.

When a small group of stormtroopers advanced in the centre Lieutenant Chambers ordered his platoon to open fire, causing the Germans to conceal themselves and return fire. Grice, on Chamber's left flank, ordered his men to open fire on the Germans. Simultaneously, more Germans appeared to the right of Chambers and they ran down the hill to charge the soldiers of 4 Platoon who were dug in there.

As the battle raged most furiously on the centre right of Ansty's front, his attention was drawn to the left, where a section of German grenadiers was working its way along a slightly sunken lane towards Grice's platoon.

The first Ansty knew of this was the sound of explosions and shouts of Grice's men, now caught in a vicious grenade attack.

"Mortar smoke now, Sergeant Major Jakes, and get reinforcements onto the left as quick as you can, man!" he ordered.

Ansty would have preferred it had the main thrust of the German assault come on his centre. Then he could have flanked the Germans on both sides behind the cover of smoke, inflicting enough damage to force a withdrawal.

Even now, he considered, so long as Captain Wadham's men on his own left flank stood firm, then his attacking sections would send the Germans reeling onto them.

The smoke shells began to fall and Ansty watched as his soldiers moved into position. Grice's platoon began to pull back and they emerged in good order through the smoke, pursued by German stormtroopers who, trained to spot weaknesses and openings, now flooded into the gap created.

"Fire!" ordered CSM Jakes. Fifteen Lee Enfield rifles and a solitary Lewis gun opened up on the Germans' left flank. "Give it to them, lads!" shouted the CSM.

The fire from the South Devons was devastating and the German attack faltered. Seeing an opportunity, Lieutenant Grice ordered his retreating platoon to drop to the ground, turn and open fire on them.

Good, good, thought Ansty as the Germans wheeled to their right under this barrage of rifle and machine gun fire. *Now come on Howard old boy, get your rifles aimed on them as they wheel.*

No fire came from the company to his left.

Ansty ran to his mortar section. "Corporal, lengthen your fire to the ground in front of our original line and switch to high explosives – and be quick about it."

"Yes, sir!"

Ansty ran forward, revolver in hand, and picked on two men from Grice's platoon. "Follow me, you two," he ordered and the three of them ran over the open ground between his own rear and that of Wadham's company. Then, as the mortar smoke began to clear, Ansty saw that the soldiers of D Company were in retreat. Why they were running away, he did not know, for they didn't seem to be under any more serious assault than were his own men; but they were running away and in so doing were leaving a big empty void for those Germans his own men were facing to pull into. "Bugger," he said to nobody. "Howard's got the wind up and pulled out!"

Ansty could see that the withdrawing Germans had split themselves into two. Whilst a few of them opened fire on Wadham's company, hurrying even more their ragged retreat, the others had formed a line just behind the brow of a shallow hillock and were waiting to fire at any pursuing soldiers. "Oh no!" said Ansty.

He had to warn CSM Jakes. Ansty ordered the two riflemen to stay put and do what damage they could, then he took a deep, deep breath. It was about 300 yards back to Jakes' position and much of it was over open ground. His chances of making it unscathed were slim. On the other hand, he thought, he had always been a fast runner. So long as he kept moving, he should be relatively safe.

"Wait until I'm at least one hundred yards away from you, then open fire on those Boche," he ordered, pointing to the Germans on the raised ground ahead of them. With that, Ansty was off.

It was slightly downhill for those first hundred yards, and Ansty ran like the wind. He heard the two riflemen behind him open fire, heard the German rifles answer them – and on he ran. Another fifty yards and he could see the CSM making ready to attack. "No!" he shouted, but Jakes didn't hear.

Thirty more yards, now he saw Jakes looking towards him; watched the CSM put up his hand to halt the men. *Good, good*, thought Ansty, *I think he's seen me.*

Then the sharp chatter of a machine gun sounded as a sudden sharp pain exploded in his legs. He fell headlong to the ground. Silence.

Ansty drifted into unconsciousness; it might have been for minutes or for hours, he did not know. Then he could hear a familiar voice. "Are you hit, sir?" shouted Jakes.

"Yes," he said, more of a whisper than a voice. He took a breath. "Yes, in the legs. Did you hold the men, Sergeant Major?"

"Yes, sir. I realised something was amiss when I saw you sprinting towards us like that, Captain Ansty. Just you stay there, sir. We're holding them now and reserves are on the way. Once it gets dark, sir, I'll send the boys to fetch you."

"Very well, Sergeant Major. I'll be waiting, keep the men safe. Carry on CSM, carry on. Good man, Jakes."

Keep Low, Move Quietly

"I keep having the same dream, Doctor. Almost every night, can't stop it."

"Tell me what happens in your dream," demanded Mary Weston.

"I'm in charge of a troop of gunners, giving them the order to fire. But we're not landing the shells in the right place. There's a house, a family inside. Then a small girl runs out and, in French, pleads with me to stop. I could. I could order the men to cease fire. But I don't, so the house goes up in smoke and flames and the parents die. The children run towards me, but they change into German soldiers and so I shoot them. Then I wake up sweating. I want to give that order to stop – it just never happens."

"Could it be based on anything that has happened?" she asked.

"In 1917, at Vimy. I commanded a troop of gunners."

"And you hit the wrong target? It happens, Marc."

Bergeron looked at her. "You never call me Marc."

"There's a time and a place for everything." She held out her hands to him, he took them into his and kissed them, softly. Then, as if remembering something, she pulled back.

"No. Well – nobody knows. You see, there was a farm destroyed by Canadian shelling. Later we found out that two children – a boy and girl – were orphaned that day. Nobody knows which gun fired those shells – who it was that got his calculations wrong, which officer gave that fateful order."

"It's not your fault. They shouldn't have been there."

"What do you mean 'shouldn't have been there'?" he shouted. "It was their bloody country – their land!"

Mary Weston simply looked at him.

"I'm sorry," he said.

"It wasn't you, Marc. You're far too good a soldier to make that mistake. Look, recurring nightmares – that's how we refer to dreams like these – are not uncommon. They'll pass, I'm sure of it."

"God, I hope so."

"Can you find out more about what happened?"

"No. It could have been any one of us. There's no way I could ever find out if it had been me."

"No, I didn't mean that," said Mary. "Could you find out what became of the two children?"

"Perhaps, perhaps," he said.

"But you've never been charged by the Boche. Never had to shoot at them with hand guns."

Bergeron looked at her.

"Have you? You're an artillery officer, for goodness' sake!"

He simply sat there and stared at her.

"Oh my God – you have! Was it so awful, Marc?"

★

"Bergeron, would you care to join us on this blasted raid? It's your show really, you know. You want my men to capture a German so that you can interrogate him. So why not bloody well come with us, what do you say?"

"Put like that, Desmond, how could I refuse?"

"Get those red tabs off, fella, maybe lose the tunic, actually. Have you got anything else with you?"

"Erm, yes an old raincoat. Will that do?"

"Wear that, I'd advise. It can get a bit muddy out there."

★

Bergeron sat in his billet and put his tunic, complete with the red tabs, down on the bed. There was no space to hang clothing. He considered what had happened to him following his exploits with the Buffs. In what seemed like just a couple of days of moving back to Amiens with Toynbee, he had been posted. That wasn't unusual. He supposed that the recommendation for a Military Medal had marked him out. Somebody, maybe Jimmy Marshall-Cornwall, he thought, had said something and Bergeron had been picked out as a potential high flyer. He was quickly moved on, not back to his regiment but to staff HQ. Once there, somebody (Jimmy again, he wondered) had obviously judged him to be fitter and blessed with a sight more initiative than many junior officers on the staff. It was May, and here he was, he thought, posted straight back to the front as an intelligence officer and now marked down for another dirty job.

Bergeron put on the raincoat. Just two days ago he had arrived at Pontavert, close to the River Aisne. There, the 50th Division was supporting a full French Army. Clearly, somebody had thought it could do with a French speaker as interpreter – a French Canadian would do perfectly. In addition, Bergeron's command of German was felt to be useful in interrogating prisoners. He was sent to join the 2nd Battalion, the Devonshire Regiment.

The 2nd Devons was in reserve positions when Bergeron reported to Lieutenant Colonel Anderson-Morshead, the CO. Anderson-Morshead was busy, he was told, and Burke, the adjutant, immediately told him to work alongside Captain Desmond Sutherland, a dour Scot acting as bombing officer with B Company.

★

Bergeron and Sutherland were standing in the cellar of a ruined house on the east side of the town, together with eight of Sutherland's soldiers. It was warm, dank and dimly lit. In the gloomy light Bergeron could see that the men were wearing woollen caps instead of their Brodie steel helmets, and each had a blackened face. They had rifles slung across their shoulders, but each man was also armed with a pistol.

Bergeron was dressed in his Mackintosh and forage cap, though Sutherland himself was wearing his usual attire. Bergeron looked on as he set out to brief his soldiers.

"Men," he began, "you must appreciate the importance of getting a prisoner tonight. We know the Germans are amassing a force over there, and we can assume they are making ready to attack us. It will help us enormously to find out just where that attack will be. One German prisoner will be sufficient, so don't hang around. Once you have your man, you just get out of there as quickly as you can with him. Absolutely no heroics, understood? Sergeant Coker will lead the raid. Captain Bergeron here is an observer from staff."

Bergeron looked at Sutherland quizzically.

"Any questions? No, well, over to you, Sergeant."

Coker stood up. He was a large, tough-looking man in his mid-thirties, with a ruddy complexion and a short-trimmed, greying moustache.

"There's a German post in the house opposite us, the one with the red roof," said Coker. "It's only 200 yards away, and the first fifty of them is the jump-off sap. I'll lead us up to the garden fence and put up a perimeter there with four men and Captain Bergeron. Then the corporal will go in with you two." He pointed to Privates Venn and Blackler. "You get in there with Mills bombs through the windows and then inside fast.

Grab someone and run like hell back to me, got it?" Corporal Hardy and the other two nodded, sullenly.

"We'll have the front line ready with Lewis guns and rifles, and as soon as Sergeant Coker puts up a flare we shall open up," said Sutherland. "So keep your heads down on the way back. Here, Bergeron." He handed the rifle to the Canadian.

"You're not coming, Desmond?" he asked.

"Me? Christ no, much too important. Do you know the casualty rate on raids like this?"

"Here, Captain Bergeron, take these." It was Coker; he handed a woollen hat and some black cream to Bergeron, who thought it resembled soot mixed with wax or fat. "Better not have a gleaming white face out there, sir."

Soon they were ready to go. Bergeron felt the urge to say something. "Keep low, men. Move quietly."

★

Bergeron lay face down on the ground. He could hear scuffling and shuffling sounds, but he couldn't identify where they were coming from. He didn't know for sure which way was back to the safety of the makeshift line that the Devonshire Regiment were occupying, and which way led to the German positions.

He had lost contact with the raiding party!

Sergeant Coker had told him to get into the ditch. "You can observe very well from here, Captain Bergeron. If we need covering fire you just open up but make sure you shoot over the lads' heads, sir."

Coker seemed confident and Bergeron was happy enough to do as he was advised by the sergeant.

He had listened as the raiding party closed in on the German position. He heard the explosions of the Mills bombs followed by shouts in English and German. Rifle fire burst out and this subdued the other noises. Then a flare went up – that would be Coker's signal, he had thought. Machine gun fire whizzed and banged over his head; all was chaos.

In that chaos Bergeron waited for Sergeant Coker and the raiding party, but they had not come back to collect him. They must, for some reason, have returned to the Allied lines by a different route.

After a while – and he could not estimate how long it took – an intense quiet seemed to descend upon the scene. Now Bergeron began thinking about how he was going to get back to re-join the Devons. It was dark, very dark, and it was impossible to see much. In any case, Bergeron had not been in this sector long enough to have been able to recognise any landmarks. Thinking he had a reasonable idea of the way they had come out, he decided to retrace his steps.

Bergeron rose to a crouch and moved as quietly as he could towards what he thought were the Allied lines, carrying the rifle in his right hand. He made a little too much noise, however, and a shot rang out.

He dived into a hollow on his left. *Good, good*, he thought. The shot had come from behind him, confirming that he was going the right way. Then a machine gun opened up in front of him, up went another flare and the sector erupted once again into a chaos of fire, smoke, bullets and noise. This time he looked at his watch. It was 0400 hours.

By 0420 the shooting had stopped. Bergeron took hold of a stone and threw it as far as he could to his left. This prompted shots from behind him.

He waited another twenty minutes, picked up a second stone and hurled it to his right. Firing came from in front of him this time.

It was no use, he was lost.

Bergeron kept himself awake until dawn. The first sign of the rising sun in the eastern sky cast a dull red glow over the shell hole he was concealed in. He knew he must make use of this definite directional aid to make an estimation of where the German lines were. He marked this by pointing the barrel of his rifle in the direction of the rising sun and the Germans. Then he took out his revolver. Directly opposite the rifle, checking for a third and fourth time the relative directions as the sun rose, he used it to make an arrow mark in the ground. Having done this, he took hold of the rifle again and this time laid it parallel to the arrow, pointing to the British lines and safety. Cautiously, he raised his head until he could see the landscape. Yes, at least he thought he could recognise it.

Bergeron dropped back into the hollow, made himself as comfortable as he could and tried to go to sleep. *It's strange*, he thought. *We all know that the sun is stationary relative to the earth which orbits it whilst spinning away on its axis – yet we still think and speak in terms of the sun rising and falling, and of it moving across the sky. So very strange.*

★

He waited until the sky was as dark as he thought it was going to get. Then, lying on his belly in line with his rifle lying on the ground, he looked ahead and upwards and found one star amongst the many that gleamed in the sky that night – the one star that would guide him home. Bergeron carefully and painstakingly committed to memory the pattern of stars. He would look at them, close his eyes and try to recall what he had seen, repeating this many, many times, yet all the time worrying that cloud would descend and hide his beacon.

At last he believed he could recognise that star anywhere in the sky. He closed his eyes, shook his head and then opened his eyes to find it. There it was! Again and again he practised this routine.

Then, as quietly as he possibly could, for his life depended upon it, Bergeron stuck the knife into his boot, slung the Lee

Enfield, and inched his way back to the 2nd Devons and to safety.

★

"What on earth happened to you, old man?" asked Sutherland.

Bergeron simply shook his head. "Got a cigarette?" he eventually asked.

"You don't smoke," said Sutherland.

"Tonight I do, Desmond. Just give me one. I thought this was supposed to be a quiet sector."

His uniform was dirty, he was as hungry as a horse and shaking with fear – but he was back.

Sutherland lit two Gauloises. "It is a quiet sector!" replied Sutherland, handing a cigarette to Bergeron. Then a corporal arrived with tea and some hot food. Slowly, slowly he began to calm down.

"You tell me what happened, Desmond. You tell me."

"We thought we'd lost you, old man. Coker and the lads got you a prisoner, but with all that hullaballoo, they came back through the old sap on our right. We expected you to crawl back in last night, and when you didn't – well, men do get shot out there. As there was no noise from you during the day, we assumed you'd been shot dead. It happens. Anyway, good to have you back, Marc."

"Good to be back, Desmond. Bloody good to be back!"

★

Daniel Hofmann was eighteen years old and he had been in the army for a little over six months. When the Tommies had burst into the dugout he was sharing with Rossler and Strauss he had fouled his underpants – he had been so frightened.

Strauss had been caught in the blast of the first grenade; Rossler he didn't know about. The dugout had been filled with smoke and noise, everybody shouting.

The Tommies had handled him roughly, but he soon worked out that they did not intend to kill him. They were taking him back as a prisoner and he decided it would be safer not to resist. Then a flare went up into the sky and machine gun fire erupted from the English positions. German fire chattered back – another flare, this time from behind him. The Tommy sergeant seemed worried; he kept looking back and asked the other Tommies where their captain was.

Soon Hofmann was pushed inside a building and told to stand. He was searched and his pay book was taken. The Tommy who searched him said something like, "This one's shat his-self, Sarge, better find him clothes", but Hofmann didn't understand English. Eventually, some clean clothes were brought to him along with a bowl of warmish water and he was left to clean himself.

Later a Tommy brought him some food: stew, French-style bread and tea – it was good. He felt better. He was taken to a small room – a cell – in which was a bed, a blanket and a bucket. Here, Hofmann spent the night.

The following day he and four wounded Tommies were walked to a town behind the lines. A Tommy with a rifle was guarding him, but there was no need. Daniel Hofmann knew his fighting was over before he had even fired a shot – and he was content with that.

"*Was Sie den Namen?*" asked the Tommy officer. His accent was poor. Hofmann had been taken directly to be interviewed by this officer, in a well-equipped office – perhaps a brigade HQ.

"Musketeer Hoffmann, Daniel. Six, double two three four seven four."

"We want to know how many soldiers you were with and what your orders were," said the English officer. He spoke reasonably good German, thought Hofmann, apart from that accent.

"Musketeer Hoffmann, Daniel. Six, double two three four seven four."

"Yes. You've told me that. What regiment are you with?"

Hofmann was putting on a show. At first, he gave no information other than his name, rank and service number. But last night he had decided what he would say, and decided that he would tell the officer what he believed he wanted to hear long before the Tommies were rough with him. There was simply no point in not doing; he didn't know much anyway.

"Sir, I serve with the 231st Reserve Infantry Regiment of the 50th Reserve Division."

"Which company?"

"The 3rd Company, sir." He watched as the English officer wrote down his answers.

"Who is your commanding officer, Musketeer Hofmann?"

"Lieutenant Nagel commands my platoon, sir. Major Schetter commands the company."

"I mean, what is the name of the officer in overall command?"

"I do not know, sir."

This went on for an hour until the English officer gave up. "Better somebody from staff question him," he said in English. Hofmann was taken to another small, cell-like room where he was kept for the rest of that day and the night which followed.

The following morning he was awoken early and taken back to the interview room. The powerful, bitter sweet aroma of coffee filled the air. *Decent coffee*, thought Hofmann. A desk had been cleared and on it was a plate of bread, butter and jam. A mug of steaming coffee was sending those lovely, inviting smells through the room.

A different Tommy officer was sitting on a chair on the opposite side of this table. He had red tabs on his uniform and a mug of coffee in his hand.

"*Hinsetzen und trinken*, we wish you no harm, Musketeer Hofmann," he said. His accent was very good, not like most English speakers when they used German. Hofmann could tell this officer wasn't a native German speaker, but it was difficult to guess where he came from.

"*Danke*," said Hofmann and he took up the coffee mug, placed it to his lips and took a long sip of the delicious drink. "*Wunderbar!*"

"You like it then?" said Bergeron. "A long time, hey?"

"Too long, too long," said Hofmann. "We don't get coffee. Just poor substitutes."

"But the food is good?"

"Sausage, black bread and cabbage. Better than at home, though," said the German.

"Been out long?"

"Six months."

"How long in these positions?"

"Couple of weeks." Hofmann scoffed the bread and jam. "This is good, sir."

"Your regiment is a reserve unit, yes?"

Hofmann looked up at Bergeron. "Yes."

"Young men?"

"Yes, and old, and some that aren't fit. What is it you want to know, Captain?"

"You are not stupid, Hofmann. We wish to know the strength and quality of the men we face. And your orders. Will there be an attack?"

Musketeer Daniel Hofmann finished his coffee before answering. "The men will fight, they are soldiers. An attack? Possibly. Probably. How should I know, I'm just a boy!"

★

Bergeron and the other officers were summonsed to HQ early in the morning.

Colonel Anderson-Morshead addressed them. "Gentlemen," he said, "our prisoner may not have spilt the beans, but I'm informed that other German prisoners have divulged information. Also, some escaped French POWs have reported heavy build-up of German forces, tanks and transport. Staff has informed me that an attack is imminent, most probably tomorrow morning. We have our backs to the wall, for sure. The battalion has been badly mauled, as you know. Now we have with us many replacements. Some are from the Yeomanry, but others are young and untried. Nevertheless, we are to be Brigade Reserve, and I have a feeling they will have to fight. General Haig has told us all that every position must be held to the last man."

The battalion, Morshead went on to explain, had been ordered to occupy positions near La Ville aux Bois, on the Bois des Buttes, a wooded sandstone hill – and were to be positioned some 1200 yards behind the front line.

"Captain Bergeron," he said.

"Colonel."

"What are your orders from staff? Are you staying?"

"Staying, Colonel."

The officers were dismissed with a tot of gin. As they left the HQ and walked away from the briefing and back to their men, Bergeron had questions.

"Sutherland," he said, "the CO looks on the young side."

"He's thirty-two. Only took over last month. He's a captain, actually."

"What?"

"Yes. Rupert is substantively still a captain, acting lieutenant colonel," Sutherland said. "He's very good though," he added.

★

Bergeron wasn't asleep, who could be in such circumstances? The tunnels that Anderson-Morshead had moved his battalion into were safe and dry, but far from pleasant. Some of the men were clearly disturbed, either by what they imagined was about to happen or by these underground havens. One soldier had pleaded claustrophobia and had been allowed to sit it out above ground.

Sutherland woke him at about 0100 hours and he immediately tuned in to the sound of explosions ahead of them.

"Better get your helmet, old son," he said.

Then they heard shouting; a gas warning. Bergeron struggled to put on the clumsy gas mask. *Funny*, he thought, *I've been carrying this bloody thing around the whole war long and this is the first time I've used it.*

The gas didn't drift over to them and soon the order came around that it was safe to take the masks off.

At around 0300 hours the German infantry attacked. "Sounds like our boys are taking a beating," said Sutherland. "We'll soon have work to do – I'll bet."

Though it was dark, from the sounds and flashes of light Bergeron and Sutherland could work out that they were being surrounded.

"They're using those blasted stormtrooper tactics again," said Sutherland.

"Yes," agreed Bergeron. "They've got it worked out well. I experienced the same with the Buffs, back in March."

From the direction that the sounds were coming from it was clear that the Germans were intent on advancing rapidly, probing for weak spots and avoiding pockets of resistance. Though Bergeron and Sutherland didn't know it, the trenches in front of them were rapidly infiltrated and overrun and the

2nd Devons were soon the only cohesive unit of any size in Bois des Buttes.

A soldier came up to them. "Orders from the CO, Mr Sutherland," he blurted. "You are to move your men out of the tunnels and occupy defensive positions the best you can, sir."

"I'm coming with you, Desmond," announced Bergeron as he pulled himself up.

Above ground it seemed to the two officers that all hell had broken loose. Sutherland saw men bearing down on them and was about to open fire when he realised they were French soldiers in a hotchpotch of uniform and pyjamas fleeing the German onslaught. Soon they were joined by wounded men from the Middlesex Regiment and later the West Yorkshires.

"Looks like we'll be on our own in this one," said Sutherland, as he began to deploy his men as best he could.

Sergeant Coker ran over to them. "The trenches have been all but blown to blazes in that bombardment, sir," he said to Sutherland.

"Get the men to find what cover they can, Coker. They'll have to put up the best show possible if we're going to halt this blasted attack."

Sutherland's men fought like tigers, living up to the reputation of the Bloody 11th, as did every soldier in the battalion. Bergeron saw that every time the enemy came close they were repelled by determined resistance and fire from rifles and Lewis guns. To Sutherland's right, the cooks and transport men had been deployed ready to fight alongside HQ company. Still, the Devons carried on fighting.

At about 0930 hours Bergeron, Sutherland and some of the company commanders had been called over by Anderson-Morshead for a briefing, when Lance Corporal Jordan, the colonel's batman, noticed something.

"Sir!" he shouted, pointing. "Look there!"

Bergeron and the others all followed Jordan's gaze. The lance corporal had spotted enemy troops marching down the road from Juvincourt. Bergeron looked and thought he could make out a couple of hundred infantry men. Behind them were tanks and guns, with transport following on.

"Bloody hell!" said Sutherland.

Colonel Anderson-Morshead took his pipe from his pocket. As he pushed fresh tobacco into the bowl he casually remarked, "Ah well, Jordan, we shall have to make the best of it! Captain Bergeron."

"Colonel?"

"Feel free to get yourself back to staff HQ. This will probably be your last chance, I fear we are about to be surrounded."

"Perhaps I could be of use here, sir?"

Anderson-Morshead replied quickly, "You're an artillery officer, yes? Experience?"

"I am, sir. Troop commander then FOO."

"Over there," Colonel Anderson-Morshead pointed, "is a troop of gunners without an officer commanding. Can you handle them?"

"Yes, sir!"

"I need them to keep firing their guns for as long as you can make them. Shrapnel – direct role, Captain. Once you feel gunfire is no longer useful, do your best to get them away. Now off you go!"

★

Bergeron ran over to the guns and soon found the most senior NCO, a Sergeant Berry.

"Any officers left?"

"No, sir."

"Ammunition?"

"Plenty, sir."

"Have the lads switch the guns to shrapnel shells. On my order, they're fire directly at the German infantry. Can your boys fire quickly, Sergeant?"

"Yes, sir. Yes, they can."

Bergeron watched and waited until the Germans were into range. "Fire!" he ordered.

He watched as the gunners pushed their fingers into their ears. Lanyards were pulled and the guns exploded in noise and smoke almost simultaneously.

"Reload," ordered Berry, and the well-drilled figures in khaki uniforms moved swiftly to reload. Shrapnel shells were passed from man to man. The gunners cursed and sweated as they reloaded. Bergeron watched as a shell went into the gun, followed by the casing containing explosive. The breech was shut and locked.

"Fire!" Fingers in ears, lanyards pulled. Another explosion of fire, smoke, noise and smell.

Soon, as Colonel Anderson-Morshead had predicted, they were surrounded. Bergeron screamed at his gunners to take up their rifles and fix bayonets and like all soldiers they responded unquestioningly to the voice of authority.

"Now, lads," he said, "you may have thought you were gunners and you might have assumed that you'd never see the whites of the eyes of your enemy. Well, you were wrong. Gunners you were and with determination and a bit of luck, gunners you'll be again – we all shall. But not today. Today, lads, I need you to fight like infantry and I need you to fight for your lives!"

Bergeron carefully peered over the low parapet of the quickly dug trench. He saw German soldiers running towards them, moving rapidly in their keenness to gain the relative safety of cover.

"This is it, boys, make sure you've a cartridge loaded in your chamber," he said quietly, and one or two of the artillerymen pulled on the bolts of their Lee Enfields.

"Present!" he shouted and the rifle barrels appeared over the parapet, pointed towards the advancing Germans. There was no point getting the men to aim.

"Fire!" he shouted.

Six German soldiers fell to the ground, the others ran on – faster now – willing themselves to the safety of the trench.

"Reload. Present. Fire!" ordered Bergeron, and another volley of bullets thundered into the German ranks.

Still they came. "Fire!" he shouted and the German troops hesitated.

"Fire!" roared Bergeron. "Reload and fire at will. Pick your targets, boys – aim well."

Then the Germans began to turn. Bergeron sprang to his feet. "Follow me, the gunners!" he shouted. "Charge!"

The men followed him, each yelling and shouting his own bloodcurdling curses.

No sooner had his men cleared the impending enemy threat with their volley fire and bayonet charge than he ordered them to stop. "Get them back to the trench, Sergeant Berry," he said. "We don't want to be caught out in the open where Gerry's machine guns and trench mortar can find us, do we?" *No*, he thought, *I've seen too often the bloody carnage that results when men are caught in the open.*

Now what to do? Bergeron looked around him. He saw that the field guns would be of no more use, and Anderson-Morshead had instructed him to save the men if he could. The only hope of rescuing his tiny band of gunners was to have them swim. First across the River Aisne and then the Aisne Canal. That route presented the one channel back to British lines – but he must act quickly before the Germans had chance to react.

"Any of you can't swim?" he asked. One soldier waved a weary arm. "What's your name?"

"Gunner Nutbrown, sir," the soldier answered.

"You'd better stick close to me, Nutbrown. Let's hope you float," and even in the desperate circumstances they found themselves in, this raised a smile.

"Come on, lads, spike those guns and we're going to have to swim for it," said the tall Canadian officer that these gunners were warming to, "and if anyone gets his weapon wet, he'll have the regimental sergeant major to answer to once we're back. As well as me."

That raised spirits; clearly this captain thought they might get back to safety.

"Move yourselves, boys," ordered Berry, and off they went.

Each man swam as if his life depended upon his swimming, for it did. Except Gunner Nutbrown who could not swim, so he floated on his back as Bergeron, his captain, pulled him through the flowing water. Eventually, they reached the safety of the southern bank of the Aisne Canal and linked up with British troops there. Their part in the battle of the Bois des Buttes was over.

A WOMAN'S WAR

Anne McKenzie closed the door firmly behind her and stepped out into the cool late summer air. Mush pulled at her leash, already expectant and craving to run freely. "Steady girl, steady," said Anne and she gave a sharp pull which brought the dog's head towards her. Mush looked up at her, crest-fallen.

The two of them, girl and dog, walked briskly along the dirt lane that led from the outskirts of Clifton to both the woods on high ground to the south, and the lake which spread out to the north of the town. Soon it would be time to make the decision, she thought, the one point in each day that she could make an unfettered choice. Today Anne turned left and made for the woods.

As soon as she was clear of the town Anne stopped, reached down and unleashed the Malamute. Mush rewarded her with a grateful bark before bouncing off powerfully into the nearest maple trees.

Anne followed the dog at a more leisurely pace. She noticed that the leaves on those same trees were just starting to curl their ends inwards and the ground around them was beginning to smell of autumn. It had been raining, that was all, she thought. The return of warmth from the sun would quickly bring back the aroma of summer.

Would it? Anne wondered. Would there ever be bright days and sunshine again? Light, carefree days of walking and sitting in sunshine? "Oh, this dreadful, dreadful war!" she shouted out load, causing the Malamute to pause and look towards her.

"Mush!" she cried. "Come, come, come!" The dog quickly responded, reassuring herself that all was well before charging off again, nose held aloft as she followed some distant scent.

Since he left for France in early 1917 Anne McKenzie had written to her *young man*, as her Aunt Audrey suggestively referred to him, regularly until August 1918. That amounted to over a year's worth of musings contained in those letters. What else could she do?

What was the role of a young woman in this war, thousands of miles distant? Aunt Audrey knitted 'comforters' for the troops: hats, socks, scarfs. Anne couldn't knit; she had neither the nimbleness of hand nor the patience. Sally, the elder sister of Anne's best friend Hannah Malport, had volunteered to go to Europe as a nurse; but Anne and Hannah were too young. Anne had read the newspaper stories about those lucky girls in Birmingham and Manchester who worked long hours in factories manufacturing guns and bullets and shells for the war effort, but there was next to no industry here in Canada.

So, whilst her father made his contribution by coming out of retirement to manage a wheat export company, whilst both of her brothers, Johnny and Charles, had joined the army and fought at Vimy, and whilst her mother simply fretted and worried her course through the war, Anne McKenzie wrote letters to Marc Bergeron.

Writing those letters was her war effort.

She wrote because she thought her letters would protect him from the effects of what he saw, what he might have to do and what might be done to him. Put simply, Anne believed her letters might help prevent him being brutalised by the war by keeping him in touch with normality. So, in her writing Anne told him about the changing seasons in Ontario, about the mundane events that rarely troubled the community of Clifton. She told him of her frustration at not knowing what was happening to him, to the Canadian army, in the war generally. Of the latter, all that she, her mother, her sisters, her friends and all those left behind in Clifton knew of the war was what they read in the *Daily Enterprise*. This tended to be two or three days after the events, and anyway was so scant that it gave as much detail about the war in Italy, Russia and Romania as it did about fighting in France which was where, she supposed, Marc still was. If he were alive, that is.

Prior to Marc joining the army and leaving Clifton in January 1916, she hardly took notice of the news. From then on, she read more avidly and tried to make sense of events. She struggled at first with the unfamiliar place names: Arras, Lens, Loos, Verdun and Ypres. She had found a reasonably detailed map of France and Belgium and could now follow events more closely. Nothing seemed to be moving.

The news from the Somme in the July and August of that first year had shocked her as it shocked everybody. The following year, 1917, was much better. The success of the Canadian Army at Vimy Ridge in April reassured her. Other successes, such as General Byng's at Cambrai in November, were much lauded in the newspapers. Following the capture of Jerusalem in December 1917 flags were raised around the town. Nevertheless, that Christmas was a difficult time for the people of Clifton, Prince Edward Island, Ontario and Canada with so many of their young men away.

When news reached Clifton of the German breakthrough in March 1918 and of shells falling on Paris, townsfolk really believed the war was lost. Later, however, news of the Paris Gun broke and headlines told them that the British and French had now checked the German advance. Ludendorff's offensive had failed.

Clifton men were dying or being horrendously wounded

in minute actions of war, so tiny that they never made dispatches let alone the newspapers. News of their deaths came to their families – usually their mothers – by telegram. Worse still was news of a missing soldier. One poor mother had been clinging for over a year on to the hope that her only son – listed as missing – might yet be alive, whilst all those around her believed him to be dead.

Mary Stewart, engaged to Tom Owens at the outbreak and just before Tom enlisted, perhaps had the worst experience of all. Evidently Tom had spoken of Mary to his mates. What man wouldn't? Mary was beautiful. Tom, Mary later learned, had been killed somewhere around Vimy in May 1917. Tom's friend, a soldier called Albert Grey, realising that his fiancée Mary would receive no official notification of his death, must have rifled through Tom's personal effects to find her address and he wrote to her, breaking the ill news.

Albert's letter had sought to conceal nothing and whilst it was nice of him to tell Mary that her love had been well liked throughout the platoon, he also bluntly related to her that Tom "had been caught in the head by a German sniper and died instantly".

Anne had often contemplated that statement and wondered if it were true. She was sure that many – perhaps most – soldiers might have died lingering, agonising deaths and Anne wondered whether Albert Grey, in a bullish way, was trying to help Mary. Soon after, Mary received another letter – this from Tom's platoon commander, a Lieutenant Sturridge – which mentioned no cause of death.

Mary replied to each of them, thanking them for giving her this information – sad as it was.

A month later Mary received back the letter she had sent to Albert Grey. It was marked *Killed in Action*.

Two months after that Mary received a letter from a Mrs Sturridge of Vancouver informing her that she too had been bereaved. Her only son Robert had been killed just two weeks after receiving Mary's letter.

"Oh, this blasted, horrible war," shouted Anne.

Within a nexus of news, no news, assumption, worry, grief and hope, the women of Clifton lived out their war. Anne knew precious little of Marc Bergeron. His letters had been short and gave little clue as to how he really was and how things were in or near combat. She excused him this, given the circumstance: war. He had sought to reassure her, telling her he was fine and was based well behind the front line.

She knew, of course, that his duties as a lieutenant in the Royal Canadian Horse Artillery meant he was indeed far away from bullets and bayonets. But she had also worked out that the German's own artillery would be trying to shell him and his soldiers.

For a while, between January and December 1917, Anne had occasional letters back – seven in total which she kept in a biscuit box in her bedroom locker. Marc wrote to her what he could about where he was, who he had met and what was happening in Europe.

In the fall of 1917 she received a letter that worried her more than anything else. Marc told her that he had been promoted and his new duties meant that he would be attached to an English infantry regiment. That sounded dangerous. Another letter had arrived in December, wishing her and her family a very merry Christmas, but giving no hint whatsoever about where he was or what he had been doing. That letter arrived on the twelfth and had been his last.

Previously, she had been able to call on Marc's elderly mother, Mrs Bergeron, and compare notes with her. Between them they made just a little more sense of what he had been up to. Mrs Bergeron, however, had left Clifton in the summer of 1917 to live with her sister in Rottingdean, England, and nobody had heard from her since. Mrs Bergeron had asked

Anne if she would mind taking in Mush, Bergeron's Alaskan Malamute, and of course Anne had agreed.

So, Anne waited. On the first Monday of every month throughout 1918 she had written to Marc. Nothing came in return. She assumed he was killed. News would have been sent to Mrs Bergeron in England, but she must have been too distraught at the loss of her only son to let Anne know. In August she had written a letter to Marc that had been so painful for her, in the knowledge that he was probably dead, that she swore to herself it would be the last. In it she explained to him why she wrote, urged him to believe that every word she wrote was true and declared her undying love for him. She sealed, addressed and posted that letter, and it had indeed been her last. Anne simply could not bear the pain of writing any longer.

All that remained of the man she loved was a biscuit tin of rather curt letters and a dog named Mush.

Anne knew nothing of the complexity of battalion, regimental and divisional commands. In the late spring of 1918 Bergeron had been moved from the English East Kents to a staff position at HQ. Later he had been attached to the Devonshire Regiment and then the South Devon Light Infantry. These postings and re-postings were almost bound to test army logistics and cause problems in the delivery of mail.

Nor did Anne know of the mix-up in communication between the administrative units of the Canadian and British armies, which caused her letters to remain in the post room of the Buffs' home barracks in Canterbury.

Anne had continued to address her letters to him at his original posting, the Royal Canadian Horse Artillery. The last letter he had received from her was the one that she had written on Monday 6 August 1917.

Whilst Anne believed him dead, Marc Bergeron assumed she had ceased to write having found somebody else.

FAREWELL DOCTOR WESTON

Bergeron was ready for the journey back to England.

He and Gerry Finn, as walking wounded officers, had seats in first class on the train bound for Le Havre. Bergeron was carrying a stout walking stick which had been a gift to him from Soignon. The French officer, now a double amputee, had no further use for the stick, but still it was generous of him, thought Bergeron. "I shall always call it Soignon, after its first owner," he had told the Frenchman before they left. "*Adieu, Monsieur Capitaine.*"

Nurse Isobel Harris was on the train too, tending to the more serious cases in a bedded truck towards the rear of the train.

"You're lucky to have been discharged, Gerry," said Bergeron. "I'll probably be back there by mid next year."

"Sorry, old man, luck of the blasted draw. At least you've got both arms." He smiled.

"Look at this," said Finn, pointing with his left hand. "Just like the bloody British army, class ridden from top to bottom. When I was taking my exams back in Blighty before being sent out to Armageddon, I remember a question that was all bound up by class. Now how did it go...?"

Bergeron had bid farewell to Mary Weston that morning. It hadn't gone at all well, he thought. He had wanted to tell her how much he admired her, how beautiful he thought she was and how he would very much like to get to know her better. He had wanted to ask if he might write to her once he was safely in England, and he might try to visit her, if she approved, upon re-joining the staff or his regiment in France.

In the event, he had thanked her for her good work in the operating theatre and, before he had uttered another word, Mary had rushed away as yet another emergency case was brought into the hospital. *Damnation!*

"Oh, I remember, something about being at a station with a platoon of men. Train gets in late and has only two carriages – first and second class – instead of the three you had been expecting. What would you do? Go on, Bergeron, what would you do?"

Bergeron looked at Soignon's stick. It was made from three types of wood: oak in the main, with a handle carved from a single piece of a rich, dark wood with natural holes that Bergeron did not recognise and with a boss made from walnut. It had game animals carved into the handle: a deer, a wild boar and some rabbits. A brass ferrule protected the narrow end and, Bergeron suspected, a rod of iron or steel must run through the whole thing giving it strength and durability.

"Well," he answered, "first I'd make sure the men all had enough room. Then I'd give the NCOs the best first class seats I could find for them."

"Why?"

"Because I know too bloody well that it's the NCOs, the sergeants and corporals that I'll be relying on once we're in action. I want them properly rested. What's more, I don't want any one of them to be holding a grudge against me."

"You're totally bloody right, of course. But you'd have failed the test. Bad luck, old man."

The voyage was rough. Gerry Finn was sick almost the whole time and Nurse Harris had to take him away so that the sounds of his constant retching and the reek of his vomit didn't prevent the others from getting some rest, though

Bergeron suspected it was a rouse on Gerry's part, contrived so that he would get to spend some time with the pretty nurse.

Southampton was busy. *The proverbial beehive*, thought Bergeron, with boats and trains coming and going. An orderly directed the wounded ensemble and their nurses towards a hospital train that waited for the officers. A private carriage was there to meet Finn, who was being discharged.

"You'll look me up in London once you're mobile?" asked Finn.

"You can count on it, Gerry," and with that Bergeron limped over to the train.

"Where are we heading?" he asked the orderly.

"Oxford, sir."

PART TWO

BACK TO BLIGHTY, 1918–19

ALDERSHOT

Sergeant May felt lucky. Lucky to be alive; lucky to have come through the war unscathed. His battalion had been one of the first to be sent back to England following the Armistice in November. Others went to Germany, some to Russia, but the 3rd South Devons were back in Blighty. Not demobilised, not yet home in their Totnes barracks, but for now, he thought, Aldershot would do. With a bit of luck, he'd be home for Christmas.

May was having a cigarette in the sergeants' mess when Tregaskis and Tucker, sergeants from A Company, came over to find him.

"Got a message for you," said Tregaskis. "Bumped into an officer in town, says he knows you and has something of yours to return."

"What's his name?"

"Bergeron. A Canadian," said Tucker.

"We told him you'd be able to pop out this evening, so he said he'd wait for you in the Rose. What's he got of yours then?"

"Dunno, but I recognise the name. Captain Bergeron was a real gent. Bit of a drinker though, maybe I lent him a bottle opener or something. Must have done, I suppose. I'll just have to go over there and find out," he said, putting out his cigarette and standing up.

"You do that, Fanny. And if there's money involved, then

just you remember me and Alf here did our bit too," and all three NCOs laughed at the thought.

★

May strolled out of the barracks and into town. The Rose and Crown was a regular haunt for soldiers on leave. He wove and forced his way through the crowded room to the bar. He saw Bergeron at the far end drinking from a small glass, and immediately caught his eye. Bergeron beckoned him over.

"Sergeant May." He offered a hand. "So pleased to see you again. How are you?"

"Fine, sir. I'm just fine. And you, sir?"

"I'm well enough, thanks. Well, to be honest I'm nowhere close to fully recovered," he pointed to Soignon, "but I'm determined to get there. This is my first time out alone, as it happens. May, I never did catch your first name."

"Francis, sir."

"And you can drop the sir, Francis."

"Thanks. My mates call me Fanny."

"Well, Fanny, I suppose you're wondering what it is of yours I have to return to you. Well, sorry to disappoint you, but I don't have anything. As a matter of fact, Fanny May, you have something for me."

May looked bemused.

"Have a drink, Fanny?"

"Bitter, please."

Bergeron ordered and they were served two drinks.

"I'm interested in finding out about the death of Lieutenant Wainwright, Fanny. I've already spoken to Bombardier Ryan. I want to hear your version of events."

May looked away. He took a long, long drink from his glass.

"Take your time, Fanny. Just tell me what happened, as you remember it, and take as long as you like."

May drank more beer before he spoke. When he eventually did speak, he did so in a slow and deliberate voice. Bergeron thought it was as though May had thought through the details beforehand.

"Me and the Lewis gun section was in reserve and the boss, Mr Wainwright that is, was up front with the rest of the platoon. At about 2130 hours, about that time – just as it was proper dark, anyway – I hear a single shot and a shout. Then more shots – sounded like pistol shots – and a flare goes up. Then all hell breaks loose. You know what it's like, Captain Bergeron. Everyone on that front is shooting into no man's land. Then there's a call goes out, 'Medic! Medic!' Next thing our Toch Emmas are going off and the Hun's machine guns join in. It took a good twenty minutes for all of that to die down. Later the medics come back with a body on their stretcher. It was Mr Wainwright."

"Bombardier Ryan told me he didn't think Wainwright was killed in an enemy raid."

Sergeant May looked worried; he took another drink. "All as I know is that Lieutenant Wainwright caught a shot in the head, Captain."

"What?"

"Yes. Yes, that's right. And not just that." May's hand was trembling. "He copped a bullet through the back of the head."

"How do you know that, Fanny?"

"Like I said, once everything was quiet again – just the odd shot going off – a stretcher team came up and it passed right by me. The lieutenant was laid on it, but they hadn't covered him. Either that or the sheet had fallen off. I shone a torch on him. He was on his back, Captain Bergeron, and had an almighty hole in the front of his face. Exit wound, no doubt about it."

"You sure?"

"Perfectly sure. Had a word with the medic. 'What did that?' I asked him. Medic turned Wainwright over for me to see – smaller hole, nice and clean, in the back of his head. No mistake, Captain Bergeron, shot in the head – from close range, I'd say."

May had finished his beer, so Bergeron bought them each a refill.

"Let me get this straight. A German raiding party gets into our front-line trench without being noticed. The first soldier they come across is Lieutenant Wainwright, who just happens to have his back to them and doesn't hear them. They shoot him... you said you heard a single shot first?"

"Correct."

"They shoot him in the back of the head at close range. Then they do a bit more shooting and clear off, without anybody seeing them. Is that right, Fanny?"

"Correct." The sergeant took a long drink of his beer and paused to wipe the froth from his lips.

"Except you've missed out Major Cross. Tell me about him, Fanny."

"About fifteen minutes before the raid, Major Cross walks past my dugout. 'Inspecting the front line, Sergeant. Care to join me?' he says. Anyway, off he goes and, as I say, fifteen minutes or so later I hear a shot and up goes the flare. Then those other shots, they were all pistol shots. I can't remember hearing a rifle go off, not at the start."

"Are you trying to tell me something, Fanny?"

"Following the stretcher party came Major Cross. 'What happened, sir?' I asked him. He told me that he saw the German raiding party, loosed off his revolver at them, fired the flare and called the medics in."

"Did you believe him, Fanny?"

"Yes. But, well, we all knew the boss was angry at the charge they'd put on CSM Tozer. He blew his fuse when he found out Tozer was dead, and how he'd died. Blamed Major Cross and Captain Wadham. You ask me did I believe Major Cross… well, I don't know for sure."

May took another long drink, this time emptying his pint glass.

"I do know this much: Lieutenant Wainwright getting shot did both the major and Captain Wadham a really good turn."

"You think Cross bumped him off, don't you, Fanny?"

The sergeant stared into the empty glass. "I didn't say that," he muttered.

"Cross. Bloody Cross, why is he always around when things get dirty?"

Bergeron looked May in the eye. "Cross is a bastard all right, but murder? No. He can't have done, Fanny, you said he invited you to come on the inspection with him."

"All for show. Well, of course I wouldn't join him, I was dry and comfy. He knew that! He knew I wouldn't, he knew I was all wrapped up with a cup of tea. Anyway, if I'd have said 'yes' what has he lost? Nothing. Would simply have done it on another occasion. Come on, Captain Bergeron, when did you ever see Major Cross doing an evening inspection? I'll bet never!"

"And you'd win, Fanny. Yes, you'd sure win that bet. Not like Cross at all, is it? The bastard!"

"I'm sorry, Captain Bergeron."

"Sorry?"

"Probably should have said something to someone at the time." May seemed frightened.

"Who could you have told, Fanny?"

"Well, that's just it. Couldn't tell anyone."

"So stop worrying over it, you're not to blame."

"What's going to happen, Captain Bergeron?"

"Nothing, Fanny. Nothing's going to happen. And listen, it'll be for the best that you simply forget what we've been talking about, understood, Fanny?"

"Yes, Captain Bergeron." Fanny May stood up and saluted. Bergeron returned the salute and took something from his pocket.

"Here, take this." Bergeron handed May a cigarette lighter. It was heavy and well-made of good quality brass.

"They're bound to ask," he said. "What will you do now the war's over, Fanny?"

"I want to get back to Newton Abbot just as quick as I can. Hopefully I'll get back my old job in Tucker's Maltings and, if she'll have me, I'll marry Maisie."

"I hope you do that, Fanny. I really hope so. Listen, you just forget about all this now, put it behind you. Goodbye, Sergeant Fanny May, and good luck."

HOSPITAL BLUES

He puffed and panted his way up the steep hill that took him from Winchester station towards Jeffries' place. The morning air was still cold and he could see his breath starching out before him each time he exhaled. It was January. The fields around Christ Church college had been covered with frost when he'd walked through them on his way to Oxford station.

Bergeron had hoped he would have been recovered by now, and he was surprised at just how unfit the injuries had made him. Soignon was a huge help. Wounded servicemen of other ranks wore hospital blues which Bergeron found garish and cheap looking. He was pleased that officers could sport their number two dress, and his attracted more than a few tipping of hats from men and inviting smiles from young ladies. Or at least he thought them inviting; perhaps it was his imagination.

The hill was steep. Bergeron stopped twice and began to wonder was it worth the effort. But he had to see Jeffries. He had written a couple of weeks previously to announce his intention, not mentioning the intended subject matter of subsequent conversation.

He knocked at the door of a large, lodge-like building which stood in front of a college.

Jeffries answered the door himself.

"Bergeron, Happy New Year!" he said. "Good to see you!"

"Likewise, likewise. I wonder what 1919 holds in store for us. Wilfred, I need to sit down, if you don't mind."

Jeffries pointed him towards a comfy chair. "Want a drink?" he asked.

"Need one, actually!"

Jeffries brought two large glasses of scotch and set them on a low table in front of a roaring fire.

"Cheers."

"Cheers, Wilfred."

"What do you want to know about? Your letter didn't give too much away."

"I'm trying to find out exactly what happened the night Billy Wainwright was killed. You were duty officer, weren't you?"

"Yes, I was the duty officer that night," said Jeffries. He was dressed in a lounge suit with a gaudy cravat around his neck. He was smoking through a long silver holder what smelled to Bergeron like a rather fine cigarette.

"As you know, Bergeron, that means I was based in company HQ – well, more of an enlarged dugout really." Jeffries lit another cigarette. "Major Cross came by at about 2030 and said he was going through to the front line to inspect it."

"Didn't that strike you as odd?" asked Bergeron.

"Not at first. He was fully entitled to, of course. Any officer commanding can go and inspect who or what he likes, you know that, Bergeron. So, to answer your question, old man, no not odd in principle. Odd behaviour for Major Cross? Yes. He didn't usually show that much interest."

"Did you ask him what he was up to?"

"Of course I bloody didn't. Who do you think I am? Wainwright's platoon was holding the front with Wadham's lads in the support trench taking things easy. Major Cross said he wanted to have a look at the condition of the front-line trench and wanted to make sure young Wainwright had sentries properly deployed. I reassured him, politely, that he needn't worry regarding Wainwright's competence. I knew Billy would be going by the book, but Cross was well within his rights to go and have a peek. He was OC after all, Bergeron."

"Where was Wadham while all this was going on?"

"I assume the captain was back in the support trenches with his men."

"What happened next?"

"For a while, nothing. Then there were some shots. Up went a flare and all bloody hell broke loose on both sides. It was pandemonium! Emma Gees, Toc Emmas, rifle fire – the works." Jeffries drew on his cigarette.

"Go on."

"Look, Bergeron, what's all this about?"

"Just trying to establish what happened to Wainwright."

"We all know what happened to poor old Wainwright. He was killed. Shot during a German raid on our trenches."

"Did you write the report?"

"Yes."

"Who did you interview?"

"A couple of NCOs. Can't remember their names."

"Doesn't matter," said Bergeron. "What I want to know is this: who saw Fritz?"

"I didn't ask the major anything, but he told me that he saw several shapes in the trench – men. He threw up the Very light. In the light of the flare, he said he saw a section of Germans making off to their own lines."

"And did the non-coms verify that?"

"No. Nobody else saw any of the Boche."

"Any dead or wounded Germans out there next morning?"

"No. Nothing."

"How was Major Cross armed when he went up?"

"Service revolver."

"Did he use it?"

"He said he'd let off a couple of rounds at the Germans."

"Jeffries, did you inspect the body, or talk to the stretcher bearers at all?"

"No. No need to… was there?"

"How did Cross seem afterwards?"

"At first he seemed flustered. Then depressed. With yet another junior officer gone I think he'd had enough by then."

Bergeron drank the remaining drops from his glass.

"Want another?"

"Please."

Jeffries topped up both of their glasses. Bergeron looked around the large, comfortable room.

"Nice place you've got here, Wilfred."

"Yes. My father is principal of the college. House comes with the job. Winchester is so very nice. You should come in the summer, Bergeron."

"Marc, please."

Jeffries thought for a few moments. He lit yet another cigarette and puffed away on it.

"Marc, let me tell you what I think happened. Only, I don't think it would be a good idea if it all came out. Wainwright's family, you know. It's probably best left alone."

"I've no intention of going to Gee-Gee, nor the newspapers – if that's what you think."

"Do you know what became of the CSM?"

"Yes."

"When you were in hospital, Wainwright kicked up an awful fuss at the way Tozer was being treated. Blew off in front of me, Wizzo and the others. Demanded all charges be dropped. The major listened to him. I think if it had just been Cross he may have taken notice, but Wadham had really dug in his heels by then. You know that Captain Wadham hated Tozer."

Jeffries paused and drew on his cigarette.

"Anyway, then we got the news that Tozer was dead. That was the day before the trench raid. Well, the major was at battalion HQ, as I said. Wainwright was all for going there to tell Gee-Gee what had happened in front of Cross. Speed and I calmed him down a bit. Wadham looked really worried."

They looked at each other, both men holding their whisky glasses. Bergeron looked hard into Jeffries' eyes, trying to guess what was running through his mind. It was Jeffries who eventually broke the silence.

"You asked about the body, about the medics. Do you know anything?"

"Yes," answered Bergeron. "Sergeant May insists that Wainwright died from a single shot, back of the head and at close range."

"Oh my God!"

"Doesn't sound like Fritz's work, does it?"

"It had to be Cross, didn't it?"

"Do you think so, Wilfred?"

"Who else could it have been?"

★

Bergeron strolled down the steep hill towards Winchester railway station. Outside the hospital on his right were soldiers in the blue uniforms of the wounded. On his left was the prison rotunda. Soon he was Oxford bound, having caught the first London-bound train from Winchester, and changed at Basingstoke to a connection for Reading and from there through to Oxford. He had dozed throughout the journey, his unsettled imaginings preventing proper sleep. Between them, May and Jeffries seemed to confirm much of what Don Ryan suspected. He didn't know the full story about Tozer's execution, but he was certain that he had enough evidence of Cross's part in Billy Wainwright's murder. As for Tozer, however, Bergeron was at a loss. Why? Why had Cross murdered CSM Tozer?

He needed to talk to Gerry Finn.

THE ONE-ARMED SOLICITOR

Oxford wasn't a bad base. The journeys to Aldershot and Winchester had been straightforward. Getting to London was easier still. Bergeron took a cab from Paddington station to Lincoln's Inn Fields. He got out carefully, putting a lot of weight onto trusty Soignon. His leg was mending, but anything more than a short walk set it off aching. These cold February mornings didn't help much, either.

He climbed the steps to the offices of Anderson & Finn, Solicitors at Law. At the polished oak reception desk, he asked for "Mr Gerald Finn, please. A personal call, tell him."

The receptionist took him up to Gerry's office. The room smelt of wax polish and stale tobacco. Gerry's desk was littered with papers, without any obvious organisation about them. Bergeron walked to the nearest bookshelf. There were the sorts of legal texts he might have expected. Then there were others which seemed to be a collection of histories of law, such as Fitzjames' *History of the Criminal Law;* Hallam's *The Constitutional History of England from Henry VII [1457] to George II [1760]* and Maitland's *History of English Law. Well, the desk's a mess, but at least Gerry keeps his books in good alphabetical order,* thought Bergeron.

He walked over to another bookcase, by the window. *Now,* he thought, *these are philosophies. What are you up to, Gerry?* Plato and the other Greeks were there. Then a collection of British texts: JS Mill, Hulme and Bentham. There were books by

European philosophers of whom he had heard: Descartes, Kant and Leibniz. There were other volumes by authors unknown to him. He moved to take one of these from the shelf – Nietzsche: *Der Antichrist*, 1888 – mainly because the title was so intriguing. Instead out popped an unbound book, or portfolio, which had been jammed in beside Nietzsche. In his hand he found a plain, red leather folder without imprint. He opened it in the middle and found poorly typed script with handwritten notes over it. Then he turned to the first page; typed in block capital letters it read *TRACTATUS LOGICO-PHILOSOPHICUS* BY LUDWIG JOSEF JOHANN WITTGENSTEIN. *Never heard of him*, thought Bergeron, and he put the portfolio back in its place.

Eventually, the door opened with a creak and Gerry Finn came into the room.

"Good to see you looking so well, Marc."

"You too, Gerry."

"Shall we pop out for a drink?"

"No, I'm still finding it painful to walk far. Gerry, have you ever been to Winchester?"

"Not recently. Why?"

"It's fascinating, actually. The hospital, prison, the barracks and the college – all four of them on the hill. I was there a day or so back and it struck me as somewhat ironic that those four institutions – the prison, the hospital, the barracks and the teacher training college – were all in such proximity overlooking the ancient city and its cathedral. Four very different institutions, yes. But in a sense, all so similar: uniforms, timetables, some in 'authority' over the rest, rules and regulations."

"You're getting altogether too thoughtful, old man. Good old Bentham was responsible for the shape of the prison, I suppose."

"Gerry, I need you to do something for me, if you can. Two things, actually."

"Just ask, old boy," said Finn.

"April 1917, France. A farmhouse near Vimy was accidentally shelled by my outfit. *Accidental*. Was any of it an accident? Anyway, I want to find out if there are any survivors. Can you do it?"

"Can you be more specific about where this farm was?"

"Yes."

"Probably, then, I expect so. It'll cost you, mind. I'll have to get a Frog associate to make enquiries. Debreux in Arras would do a good job for us."

"Don't worry about the cost, Gerry. Just find out for me, please."

"You said there were two things."

"Yes. I need you trace somebody for me, Gerry."

"Who?"

"A Mrs Wainwright. Her son, William, was a subaltern in the SDLI. I need to speak to her – about her son, I promised him. Find her for me, please, Gerry."

"I'll try."

Bergeron stood up; Finn followed suit and these friends, united by war wounds and common experiences, shook hands awkwardly.

"Thanks, Gerry. I do appreciate your time and advice. By the way, can I use you as a forwarding address? You know I'm a bit of a loose cannon just now. No fixed abode. I'm hoping to get out of that bloody hospital soon, but little idea of where I'll be staying afterwards."

"Of course you can, Marc. Of course." Gerry Finn took a card from the top of a small stack of business cards on his desk.

"Take this," he said, and handed Bergeron a card.

"Father's offered me a full-time job once I'm properly fit. You'll always be able to get me here, and we just had a telephone fitted. You never know when you might need a lawyer, or a friend."

"Thanks again, Gerry."

DEVON CREAM

He just hadn't anticipated Sarah Wainwright and as he lay in bed – still unable, or unwilling, to sleep – he reflected on the day.

The spring of 1919 had turned to summer uneventfully for him. At last good old Gerry Finn had contacted him to say he had found Wainwright's mother. Mrs Wainwright had moved in with her brother and sister-in-law. Collingwood advertised himself as purveyor of fine meats, pointed out Finn, sarcastically, and was based in South Devon.

Bergeron had written to Collingwood posing as Lieutenant Marcus Berg. He said he had been a friend of Billy Wainwright in France and was searching for Mrs Wainwright. Collingwood had immediately invited him down.

Cyril Collingwood's man had been waiting for Bergeron at Diptford station, in an old but perfectly serviceable one-horse carriage. It had taken all of ten minutes; they could have walked the distance in fifteen, to reach the Collingwood household – a fine early Victorian townhouse which looked a little out of place in what was an unpretentious village. Bergeron suspected the carriage was for show.

"It must be Lieutenant Berg? Come in, my dear boy, come in," greeted Collingwood. "Come in, Lieutenant, make yourself at home, you are most welcome in my house."

The room was large, with fireplaces at both ends and heavy wooden panelling all around reaching up to shoulder height.

At one end was a three-piece suite, upholstered in brown leather and a high-backed chair in dark wood with red velvet upholstery. Heavy red curtains hung from the windows of the two large bays.

The other end of the room, where they now stood, was evidently the family dining area, dominated by a long table and six chairs.

Bergeron found himself scrutinised by two women. The first, who looked to be something close in age to Collingwood, with grey hair and wearing wire-rimmed spectacles, was, he supposed, Collingwood's wife. She was dressed most bizarrely in a floor-length dress which seemed homemade of a floral print material. Standing to her left was a younger woman – possibly in her late thirties or very early forties. She was tall, slim and rather elegant looking, thought Bergeron. He could tell from the way these women looked at him that he was clearly the object of their immediate interest.

"I'll make the introductions," said Collingwood. "This is my wife, Susan. Susan, meet Lieutenant Berg," with which Collingwood turned to the younger woman on his left.

Mrs Collingwood stepped forward and offered her hand. Bergeron took it and gently pressed his large fingers around hers. "A pleasure, Mrs Collingwood," he said.

"Susan, Susan, please – we seldom stand on ceremony in this house." Mrs Collingwood smiled, revealing wonderfully attractive creases at the corners of her mouth.

"That's right. That's how we do things," said Collingwood.

"Then please call me Marcus," said Bergeron.

Susan Collingwood had jet black hair which she wore pulled back from her face. This served to emphasise her dark brown eyes whilst accentuating the fine lines of her nose and jaw. She was modestly dressed in a full-length black skirt, a white blouse and a black cardigan.

Collingwood then turned to the older woman. "And this is my twin sister, Dorothy Wainwright, whom you have come to see."

"I'm so pleased to meet you, Mr Berg... Marcus," she said, offering her hand.

Just then a young woman ran into the room and Collingwood announced, "and this is my niece, Sarah. Meet Lieutenant Marcus Berg, Sarah."

He guessed that she was about nineteen or twenty years old. She was of medium height, fair-haired, full-lipped and utterly, totally beautiful, thought Bergeron. Complementing her mother's style, Sarah Wainwright was also dressed in an untypical fashion: floral dress of a similar print to her mother's, but in Sarah's case much shorter. Shorter than would be considered decent in London, thought Bergeron. But this was Devon; fashions were different everywhere.

Bergeron offered her his hand. "I am delighted to meet you," he greeted and he felt himself blush ever so slightly.

The girl took his hand, and squeezed it firmly. "It's nice to meet you too, Marcus," she said, taking slightly too long to let go of his hand.

"It's such a lovely afternoon," said Susan Collingwood. "Why don't we take tea in the garden?" she asked, rhetorically.

Later, in their garden, the Collingwoods, Bergeron and Dorothy Wainwright sat on powder blue-coloured chairs. They were seated around a similarly coloured cast iron table that was covered by a lace tablecloth. On the cloth were Wedgewood plates bearing scones, jam and Devon clotted cream. There were matching teacups.

Beside them, Sarah lay back in a deck chair. She had her eyes closed and was showing her knees, her ankles covered by tiny white socks.

The scene was perfect, the late summer sunshine glorious and so too were Sarah's calves, thought Bergeron.

The girl opened her eyes, caught Bergeron looking at her and smiled. He smiled back at her.

At last a maid brought out a steaming pot of tea.

"Dorothy, please do us the honours," said Collingwood.

"Do you take milk, Marcus?" asked Collingwood's sister.

"Yes please."

She went on to pour milk into each cup, which Bergeron thought odd as both his mother and Aunt Maude always poured the tea first. He thought that was the English way.

Fussing around the tea helped to take his mind off Sarah.

Susan Collingwood offered him a plate on which she had placed two halves of a scone. "Have you encountered clotted cream before, Marcus?" she asked.

"No, I'm afraid not," he said.

"Then do help yourself," said Susan. "There's a lot of gossip about the order we do the cream and the jam, but it doesn't really matter."

Bergeron pushed a small spoon into the cream. It was thick, with a crust. He took a large portion and spread it roughly onto half a scone. Then he dived into the jam pot and placed a dollop of red jam on top of the cream.

"I'll say it matters, Susan. Jam first is Cornish. Cream first if in Devon. Look at Marcus, he does it right without thinking," pointed out Collingwood.

"Magnificent house, Cyril," said Bergeron.

"Indeed, indeed, and I know what you're thinking, my boy. How does a butcher afford a house like that?"

"Marcus, my husband is not a butcher, though he once was. He is a businessman." Susan over-emphasised the last word.

"Used to be a butcher," said Collingwood. "Used to own a butcher's shop in Aveton Gifford. Shop was left to me by my father, Francis Collingwood. He taught me all I know about butchering."

Bergeron took a sip of tea and tried to look interested.

"Problem was there was another butcher in the village and not enough custom for each of us."

"So, Cyril bought him out and closed his shop," interjected Dorothy.

"That meant I got all the business. What's more, I could let out the other premises as a shop with accommodation – with a clause in the lease to prevent any butchering or selling of meat to carry on there. I get a reasonable rent."

"Reasonable? Come on, Cyril," said Susan Collingwood, "your income shot up!"

Collingwood smiled and nodded; he didn't quite rub his hands together, but Bergeron would not have been surprised if he had.

"So I decided to expand. I started to buy butchers shops in many of the villages around here."

"Then you had your best idea, Cyril. Tell Marcus."

"My second-best idea, actually. My best was marrying you, dear." Collingwood smiled genially at his wife. "Well, the one problem I still had was that I was always having to pay over the odds to the abattoirs for fresh meat. To solve it, I decided to set up my own abattoir and a wholesale business selling meat and meat products. Now the canny thing I did was to make sure my own shops got a better price than my competitors. They began to struggle. I moved in to buy them out. Where there was more than one, I'd close down the others in the same way as I did in Aveton Gifford."

"Sounds a very good business model, Cyril."

"Oh yes, made me thousands. But I always kept the original butchers' name. Try as hard as you will, Marcus, you'll only find one Collingwood's butchers' shop in the whole of the South Hams, even though about seventy per cent of them belong to me. That's the one in Aveton Gifford."

Dorothy took off her glasses and rubbed the bridge of her nose. "You were in France with Billy, Marcus?"

"Yes, I was."

"Were you with him when he was killed?"

"I'm sorry to say that I wasn't, but I did speak to him shortly before he was killed. He was in very good spirits," he said.

"I have always wanted to know how he died. Can you understand that?"

"I can try," he answered.

"Now, now, Dot. Don't go bothering Marcus with that!" said Collingwood.

"It's fine, really, Cyril. Do carry on," said Bergeron.

"Sarah, please come and help me with these hydrangeas," said Susan.

"No. I want to listen."

Susan Collingwood rose and left the table. Sarah started, rocked the deck chair, got to her feet and sat in the chair next to Bergeron.

"Then I'll leave you three alone," said Collingwood as he followed his wife. "By the way, you will stay the night, Marcus?"

"I couldn't possibly."

"Oh, but you must," said Dorothy.

"Yes, do stay! Please!" said Sarah.

"She likes the idea of having somebody her own age around, with her brother dead," said Dorothy.

"But I didn't bring any things."

"I can loan you some pyjamas and a dressing gown. The housekeeper will get your clothes washed and dried by the morning. It's no bother," said Collingwood.

Bergeron thought of the journey back to Oxford and the rickety cast iron bedstead there. Then he considered a comfortable, warm bed in Cyril Collingwood's house. "That would be grand, Cyril. Wonderful! Thank you so much."

"Do you know what I did in the war, Marcus?"

Bergeron felt and no doubt, he thought, looked awkward.

"Of course, you don't, how could you? Silly of me to ask. I supervised the collection of Sphagnum moss from the moor. That was my war effort. Got scores of women from all over the South Hams – Totnes, lots of them were from – and we collected, cleaned and packaged Sphagnum moss. Literally tons of it!"

"It was very useful to us, as a wound dressing. Your work was indeed very important."

Dorothy Wainwright looked at Bergeron, studying his expressionless face.

"I received a letter. From my son's commanding officer. I always carry it with me, but it's vague. I wonder if you might…"

"Yes, of course."

She fussed around in a handbag. Bergeron had long wondered just what these things were that women filled up their bags with. Eventually she brought out an envelope which she offered to him.

Bergeron hesitated. He looked at Dorothy. Collingwood had said she was his twin, but now he thought she looked much older than her brother. That was what war did – to those left at home as well as to those who suffered at the front.

He took the envelope.

"Do open it, Marcus."

Bergeron opened the envelope and took from it a letter which he unfolded and began reading.

Battalion HQ
3 South Devon Light Infantry
27 August 1918

Dear Mrs Wainwright,

It is with the deepest regret and sympathy that I write to you about your son, Lieutenant William Cecil Wainwright, who was killed in action whilst under my command. William was a fine officer, popular with his fellows and respected by his men.

If it is any consolation to you, Mrs Wainwright, I would have you know that your son was killed instantly. I have spoken with his men and they inform me that he was shot through the heart whilst leading them in repelling an enemy raid on our lines. I am sure he did not feel a thing.

Your son, my lieutenant, was gallant to the end, Mrs Wainwright.

Yours sincerely,
Major Malaby Cross, Officer Commanding D Company, 3 SDLI

"What I want to know is this, Marcus: when the major writes that my son, William, was killed instantly and did not feel a thing, well, is he telling the truth? Or is this what every mother reads?"

"Mrs Wainwright, I do not know what every mother reads. Yet I am sure of this: his men told Major Cross that your son was shot through the heart. In that case, he would have died instantly, I have seen it. I am sure that he felt nothing."

Susan Collingwood came back over to the table holding some cut flowers. She smiled at Bergeron.

"Hold these, Sarah. I'll go and fetch a vase," she said.

"Dorothy," asked Bergeron, "do you have anything else of Billy's? I remember he kept a diary – he was rather keen on it, actually. I just wondered if it had made its way safely back to you."

"About a month after he died we received a parcel from the military. I wouldn't open it. I left it to Sarah."

Bergeron looked at Sarah, trying not to make it seem obvious. She was an incredibly pretty girl, that was for sure. He had thought upon meeting her that there was something else, something about her features which puzzled him. Now he realised what it was: Sarah Wainwright's face was the exact feminine likeness of her brother's.

"I still have it," said Sarah. "That parcel. Perhaps, we can have a look together if you would like to, Marcus."

"Well… I don't wish to intrude, I was only concerned that the family had received Billy's things."

"Go and look, Marcus. If there is anything there that you would like to hold onto as a memento of Billy, then you have my blessing to keep it," said Dorothy Wainwright.

Sarah was on her feet. "Come on," she said.

★

They went into an inside room with a table and chairs, where Bergeron waited until Sarah Wainwright came in with the parcel. It had obviously been opened.

"There's not much in the parcel," she offered. "Billy's tunic and cap, a few papers. Here." She handed Bergeron a paper. He took it and read it quickly.

"He was going to send this to your mother. Has she read it?"

"No, I told her about it, but she insists that she doesn't want to see it."

"May I?" He took hold of Lieutenant Wainwright's jacket.

"Of course," said Sarah. "Don't you think it odd, Marcus, that there is no blood on it? The letter says Billy was shot in the heart."

"This won't be the one he was wearing," he lied.

Bergeron held up the jacket. *Thank God it's not blood-stained*, he thought. He examined the pockets of the tunic. Nothing in the four exterior pockets, as he thought, for surely Sarah would have searched through these.

"No diary?" he asked. "I think it was green."

"Yes," she replied. "It's here."

Sarah Wainwright looked intensely at Bergeron. "I've read every word inside it. Take it, you can give it back tomorrow before you leave."

★

After tea Cyril Collingwood took Bergeron to one side and offered him tobacco.

"You'll have to excuse my sister, Marcus," he said.

"Not at all, Cyril."

"It's not just this thing with her son, we can all understand that. But Dorothy isn't like the rest of us, she's much more, erm, Bohemian, I think the word is. She married an artist, you see. This Wainwright chap was from London. He moved down to Salcombe to paint. Odd man – had an influence on my sister. They brought the children up to speak out – be themselves and say what they thought and bugger everyone else! Since her husband died, well, Dorothy has become something of a 'free spirit' – and the girl, she smokes!"

"Oh, really?" Bergeron took Gerry Finn's card from a pocket. "By the way, Cyril, could I possibly make a telephone call from here?"

"Sorry, not a hope, Marcus. No telephone lines here."

★

The room that Susan Collingwood had shown him to was small and wonderfully cosy. The single bed was comfortable and he was snug under its blankets and cream-coloured candlewick bedspread. Yet Bergeron dared not allow himself the pleasure of sleep.

He dared not sleep for fear that he might dream, and in his dream – his nightmare – he might shout out loud and wake the household. True, this room was tucked away at the rear of the house, and it seemed to be a long way from any of the other bedrooms. It had probably been a servant room, but these days the staff went to their own homes at night. Still, he didn't want to take the risk.

Anyway, he had things to do.

At first his thoughts kept him awake. Bergeron began to fit things into place. Bergeron had never seen a man shot through the heart, but no matter, that had been a 'white lie' meant to make living easier for Mrs Wainwright. Nor had Billy Wainwright been shot through the heart, but that was a needless lie by Cross. He felt sure enough that Cross had not spoken to Wainwright's men – not his style at all. Yet there was some truth in the words of Cross's letter to Dorothy Wainwright. Her son had indeed died instantly and could not have known anything about it.

Then he needed to read Wainwright's diary. He scanned through the pages, quickly at first. Everything about Wadham and Tozer was here. Billy had been both thorough and succinct. July, August. He slowed down now. *It was all here*, he thought as he looked at each page. *It must be close now*, he thought as he turned the next page. There it was, written in Billy Wainwright's hand: MO attended two days later – Capt. Feltham, RAMC. *Two days later! Well done, Billy, well done!*

There came a light knocking at his own door.

Before responding he glanced at the clock by his bed. Almost midnight. Who on earth could it be? he wondered.

"Yes?" he whispered, the air catching in his throat.

He saw the doorknob turn, the door was gently pushed towards him and Sarah Wainwright stood in his room.

"I'm sorry to bother you, Marcus. I saw that your light was on. I wanted to talk to you."

Well, he thought, *you may have seen that my light was on, but we both know that you must have already made a trip from the other side of the house to see it. And why was that?*

"That's no problem. I was reading your brother's diary. I'm afraid that I suffer a little from insomnia," he lied. "The diary is most interesting. It is a complete record of Billy's war."

"Did you find anything of particular note?"

"No, no. I was just interested."

She walked towards the bed. "I know you didn't know him, he was a wonderful young man. All of the girls around here, well they..."

"Yes."

"Some of them, my friends, well, they would talk to me about Billy, they all wanted to be introduced to him."

"I expect so," he said, awkwardly.

Sarah Wainwright looked him in the eye. Her full cheeks seemed reddened in the half light of the gas lamp. She sat on the bed.

"I saw you blush... when we were introduced," she said. Bergeron did not reply. "And I saw you looking at me. Do you think I'm pretty, Marcus?"

Sarah Wainwright was wearing a white calico nightdress that covered her shoulders, leaving her long arms bare. It was intricately embroidered around the neck and chest, with small marbled buttons which came down from her neck as far as her navel. To Bergeron's amazement Sarah seemed to be taking great delight in slowly, very slowly and deliberately unfastening each one, beginning at the top. As she did so, she contrived to push forward her chest and move apart her hands so that – slowly and provocatively – she revealed more and more of her skin to him. Pale, translucent skin which he now just longed to touch.

"Sarah, you must stop," he said.

Sarah looked at him and found that it was her turn to blush. She quickly buttoned up her nightdress.

"I'm sorry," she said.

"It's nothing really. Look, you are very beautiful, Sarah, but..."

"There's somebody else. I understand."

Bergeron said nothing.

"Look, I just want to thank you for speaking with my mother about Billy. She is so, so saddened by it all. I think it's the not knowing. It will have done her good to have spoken to a soldier about it."

"There must be ex-soldiers here."

"Not those she can talk to. Major Cross lives in India now. But Mother could never approach him anyway."

"No?"

"No, the major is of a different kind to us, a different class. He hunts, shoots, and the men from my brother's, erm, company…"

"Platoon. I expect you mean his platoon."

"Yes. Well, they're working men and Mother…"

"I understand. It must be hard. Here." He handed Billy's diary to the girl. "You should keep this safe."

Sarah took the diary and turned to the door.

"Sarah," he said, "please can you try to help me with something else. There's one of the soldiers I'd like to speak to, a man called Eber Trant. Could you help me find him?"

"But everyone knows the Trants," she blurted. "Why, they're the black sheep of Ugborough. Mother Trant lives on Donkey Lane, by the church. Just ask in the shops or the pubs, everyone knows the Trants."

"Thank you so much, Sarah," he said.

"It's no trouble, Marcus. I do hope that you will visit us again," she said, and she kissed him softly on the cheek. Sarah Wainwright rose and stepped towards the door. As she left him alone in the bedroom, she smiled somewhat cheekily.

Well, well, Sarah Wainwright, he thought, *the cream of Devon, and who would have thought it? Your uncle thinks you're a free spirit – somewhat Bohemian – but does he know the half of it?*

★

Back in Oxford the next day he wanted to telephone Finn. Search as he might, however, Bergeron couldn't find the card

Finn had given him. Bugger, he thought, I must have left it at Collingwood's house.

He walked over to the City Library and found the most recent London directory he could. There he found Anderson & Finn's number and called Gerry.

"Captain Feltham, Royal Army Medical Corps. I have no idea if he is still in the army or has been demobbed. Find him for me, Gerry."

"What on earth are you up to, Bergeron?"

"Gerry, this is business. I'm paying so just find him for me. Any news on the French children?"

"No," said Finn, and Bergeron thought he sounded slightly hurt.

A Consultation with Dr Feltham

He was early and his leg ached.

Bergeron stopped at the street corner. Signs of the onset of autumn were clear. The September chill and recent winds had brought down thousands of leaves in the parks and squares of Leamington Spa. He looked across the road towards number 102. St James's Crescent was situated in a salubrious part of Leamington, close by the pump and Assembly Rooms. It was only a short stroll from the railway station and it had taken less than fifteen minutes for him to walk there.

Bergeron balanced his stick against a doorway and took from his jacket pocket the crumpled piece of paper that Gerry Finn had handed him. He read it once more: *Dr Julian B. Feltham (Psychoanalysis Specialist), 102 St James's Crescent, Royal Leamington Spa, Warwickshire. Consultations by prior appointment only.*

He had found Feltham's telephone number in a directory and called a few days previously to book an appointment. Bergeron gave his own name, as Feltham didn't know him, and he gave an address in Birmingham.

He wondered why Feltham had set up as a psychoanalyst here in the Midlands. London would have been more obvious – much more money and people with nothing much to do but spend it – but here? He supposed that following the war there must be enough wealthy, but frustrated, women and shell-shocked officers to generate enough business just about anywhere, and it was one of the latter category that he purported to be.

Bergeron walked across St James's Crescent and rang the bell of number 102. Eventually the door was opened by a young woman dressed in a uniform like that of a nurse, but not one he had seen before. She asked his name, showed him to a waiting room. Then she disappeared.

He glanced at the small selection of reading materials on the table by his side. He picked up a copy of *The Muse in Arms*, opened it and noted that it was a 1918 reprinted edition. As he thumbed his way through it, recognising some of the poems therein, reading others for the first time, the door opened and into the waiting room stepped a tall, thin man of about his own age.

"You must be Captain Bergeron," said the man. "Interested in poetry, then?"

Bergeron looked up. "Dr Feltham?"

"That's me. Thanks for being prompt. Care to come through to the consulting room?" he said. He didn't offer to shake hands.

Bergeron followed Feltham through to the consulting room. It was a small room with one window overlooking a garden at the back of the building. The window was open. The room was simply furnished: a small desk, an office chair – now occupied by Feltham – a bookcase. Bergeron quickly took note of volumes by both Freud and Jung. There was a couchette-type set-up which looked like the sort of thing Bergeron had seen in his dentist's surgery, but nicely upholstered. A kind of *chaise longue*, he thought.

"Take a seat," said Feltham, pointing towards the *chaise longue*. "So, poet type, are you?"

"Me?" Bergeron looked surprised. "No, not at all," he said.

"But you do like poetry?" asked Feltham, pointing to the magazine in Bergeron's hand and only then did the Canadian notice that he had brought *The Muse* into the consulting room with him.

"Well, yes. Some… I suppose. I know this one." Bergeron pointed out Sassoon's *Before Action* in the magazine he was holding.

"*At dawn the ridge emerges massed and dun, glowering in the morning sun*," quoted Feltham from memory. "Sassoon's poems are very good, aren't they? But do they really represent your experience of war? I mean, is that what it was like for you, out there?"

"Hardly. Artillery, you see. I didn't get so close to the action. The poems, not just Sassoon's, are all so melancholy. Do they tell the story of your war, Feltham?"

"Not a bit. It wasn't all that bad, was it? Not for me anyway. Of course, men were killed and badly injured. And some of us – well, not me, but men – killed, too. We also had laughs, saw Europe. We made new friends. Without the war, I expect I'd still be a virgin, as a matter of fact."

"French whores?"

"Belgian, actually," said Feltham.

"Anyway, he was round the bend, wasn't he, Sassoon?" said Bergeron. "Ended up in a loony bin, didn't he?"

"Do come on, Mr Bergeron. You can do better than that. After all, you're a well-read fellow, aren't you? In any case, Sassoon hardly *ended up* there."

"And how would you know that I'm well read, as you put it?"

"I always research my patients. Prospective patients – sorry. A friend of mine, Alan Toynbee, told me all about your eclectic reading interests. You are positively the *Renaissance man*, he tells me."

"Toynbee! I haven't seen him since France. What did he have to say?" asked Bergeron.

Dr Feltham ignored the question. "A bit of a poet himself, actually," he said.

"Yes, he tries hard. Getting better as he goes along."

"Well, he isn't published, yet," said Feltham. "He's got plenty of talent though. So, how shall we proceed?"

"I rather hoped you'd tell me that."

"I mean, what exactly brought you here? How do you think I can best help you, Captain Bergeron?"

"So, you don't know why I'm here?"

"Frankly? No. Toynbee hadn't a blasted clue. But he's quite sure that you're no neurasthenia case."

Bergeron looked at the doctor long and hard. "You can answer some questions for me. If you would," he replied.

"I thought it was the doctor that asked questions of the patient," said Feltham.

"Not in this case, Feltham. I'm investigating an incident, last year, out on the Western Front."

"Toynbee didn't tell me you've turned private detective."

"Let's keep Toynbee out of this, eh? Let's just say that I'm investigating on behalf of some friends of the, erm, of the deceased."

"Well, there were bloody thousands of deceased."

"I'm only interested in one," said Bergeron. "Tozer. A warrant officer in the SDLI. I believe you were there at his death."

"CSM Tozer. Yes, I remember him. Firing squad. But you're wrong, I wasn't there at his death. I was called in a couple of days later – somebody needed a certificate signing off."

"Should you have been? I mean, should a doctor have been present?"

"No. Nothing in the orders to say that. Have you ever been near an execution, Mr Bergeron?"

"No."

"I have, twice. I'll tell you what happens, if you like."

"Go on," said Bergeron.

"It's usually at dawn. Again, nothing in orders says it must be, but it's a quiet time and spectators aren't welcome. It also gives less time for the men forming the firing squad to think about it. So, a squad is selected, usually from a different regiment, or at least a different company – funny, the lads don't seem to like shooting their mates!"

Feltham picked up a pencil and began doodling on the pink-coloured ink blotter that half covered the top of his small desk.

"Usually twelve of them with an NCO in charge and a lieutenant or captain overseeing the whole bloody thing.

"The squad comes out first, the men lay their rifles on the ground, turn and march a few steps away. With the men's backs to their rifles, the NCO or the officer removes a bullet or two – so that nobody knows who fired the killing shots. Codswallop, I say. Any soldier knows if he's fired a bullet!

"Then the convicted man is led out. He's blindfolded, tied to a post or a chair with a piece of paper pinned to his chest. On the orders of the NCO the men take aim and fire. If the poor old convicted isn't killed outright, then it's the duty of the officer commanding to put a shot through his head, putting him out of his misery."

"So, tell me about CSM Tozer."

"I was asked by a major in the SDLI to look at the body of Warrant Officer Tozer and certify him dead. I was told he'd been killed by a firing squad. The body was lying in a hut and was beginning to decay. Men were digging graves close by. I inspected the corpse as requested and signed off a death certificate."

"How did he die?"

Feltham fiddled with the pencil. "Single shot to the side of his head. Close range, pistol I should say."

"The rifle shots didn't kill him?"

"There were no other bullet wounds on Tozer's body."

"What?"

"Just the head wound, Bergeron. One bullet through the head killed him, there were no other injuries."

"Isn't that rather odd?"

"I spoke to the officer who commanded that firing squad. A Captain Wadham. He told me that he'd mixed up the rifles as well as removing two bullets. That meant the men were shooting with rifles not zeroed to them. They all missed. Wadham said that rather than reload and make the lads fire again, he shot Tozer through the head as army orders demanded."

"Hold on, if Wadham removed two bullets that's still ten loaded rifles. And they all missed?"

"The men would have been full of rum and, as I told you, Wadham said the rifles weren't properly zeroed. It's perfectly plausible, Bergeron."

"Do you know what unit the firing squad was drawn from?"

"Wadham said they hadn't dared use men from their own battalion. I'm not surprised. He told me the firing squad was formed of men from a nearby battalion of Highlanders."

"Did you corroborate that, Feltham?"

"Bugger off, Bergeron. I'm a doctor, not a bloody detective."

EBER TRANT

Bergeron considered his face the mirror; only a few cuts. Not bad. It had taken him five weeks, or thereabouts, to grow a convincing beard, and only fifteen minutes to shave it off.

Bergeron had travelled down to Devon again, this time sporting his full set. He was dressed in a hotchpotch of flamboyant clothes that he had purchased from a theatrical outfitter in Soho and which he thought rendered him continental looking. He alighted the train soon after South Brent, at the Kingsbridge Road stop, not wanting. to be recognised by any of the Wainwrights or Collingwoods. He strolled along the lanes from the station to Ugborough and booked himself two nights at the Anchor Inn, putting on what he thought to be a convincing Italian accent and giving the name Marco Bergamon.

Then he made use of the last two hours of daylight. He first went over to the church. Judging by the size of the church compared to the small village, Ugborough had once been a wealthy rural parish. Plenty of money in sheep, he supposed. Then he walked along Donkey Lane to try to find the man he was looking for. Nothing.

Bergeron ate a meal of game stew that was mostly rabbit in the back room of the Anchor, then went through to the bar for a pint of ale and to see who was there. Empty.

"Quiet," he said to the barman.

"Always quiet on a Wednesday night, sir. Euchre league down at The Ship. All they locals drink there on account of the free sandwiches."

Bergeron said nothing, finished the beer quickly and made his way to The Ship at the other end of Ugborough Square. He gazed over the company of men gathered around the bar and tables. Nothing. He decided to wait.

★

Eber Trant hated early morning starts. He hated early mornings altogether and didn't particularly enjoy late mornings. Especially now as an autumnal mist hung over the valley and the grasses of the meadows were coated in a glistening, white frost. The air was still. *Bloody mist will last half the day*, he thought.

The fact that the morning mist obscured everything more than fifty yards away was irrelevant to Trant. He knew very well where his snares were placed; he'd been taking rabbits from the fields above the Erme water meadows ever since he was a teenager.

It was important to set the snares early, as this would allow the smell of his hands to wear off before the rabbits came out of their warrens to feed, which would not be until dusk. He set hoop snares, as these worked best in the relatively dry soils of early autumn following this year's fine summer. Pegs were better after a rainfall.

Taking a piece of wire about five feet long, Eber Trant carefully bent it into a loose letter U shape. He then attached a regular snare onto the side of the hoop and pushed the two legs of the hoop into the ground until the snare was set at a good angle. He examined the snare and satisfied himself that it would work, then he walked about fifty yards to the west and set the second trap.

The mist had begun to lift. It was quickly being replaced by more of a light but low cloud with distinct breaks in it. Trant looked around and saw a watery sun between the clouds to the east. *Time to go*, he thought, and he walked briskly the mile and a half to Ugborough.

"What's for breakfast, Mam?" he called as he closed the back door that family always used – less people to see your comings and goings that way.

"Bread and cheese in the kitchen, Eber. Help you'm self, boy. I's busy 'ere."

He cut a large slice of his mother's home-baked bread and took some cheese. Munching the sandwich, Trant walked round to Eggy Pearce's workshop for he had an afternoon's work promised. Eggy set him to cleaning old bridles and shoes; bits that could be recycled having been sorted from the iron and leather that was of no use.

"Playing Euchre tonight, Eggy?" asked Trant.

"Try to keep me away. Avonwick. Proper job! You'm going down?"

"Happen I will, yer, once I've checked my traps," he said.

"If we win, which we shall, I'll stand you a pint. Two if you fetch me a plump doe, and that's a promise," said Eggy.

★

Eber Trant went back to the field after work. Two of his snares had trapped rabbits; the others were empty. He took hold of a rabbit. It fought his grip in a futile effort to gain freedom, but Eber broke its neck with a snap and placed the body in his sack. Likewise, he dealt with the second rabbit. He would take both home to his mam, he thought. Eating was preferable to drinking.

★

At eight, after eating from the stew pot that Ma Trant kept going almost perpetually on her stove, Eber Trant made his way to The Ship. He nodded respectfully to the older men and knowingly to his peers as he approached the bar.

"Nothing for you, Eggy," he called to the men playing cards, "sorry."

He bought a pint of cider and sat in a corner, gazing at the stranger he noticed in the opposite corner. As Eber quickly drained his glass, the bearded man rose and walked over to him.

"Will you let me buy you another, Eber?" he asked.

★

"Why the disguise?" asked Eber Trant.

"I don't want anyone recognising me, Eber, and I'm trusting you not to blow the whistle."

"You know you can trust me. If it weren't for you I'd be pushing up poppies in France. I owe you, sir."

"Cut out the formalities, Eber. I'm an Italian visitor and if anyone asks you, say I was quizzing you about horses. Got that? Some horse dealer from foreign parts."

"I've got that, boss, and I could tell you a thing or two about horses round here, boss. Back in '14, just after the war broke out, I was a nipper, but I remember."

"Tell me, Eber."

"I went to Kingsbridge in August with my dad. The quay was crammed with horses. Must have been between 800 and 900 of 'em brought for inspection by the army. I never saw so many horses before nor since, boss. Carriage horses, hunters, hacks, light and heavy. It being early closing day, shops were shut and everybody turned out to see such a sight. I saw fifty-odd of 'em – splendid animals they were – being entrained at Kingsbridge station. Dad said they was destined for Bulford

Camp on Salisbury Plain, to be trained for heavy field artillery before being sent to the continent.

"Oh, how people tried to hold onto their steeds. Some turned proper devious, they did. My brother Josiah worked at the Stowford paper mill in Ivybridge. Well, he told Mam when they heard about a visit by a military requisition team, them at Lodge instructed Josiah to take one of the best stallions and hide it near the railway viaduct." He took a long draw on his cider.

"Not everyone was pulling together, though. Oh no," continued Eber Trant. "Then as now, rogues and nae'r-do-wells were out to take advantage. I remember talk of men coming down 'ere from Wales an' posing as War Office officials. They was a buying beasts a plenty, and at knock-down prices. Bought they best mares for thirty quid and sold 'em on for fifty; bastard Welsh!"

Bergeron went up to the bar and returned with more drinks. "Eber," he said, "I want to know something. Tell me about Major Cross and CSM Tozer, would you?"

Trant looked around him and fidgeted. "Not here, boss," he whispered. "I'll leave now and wait for you outside. Follow on in two or three minutes. We'll have to go back to my mam's place."

PART THREE

REVENGE, 1920

PART THREE

Always Time for a Drink

He took hold of a fountain pen and dipped it into the pot of raven black ink. Then he took the sealed envelope and began to write the address:

Mr D Ryan
Mahon's Bar (on the road to Enniskean)
Ballynacarriga
County Cork

From a small pile of stationery at the back the dark brown, heavily polished writing bureau, Bergeron took a postage stamp. He placed it on his tongue, savouring the sweet taste of the glue. Holding the stamp in his left hand, he offered it up to the top right-hand corner of the envelope, making sure that the margin between the top of the stamp and envelope precisely matched the gap he was leaving along the edge. He pressed firmly down with his right index finger and checked that the stamp was stuck fast.

Bergeron placed the stamped and addressed envelope on top of the writing bureau. He would go out shortly to post it, so that it would catch the five o'clock collection, he thought. But he would have to be sharp, he could hear the paperboys already beginning to hail the evening headlines.

There was time for a drink, he thought. *Always time for a drink.*

From the sideboard he selected a small cut glass tumbler. He poured himself a large measure of whisky to which he added a smaller amount of water. He took a long sip and smiled.

Glass in hand, he walked over to the window. Bergeron had moved into rooms at the Russell at the beginning of the year. It was expensive, but that didn't worry him. He had needed to rest. Touring half the country in search of May, Jeffries and Feltham – not to mention those two trips down to Devon – had left him tired out. His leg was still a problem. He had needed to rest and the luxury of the Russell was welcome.

He gazed out of his window. Green grass smothered most of Russell Square and spring daffodils, together with other flowers that he could not name, added a blush of colour to the park's borders. Young ladies were out strolling with their mothers or friends, some pushing perambulators, all looking beautiful. Occasionally a couple would saunter along, carefree. Soon the office boys would be rushing around, making their way home, pausing only to buy copies of the early editions; others would wait patiently for buses.

It was all so normal. Almost eighteen months since the war had ended and it seemed as though it had never happened.

Bergeron again sipped his whisky, his thoughts now racing. *So, the bastard's back. About bloody time!*

AT HOME IN BRENT

The windows of the Victorian conservatory of Lower Aish House faced west, offering a view over Ugborough Beacon, and beyond it to the vastness of Dartmoor.

"Best view in the world, what?" asked the older of the two men now standing looking out.

"Yes," agreed the younger man. He was not yet out of his twenties and had just walked from his home near the parish church. It was not far – perhaps half a mile – and only slightly uphill, but because of his limp it had taken him nearly forty minutes to get to Lower Aish House. He was tall, rather thin and with a pencil moustache. He wore a dog collar and he was paying a social visit. He turned away from the windows to face his companion. "It's so good to see you back, Major."

"Believe me, it's good to be home, Ansty. Very good indeed."

"How is Mrs Cross?" asked the vicar.

Cross rang the service bell. "Virginia's well, considering. Thank you for asking. Caught a touch of the malaria in India, but she's coping. Keeps muttering that the house is too big for us, she always thought that. Wants to move."

"Will you?"

"We'll see," said the older man. "We've lived at Lower Aish since my father gave the house to us as a wedding present in 1905. It's served us very well as a family home ever since. I'm for staying. Don't worry though, if we do move, it won't be far away so we'll still swell your Sunday congregation, Ansty. Better have some good sermons planned, eh?"

Both men smiled. The maid arrived.

"Bring us a pot of tea, Nancy, and some crumpets." Major Malaby Cross stood and walked to the window as Ansty watched him. Cross was built like an ox, thought Ansty, and he recalled that in his day the major had been quite a remarkable sportsman. Not only had he played cricket and rugby for his college, but he had rowed at stroke in the Cambridge eight on two occasions. He had also been a track athlete and had come very close to national selection in the 200 yards. All of that may have been many years ago, but Ansty could see that he still looked fit.

"There's a cricket match on Sunday, Major. Will you play?"

"Yes, Baker Pearse invited me already. I'd love a game. Are you playing?"

"Yes, rather!" Ansty agreed. "I'm looking forward to it. First game of the season – weather's bound to change soon too. I'm down to keep wicket. What about you?"

"I expect I'll open the batting with Pearse," he offered. "Pearse also said I should be skipper for the next few games. Take it that's all right by you?"

Ansty didn't answer. Major Cross must be well over fifty years old, he thought. He certainly retained the commanding bearing of a military man – *I expect he* told *Pearse that he wanted to be captain*, grumbled Ansty to himself. *Oh well!*

The maid came back with a tray. On it was a pot of Darjeeling tea, two cups, a plate of muffins and the butter dish.

"I said crumpets, Nancy."

"Sorry, Major. Cook hasn't got crumpets. She says she'll make some for tomorrow, but will muffins do for now, sir?"

"Have to, I suppose. Carry on," he commanded.

She poured the tea as though the men were incapable.

"Thank you, Nancy. That's everything for now. Tuck in, Ansty."

The major cut off a thick wedge of butter and took his time in spreading it onto one of the warm muffins. Then he passed the butter dish to the vicar who helped himself; to rather less. As they ate and sipped their tea, Ansty asked him, "How was India, Major? Rather hot, I expect."

"Rather! In more ways than one – literally and metaphorically, if you follow me. I take it you know what I was up to out there?"

"No. No I don't, actually. You see, after the war I went straight back up to Corpus Christi to complete my final year," replied Ansty. "Almost as soon as I finished Father died."

"Yes, I heard about that and I'm very sorry. He was a good sort, your father. Sad loss. How old was he?"

"Just fifty-six," replied Ansty. "I've been here since. Please, do go on and fill me in about India."

"Yes. Well, I landed there in December 1918. I'd been back to Blighty for a few months in August, to recuperate. Applied to go back on active service. I just couldn't stand the thought of being here, not with you and the rest of the battalion still out in France. I was keen to resume my post, but the regiment wasn't." He paused to take a sip of the tea. "Anyway, they compromised. Posted me to the 6th Battalion out in India, the Punjab. I took over a company there. Ruddy heat!"

Cross took another sip of tea at the thought of the Indian heatwave.

"I wasn't demobbed at the end of the war in France, not like you lucky lot. No. We were out there 'till early this year. There were some ghastly goings-on in Amritsar. Read about it, I expect, it was all over the papers."

"Yes, I read about. Were you actually there at the time?" asked Ansty.

"No. We were sent in afterwards to sort out the bloody mess left by General Dyer. Not pretty work. Three hundred and seventy-odd killed and well over 1,000 wounded. We were forced to carry out some drastic measures to keep the natives in order. Dyer was torn off a strip – but what else could he do but shoot at the buggers? Anyway, the Hunter Commission will be reporting publicly so we'll soon get to know what they think. Well, I'd had enough. I applied to leave and came back to England."

"Well, as I say, it's good to have you back," smiled Ansty and he sipped his tea.

"I feel out of touch, you know," said the major. "Not having been around much, I've missed out on all the news and small talk so I've been catching up on what I've missed. Matter of fact, look at this, will you?"

When Ansty arrived, the major had been reading the *Western Morning News*. Now he passed Ansty the newspaper.

"Events in Ireland look worrying. What do you make of that, Ansty?" he asked.

Richard Ansty was hard pressed to answer as he had not been given time to take in the report, but he could see from the headline that there had been a shooting in Ireland. The question turned out to be rhetorical.

"Those Fenian bastards have killed another police officer in the South of Ireland. County Cork. It says here that some of them are ex-military. Why would any former British soldier want to join with those blasted Fenian swine, Ansty? Tell me that if you can."

"Well, I do remember that several the Irish lads who joined us in 1916, especially those from the south, were always talking about the Easter Rising, and the way it was put down." Cross had paused long enough for the vicar to speak. "I distinctly recall one of them questioning whether he was fighting on the right side."

"Do anything?"

"Well of course I did! I got an NCO to shut him up straight away. Couldn't have any of that kind of talk. They made good soldiers, though, the Irish."

"Good soldiers be damned, Ansty!" thundered Cross. "They're guilty of ambushing and murdering our men over there."

A long silence allowed Ansty to drink.

Eventually, the vicar rose from his chair. "You won't think it rude if I leave you now, Major?" he enquired. "I've got to go over to Mrs Roebuck. She's been unwell for some time now."

"Of course, not, old man," replied Cross. "Off you go on your rounds. I'll see you in church, eh?"

Ansty offered his hand and the two men shook and parted company.

WEST CORK

Patrick Casey was supposed to sort the mail in the early morning so that he could complete his delivery round before noon. But Patrick was lazy.

The postman had a well-rehearsed routine that worked well. Especially for Patrick Casey. Each morning he had an extra hour and a half in bed, followed by a nice breakfast. Then he would go out on his rounds delivering yesterday's post. The sorting he would leave till late afternoon, so that it was ready to go the next day. This method ensured two things: first, that the people of the area of west Cork that the elderly postman served received their post a day later than most; second, that Patrick had a fat belly.

There were never any complaints. Around the villages of Ballyneen and Enniskean the people generally received their letters and parcels well before noon. It just happened that the post was a day later than it ought to have been. If they knew, nobody seemed to mind.

Today was a Saturday and Patrick Casey was eating a breakfast prepared by his granddaughter, Mairead. The bacon smelled wonderful. Black and white puddings. Fried bread, crisp and browned. Two eggs – now that was a rare treat. A pot of fresh-brewed tea. Soda bread and butter. Lovely!

"Mairead!" he called. "Are we in the money, girl? Two eggs? It doesn't grow on trees, you know."

"Mammy got them from Farmer Cronin. His hens are a-laying well, she says."

Aye, he thought, *and is Farmer Cronin laying your mammy in return? There again, with her husband Daniel taken in the war, what did it matter?*

"That's nice then," the old man shouted.

Casey pondered this morning's round, which he had sorted yesterday. A bunch of letters for Dooley the grocer – bills he expected. A small parcel for Mrs O'Donnaghue. Several letters from Dublin and Cork for the villagers. Usual stuff. But what about this one? Casey took the manila envelope in his hand and he wondered what it might be. He carefully examined it, noticing that the postmark was from England and the recipient one of Mrs Ryan's boys.

Most unusual. He would leave the delivery of this letter until after his dinner.

Patrick Casey looked over his bicycle, which was elderly, a little rusty in places, but serviceable. He took a small oil can and applied a little lubricating oil to the hole in the chain guard whilst spinning the rear wheel. He smiled at the whirring sound. He first wiped off the excess oil with a once-white cloth that he kept specifically for this task, then wiped his hands and was off away on his morning round.

At half past twelve, Casey arrived back home and sat down to dinner with Eileen and Mairead. The stew and dumplings was very good, though he knew it would rest heavily on his stomach. No matter, there was work to do!

At precisely two o'clock Casey donned his cap once more. He put his bicycling clips around his ankles, his postbag over his shoulder and set off.

He whistled to himself as he cycled slowly along the road leading from Enniskean to Ballynacarriga, and turned off right just before the village. Patrick Casey was heading down to the Randal Óg, for that's where he would most likely find Doncha

Ryan playing in the pre-season friendly against neighbouring Ballygurteen. Friendly was a misnomer, for following the breaking of Mick O'Brian's left leg in 1909 this had been a grudge match and Postman Casey was eager to get to it.

No doubt, the wind had met the drizzle at some point to the west, over the Atlantic Ocean. There, it had picked up the light rain and was now lashing it horizontally across the open field that served as the Randal Óg Gaelic Athletic Association ground.

Postman Casey could hear the muted shouts of young men and the dulled thump of wood against ball; it was as though the sounds were themselves absorbed by the rain. There was nothing to break the force of the wind and Casey screwed up his eyes as he peered into the rain to see if he could catch a glimpse of Ryan. There he was! With his hurley at hand, practising goal strikes with some of the other lads.

Casey stopped the bicycle by the shed that served as a changing room for everyone: the officials, the home team and the visitors. As he clambered off it and leant the bicycle against the shed wall, Casey saw the referee appear. *They're about to start*, he thought, *I'll wait 'till the half time.*

A whistle blew. The sounds of young men shouting and of hurley on ball reverberated across the field. The players ran, steamed, squelched and slid around the field.

"The boys are improved," said Casey to Sid Simes.

"Sure," replied Sid, the second team coach. "Sure, they're coming along nicely, but they miss Connor O'Keef, so they do. With him away to England, they'll not be doing so well this season."

At that, a goal against the run of play put the visitors from Ballygurteen in the lead.

"Oh no," said Casey, "I sure put the mockers on them saying that. I'll need to keep my big mouth shut."

On and on went the game. *It must be near the interval,* thought

Casey. Then, from a longish build-up of play, Billy Cummins, the Randal Óg team captain and their centre forward, scored a goal. The home side cheered Cummins; Doncha Ryan shook his hand.

"All square, that's good," said Casey to Sid Simes.

Doncha Ryan picked up the ball just inside his own half. With a jilt and a swerve, and bouncing the ball on his stick as he ran, the little fellow jinked and twisted his way by two defenders and passed the ball left to Gary Regan. Ryan carried on his run and Regan, with a deft flick of the hurley, passed back to him.

From the side-line, both Casey and Sid Simes could see that Ryan was within shooting distance and they guessed what was coming.

"Come on, boy. Come on," muttered Casey.

Ryan paused as he took his back swing.

"Steady, Doncha, son. Steady," said Sid Simes.

What happened next seemed to the two older men to take place in slow motion. Ryan continued his back swing until the hurley was level with his shoulders. As he did so Micky Concannon, a burly and robust Ballygurteen defender, ran towards him to close him down. Ryan launched his stick at the ball as Concannon slid towards him. Ryan's hurley descended and met the ball with a crack, sending it soaring high, as Concannon's hurley crashed into Doncha Ryan's right leg.

Slowly and gracefully the ball passed just to the left of the stumbling Ballygurteen goalkeeper. It had missed the left-hand post by a whisker. Ryan, felled by Concannon's clumsy challenge, lay still on the ground. He slowly raised his head. "What the bloody hell do you think you're up to, you bastard?" shouted Ryan.

"You slipped, I never touched you," said Concannon.

Ryan jumped to his feet. "Never touched me? Well now, tell me just what this is, then?" He pulled down the sock covering his right shin, which was badly grazed and bleeding. "You just ploughed into me, you fat lump!"

"Just piss off, you wee runt," said Concannon, turning his back on Ryan and jogging away.

Ryan ran after the bigger man. He caught Concannon's shirt and swung him around. The big Ballygurteen defender threw a punch, which missed as Ryan ducked. Then Ryan launched himself at Concannon, his hurley thrashing around.

The whistle sounded. The referee, supported by players and officials from both teams, rushed in to stop the fight.

"That's half time, lads," shouted the referee. He spoke to Ryan as everyone walked off the field. "Now listen, son," he said, "I blew up a good minute early. Now you calm down, otherwise I'll be sending you off."

"Yes, sir," said Ryan, sullenly.

"Doncha! Doncha Ryan!" called out Postman Casey as he walked towards the field of play waving the letter furiously as he did so.

Ryan smiled at the old man. "Good afternoon to you, Mr Casey," he shouted back, "and what can I be doing for you this fine March afternoon?"

"The afternoon isn't fine, you're a might too quick with that stick of yours, and it's what I can do for you that you should be asking," said the old man as he held out the letter.

"For you. From London. Posted the day before yesterday."

Ryan jogged across the wet grass to the postman, taking the letter from him. He recognised the handwriting immediately. "And what does it say?" he asked.

"Now, how on earth would I be knowing what it says?"

"Well, you seem to know most everything else about it," answered Ryan with a grin. He opened the envelope and quickly read the letter. Two guns and nice trip, he thought. That will suit me just fine, Captain.

"Thank you very much, Mr Casey," he said. "Now I must be back to the game. Are you staying to watch?" he asked.

"No, no, son. I'll be away home now. Just you make sure you win, that's all."

"Sure will, Mr Casey," said Ryan as he made his way over to the shed to get his cup of tea and a team talk from Matt Dacey, the Randal Óg first team coach, and he broke into song as he walked.

"Bugger me, Doncha," shouted the postman. "If the Peelers catch you singing a rebel song like that they'll shoot you as soon as look at you, so they will."

Ryan swung around and shouted back, "Sure, but it's not a rebel song that I'm singing. It's more the Irish history, you know. Father Murphy and the Wexford boys and all that there. In any case, even if the ditty were rebellious, then you'd not be a tellin' on me now, would you?"

"And no more fighting, you!"

"Sure thing, Mr."

Ryan took his wet duffle bag from under the bench and stuffed the papers into it. Sid Simes swore at him for being late for the team talk, and for his fighting.

"Sorry, Mr Simes. Sorry."

"… and if you are going to hit Mick Concannon," said the coach, "then you're to get him with your stick when the bloody referee can't see you doing it!"

Postman Casey got back onto his bicycle and began to peddle out of the sports ground; soon he was back on the road to Enniskean.

★

Murphy's bar was off the main street in Clonakilty. The smoke hit Ryan as soon as he set foot inside. Cheap tobacco mingled with peat smoke. The atmosphere reminded him of the wartime dugouts, though the smell was sweeter. Anyway, he didn't want to be reminded of that. He removed his cap and thrust it into his pocket and stood at the bar examining the green porcelain tiles and nicotine-stained wallpaper. Connor Sexton, the barman, waited expectantly.

"Pint of Wristler, please, Con."

"Coming up."

The walls were littered with an eclectic display of artefacts: Toby jugs, bottles, ornate trays, pewter tankards, pictures – of boats mainly – advertisements for 'Deaseys Clonakilty Ales and Stouts'.

"I'm looking for Tommy."

"He's in the snug." Sexton gestured with a nod of his bald head as he said this, indicating the general direction of Tom Deans' hideaway. "I'll bring this over to you once it's settled, if you like."

"Thanks, Con," he said as he turned and walked over to the snug where he found Deans smoking and reading a newspaper. He didn't look up, so Ryan sat down at the same table.

"I need to be away, just for a few weeks. That all right, Tom?" he asked.

Deans didn't speak, but looked up from his newspaper and met the gaze of Ryan. The two men stared at each other. Ryan noticed Deans' peculiar small eyes. Small, light grey eyes, sharp as a knife and crystal clear, eyes that didn't leave his own as Ryan spoke.

"I'm sorry, but this is important, Tom. It'll only be for a wee while."

Con Sexton brought over the porter. Ryan took a long drink then gazed into his glass at the black liquid. He was relieved at the opportunity to look away from Deans.

Deans put down the paper and stubbed out his cigarette in a heavy, darkly coloured, ceramic ashtray. "I need you here," he said.

"Look, Tom, I need to be away for a few weeks. No debate. No questions, either, eh? This is personal. And I'll need a gun."

"You've got a bloody gun," pointed out Deans.

"I need another."

"Then you'll have to tell me what it's all about, Donny."

Ryan paused. *How much is it necessary to reveal?* he thought.

"I've a score to settle. From the war."

"So, it's Corporal Ryan is it, now?"

No answer. No response for fully two minutes. Ryan simply stared at him. *What game was this?*

Then he said, "Bombardier Ryan, to be accurate, Tom."

"No, Don. No personal scores. That's not what this is about."

"If it helps, it isn't in Ireland. If it goes wrong it won't implicate you or the boys at all. But it does involve killing a British Army officer, so it will be helping the cause, so's to speak. Anyhow, as you say, I do have a gun, so perhaps I shouldn't have bothered you at all, Tom. I'd better be off."

Deans studied him carefully. "Oh yes, that old Mauser of yours? Surprised you've still got ammunition for it, Don."

"Stole the ammo when I pinched the gun."

"While you were fighting for the King, wasn't it? While some of us were fighting here in Ireland, for Irish liberty. While Pearse and Connelly were fighting in the GPO. Dev in Boland's Mill. While I was at the side of the Countess – God bless her – at St Stephen's Green. That was when, wasn't it? While Irishmen were dying for their country's freedom, you were fighting for the King of England. And now you want to desert the cause to settle an old score!"

Ryan rose silently from the table. He raised himself to his full five feet four inches. He lifted the glass and, although it still contained almost a pint of porter, finished the drink in one, all of this time his eyes never leaving Deans'.

When he eventually spoke, Ryan's voice was loud. Too loud – he was almost shouting.

"Commandant Deans, sir. I have never, ever deserted you nor anyone, anywhere, as well you know, sir."

Ryan took a deep breath and seemed to calm himself.

"If you're asking me why I joined up, Tom, well, I'd say for pretty much the same reason as lots of us did. Aye, including Tom Barry. I just decided to see what this 'Great War' was all about. I can't plead that I went on the advice of politicians – that if we fought for the British we would get home rule for Ireland. To tell you the truth, I can't honestly say I understood then what home rule meant. And, since you're interested, no, I wasn't at all influenced by sentimental appeals to fight to save 'Poor Little Belgium'. I didn't know where Belgium was."

Ryan paused to take his cap from his pocket, unfolded it and put it on his head.

"No, I went to the war for no other reason than this: I wanted to see what war was like, to get a gun in my hand, to see new countries. I'd lived in Ballynacarriga all my life, Tom. You know what that's like for a young man. Sure, it's a pretty enough place. It's got a lake and a castle and a church and a shop and a bar and a shrine to the Immaculate Conception." Ryan paused to cross himself. "It's got a few girls and it's got Randal Óg, for which I'm eternally grateful, for without sport I don't think I'd have stuck it, Tom, really I don't. I went to war because I wanted to feel like a grown man. I was posted to the Artillery – had no choice in the matter. Well, it suited me – I like big guns! They just happened to be the Royal Artillery. Well, that there can't be helped."

There was a deathly silence in Murphy's. Connor Sexton polished glasses, head down as if searching for the tiniest mark still to be erased by his white towel. Other customers in the bar area gazed at their drinks. A game of darts had stopped. Ryan lowered his voice.

"Well, 1916 changed all that. The way those so-called Rebels were treated and all. That's what brought me to Republicanism, brought me to the Volunteers and brought me to you, Tom.

"Anyhow, seeing as how I am a volunteer and seeing as how I don't get any pay, well, I don't really think you can stop me going now, can you? Not unless you're going to shoot me, that is. So, if you don't mind, or even if you do, Tom, I'll be off tomorrow."

Deans stared at him. "Sit down now, Donny, and calm down," he said. "I'm only playing. Here, have a cig." He offered the open packet of Woodbines to Ryan.

Ryan took one and slowly regained his seat. "This isn't a game, Tom. You were testing me. Please," he paused and looked Deans in the eye, "never do that again."

Deans took out his matches. He first lit Ryan's cigarette and then one for himself. He took a long draw on the cigarette, filling his lungs with the fumes. He turned his head to the left and exhaled the stale smoke away from Ryan's face.

Deans shouted to the barman, "Connor, two more drinks in here, please." Then, to Ryan, he said, "I'll get you a gun. What kind do you want? Tom Barry tells me that the new Thompsons are very good."

Just the hint of a smile broke out on Ryan's face. "A pistol, Tom. Just any pistol will do. A revolver or an automatic, it doesn't matter… I expect it's more for show. Bluff. You know the sort of thing. The broom handle – the Mauser – will do the dirty work."

"You expect it's for bluff? You don't know? Who's running this show?"

"No names, Tom."

"It had better be somebody you can trust." He took another long draw on the Woodbine, already reduced to half its original length.

"With my mother's life, Tom."

Both men had now leant back slightly in their chairs. They concentrated on their smokes rather than on each other. The noise in the bar had started up again. The darts players resumed after their impromptu break.

"Tell me, Doncha. What's the score? Where are you going?"

"I don't know yet, but first England, that's for sure."

"How will you get there?"

"Boat to Wales then a train, I suppose."

"You won't make it. You won't get a weapon onto the boat at Dublin. The Peelers are searching everyone. I mean everyone. I could get someone to meet you in England with weapons, though. If it's that important to you. They might be followed, of course."

"If you like, you know best."

"No. I know. I could get you there in a fishing boat."

"A fishing boat?"

"Yes. We use them a lot for that kind of thing. You know. The sort of stuff we can't get through Dublin. It's not widely known, even amongst the Volunteers. So don't blab. What do you think?"

"I'll take the deal. Thanks, Tom," Ryan smiled.

"You can be dropped off somewhere on the Welsh or south west coast at first light. You can make your own way on from there. You'll have to get back yourself, though. That might mean ditching the guns." Deans looked at Ryan thoughtfully. "But there's a condition," he added.

Ryan stubbed out the cigarette. "What condition?"

"That you don't go so soon. I've a job for you here first. An ambush at Bantry. Then you can go – I'll even get you out! What do you say, Donny?"

"That sounds just fine, Tom. Thanks a million!"

CONTEMPLATING MURDER

He had killed before – many times. It was impossible, he thought, to know just how many. An eighteen-pounder field gun has a range of more than 9,000 yards. If any such gun happened to be placed in Trafalgar Square it could, hypothetically of course, fire a shell that would land as far away as Putney or Hammersmith Bridge, say. Or Lewisham in the other direction. It was a truly enormous range that never failed to impress him. Those who fired these guns seldom saw the consequences.

Perhaps thousands of men had died upon his orders.

He sipped his whisky and pondered the possibility for the thousandth time. He tried to recall as much detail as possible.

"Somebody over-cooked the job the other day. In fact, we badly overdid things," said Major Moncrieff when he debriefed them afterwards. Moncrieff looked worried. He had received intelligence that something had gone wrong. The Canadian shells had landed too far behind the German lines. They had destroyed a farm, rendering two French children homeless orphans. Bergeron supposed he would never know if the carnage had been caused by shells from the guns of his own troop. Guns he had aimed and ranged, shells he had ordered to be fired.

He had finished the drink. It was early, but what the hell? He poured another glass of whisky, his mind still back in the war.

Though he seldom brought up the provenance of his Croix de Guerre and Military Cross, the decorations were testament to the fact that he had also killed at close range. He wouldn't exactly say he had 'smelled the fear and the blood of his adversary', but he'd been close enough.

However, those killings had been done obeying orders or in self-defence, or – just possibly – by mistake. The next time would be different. He would have to take a man's life in cold blood, not as an order obeyed or a mistake made. Some would no doubt consider it murder.

This presented Bergeron with an immediate set of problems. First was the obvious moral question. *Is it right to kill a man now the war is over?* he asked himself. *Yes, in these circumstances.*

Then to logistical issues. Where and how to kill him? Moreover, how was he to do it and get away with it? How to never once be suspected?

Swallowing a large mouthful of whisky and waiting until the fiery sensation it produced in his chest had subsided, Bergeron smiled. He always enjoyed the peat flavoured spirit. His broad smile disappeared as quickly as his thoughts returned to the immediate reality. "Blast the whole rotten business!" he shouted, and banged the glass down.

Let me think – when did it begin? When does anything begin? With the deaths of Tozer and Wainwright? Surely. Oh, had it not been for that bloody dreadful war, none of this would have happened. So, was it that blasted assassination in Sarajevo that started the war, after all?

No, don't be damned silly, he told himself, *that sort of thinking diminishes the evil work of the individuals concerned.* Had it, then, begun with the birth of Malaby Cross? Or earlier, when his parents copulated to spawn the bastard!

This was getting him nowhere. He took another drink of whisky in an attempt to rid himself of the thought.

What was totally indisputable was that things had come to a head last Tuesday. Bergeron had been sitting reading a morning paper – *The Times*, as it happened. Not that he usually read *The Times*; the paper just happened to be lying around in the lounge at the Russell. He didn't much care for the Russell Hotel. It was too dark. The mock Georgian alabaster work above the fireplaces and bookcases did little to lighten the gloomy atmosphere of the place established by the deep red carpet, flock wallpaper and oak panelling. *Yet, for all its ills,* thought Bergeron, *I* live *here now. Oh, how bloody depressing.*

He had sat down to enjoy a nice pot of coffee at about ten o'clock that day. He turned over the first page of the paper and scanned the news there. And there it was, staring him in the face. Shocked, Bergeron jolted and sent a half cup of hot coffee down onto his lap. The scalding heat made him jump to his feet and shout out. He dropped *The Times* onto the floor.

"Are you all right, Captain Bergeron sir?" asked the concierge.

"Yes, Bill. Quite all right, thanks. Sorry to have startled you."

So, he was back. Bergeron stared down at the newspaper on the plush red carpet – and the headline glared back at him in dull black on white:

Major Malaby Cross, formerly of the South Hams Rifles (Volunteers) and 3rd Battalion, the South Devon Light Infantry, returned to the UK on Sunday from service in India.

Bergeron had been looking and waiting for Cross since August 1918. He knew very well where Cross had gone, but a trip to India was impractical. His fellow officers had always considered Bergeron something of a planner and an organiser, and they constantly ribbed him for it. They may well have been right, for immediately upon discovering that Cross was back in the country, his thoughts had turned to planning what he would need to do.

Cross would have returned to the family home, of course – Lower Aish. *Well*, he thought, *that made things relatively straightforward*. What he needed were an alias, an alibi, a train ticket and Doncha Ryan.

The alibi was solved in an instant. He would simply tell people he was spending some time with Aunt Maude on the south coast. What about an alias? Turning back to *The Times*, he found again a short article about an archaeological dig at Avebury, Wiltshire. *Well*, he thought, *if archaeologists can dig there, so they can on Dartmoor*. That meant he also needed a tent and some camping gear.

A plan was quickly sketched.

He had written to Ryan, his would-be accomplice. Bergeron hoped to God that Ryan would be able to join him. Not simply to bring the weapons. Don Ryan was the only person he could trust to help him.

The following day Bergeron went out and bought a second-hand, medium-sized wood and leather trunk. He packed into this his bulkier items: tent and stove, other camping equipment, a well-used army pack with some clothes stuffed into it, binoculars and those sorts of things.

He had also thrown into the trunk some military trousers and a waist belt which would match well with a couple of civilian shirts and, perhaps, a tweed jacket. He would need to get one later. Lastly, he carefully stowed away his Prussian knife.

On Saturday Bergeron had been very busy. He had arranged for the trunk to be sent off to the post office at Princetown, Devon. A covering letter outlined that this would be collected later by one Dudley Spring – the name came from the obituary column in *The Times* – a student of archaeology at the University of London.

Then he went shopping. He had prepared a list: tweed jacket, map, compass, notebook and pencils, wire, a small trowel and a tape measure. A guidebook of some kind would also be of use.

Most of the equipment had been easy to come by in the shops around Leicester Square. But the jacket and guidebook had presented problems. It would hardly look authentic to arrive with either of them obviously brand new.

Part of the problem was solved in a second-hand bookshop on Long Acre, where Bergeron found a copy of William Crossing's *Guide to Dartmoor*, 1912 edition. It had been well thumbed through, which was good.

The tweed jacket, however, had to wait. It was already eleven thirty and Bergeron hoped to catch Gerry Finn before the lawyer finished for the day, though he hadn't made an appointment. He walked quickly from Long Acre to Lincoln's Inn Fields and found the offices of Anderson & Finn, Solicitors at Law. At reception, stood in front of a highly polished oak desk he asked for "the younger Mr Finn, please. A personal call, tell him."

"I'm very sorry, sir, but Mr Finn is away. You can't possibly see him till the week after next."

That's bloody awkward, he thought, but it couldn't be avoided.

"Then I'd like to make an appointment to meet him, let's say the Tuesday after next. When is that?" As he asked, Bergeron took a small, red notebook from his pocket.

"That will be Tuesday March 9th, sir. What time would you like?"

"Let's say two," said Bergeron.

"Two o'clock it is. Personal visit again, sir?"

"No. Business."

"And who shall I say it is?"

"Captain Bergeron, RCHA."

"Certainly, Captain."

This would mean a trip back from Devon, but at least he could double up and check for any post from Ireland.

Bergeron was hungry and still worried about how to obtain a good quality, used and slightly shabby jacket. His stomach won the dual and so he doubled back to Covent Garden and straight into the Nag's Head.

The Nag's had become a favourite of his recently, not least because of Lizzie the waitress there. He sat at a table in a small booth, well away from the bar but with a decent view of it – and of the girl working behind it. He liked to look at Lizzie – her sharp features, her long dark hair and her curves.

The waitress walked over towards him, her eyes cheekily fixed on his. "What can I get'cha, Mr Bergeron? Whisky as usual?"

"No. I'm starving, Lizzie. What's the *biggest* thing on the menu?"

"Chops and mash. Mutton chops fresh in this morning and Josie has made a really good horseradish mash – I'll tell her to put you an extra big lot out, if you like?"

"That'll do grand, Lizzie. And a pint of, of…"

"Ale, bitter? You Americans! You don't know nothing, do ya?"

"That's it, a pint of bitter, please, Lizzie."

He watched Lizzie's rear as she sauntered towards the kitchen, hips rolling as she did so. *What a girl! But can she get me a used jacket? I wonder what her father wears, and is he anything like my size?*

Soon Lizzie came over to his table with beer and an enormous plate. Chops and mash, swimming in rich, dark gravy.

"Thanks, Lizzie. It smells delicious!"

He ate hungrily, and the meal was soon finished and so he sat contemplating the bar area from his table in the back corner of the Nag. The clinks of glasses rang out above the noisy hubbub. The bar was very busy. All the customers were men and their boots banged on the polished wooden floor. Bergeron guessed they were mostly porters from the market who were popping into the pub for a swift drink between jobs.

Suddenly an idea came to him. As luck would have it, most of the porters and other workmen were wearing jackets. *That's it*, he thought, *but I'll need to hurry. They'll knock off work soon.*

As he finished his beer, Bergeron watched the porters intently. Eventually he settled on a tall fellow – around about his own size – wearing a brown tweed jacket. The jacket had clearly seen better days, but it was of fair quality and would certainly do the job. *A hardworking, though no doubt underpaid, chap will snap up the chance of pocketing two quid for an old coat*, he thought, *but I don't want him to 'blab' about the deal.*

Instead of calling Lizzie to fetch him another pint, Bergeron strolled over to the bar, stood behind the porter and deliberately bumped into him as he stood there, making sure a good portion of the drink he was holding spilled.

"Oi! Look out, mate!" The porter span around. "Look what'cha done! You clumsy so and so. That's my beer gone!"

"Sorry, sorry! My fault entirely." Bergeron was careful to disguise his North American accent. Now he adopted the best upper class English cut glass he could muster – good enough to take in a Covent Garden porter at least.

"Let me get you a drink. What will you have?"

"Don't mind if I do, guv. Thanking you very much. Mine's a pint of draught mild, please."

"I say there." He caught Lizzie's attention. "Mild for him and bitter for me. If you don't mind," he ordered, wondering why she was giving him such a quizzical look.

Lizzie placed the two pints of beer on the bar and Bergeron thrust a note in her hand, winking as he did so. "Keep the change, dear," he said.

The two of them, now bosom friends – the porter and the toff – sat down at the table at the back of the pub, which still housed Bergeron's empty plate.

Mr Porter took a long, slow drink of the beer. Clearly, he wasn't stupid, this man, for he immediately took the initiative. "What can I do you for then, guvnor?" he said, wiping the foam from his lips.

"Two pounds for the coat off your back, friend, but not a word to anyone, eh? What do you say?"

Bergeron had considered this was no time to beat around the bush, as the English say. As he asked the question he offered the porter two crisp, new £1 notes. The porter looked at him, but didn't take too long to make up his mind. He took the money, took off his coat and handed it over. Then he took another long drink from the pint glass, looking at Bergeron quizzically as he did so.

"Doing a spot of gardening, you see. Don't have one myself – not anything I would like to get dirtied up, if you see what I mean."

"Yes, sir. Understand you completely," said the porter, in a sarcastic way that suggested he understood nothing save the value of £2.

Of course, Mr Porter would talk, but only to his mates, about how he had fooled a city gent that an old jacket for the garden was worth two quid.

He finished his drink, stood up, and offered his hand to Bergeron – who shook it firmly – and left without a word.

Once the porter was gone, Lizzie came back to the table. "Why was you talking all funny to that geezer?" she asked. "You sounded like a proper toff!"

"Ah, that. Just, erm... just joking," he answered unconvincingly. "I have to be off now, Lizzie. Here, this is enough to cover the drinks and tucker. Keep the change."

"Thanks. Will you be back in tomorrow?"

"No. Actually I'm going to be away for a few days, maybe a week – not sure."

"That's a shame." She blushed slightly and looked genuinely disappointed.

"But I'll be back, don't worry," he added, as he got up to go.

What a bloody time to be going, he thought. *What a pity.*

He blew Lizzie a friendly kiss and made for the door. Carrying his new (and less than new) possessions in a handbag, he took up a northerly course back towards the Russell. Soon he was walking along Lambs Conduit. This street had long fascinated him. He wondered if it really did mark the line of a nineteenth-century waterway, a theory he had picked up from somebody. He couldn't remember who. An enclosed sewer or something, he supposed.

It was about half past four by the time Bergeron returned to his room at the Russell. He poured a glass of whisky then laid out all his kit. *Good enough*, he thought. *I should be able to pass myself off as Dudley Spring, student of archaeology from the University of London.*

He then emptied the room. With his usual meticulousness, Bergeron packed away everything of his which he did not need for his expedition, cramming his unnecessary belongings into two army holdalls. He was undecided about Soignon.

Soignon was heavy, but might come in very handy for aiding hill climbs, clearing thickets and defence; but it was also strikingly unusual and no doubt very easily recognisable. He decided to take it.

The London to Plymouth Express

The sign immediately in front of his eyes as he departed the lavatories at Victoria station made him smile. He marvelled, not for the first time, at the oblique and ambiguous predisposition of the English: *Gentlemen, please adjust your dress* read the sign.

So, after checking his trouser buttons, Dudley Spring walked nonchalantly across the concourse.

Earlier that day, Bergeron had awoken early. He made five laps of Russell Square in quick time, sprinting the two shorter sides and jogging along the others. He went back to his room, bathed and then had a good breakfast in the dining room.

He settled his account with a pompous-looking, middle-aged man at the hotel reception. He explained that he wanted to pay to keep the room, but was going away for a while. Bergeron had left just one bag in the room, he told the man.

"How long for, Captain?" asked the receptionist with a frown.

"Look, I don't really know, a week or two, I think, but I shall keep you informed."

Then he made arrangements with Bill, the concierge, to send the holdall he had brought down with him to an address in Rottingdean, which was his Aunt Maude's.

"I want to travel light," he explained, dangling the handgrip in front of the concierge. "Please would you get me a cab to Victoria, Bill? I'm off for a well-earned rest by the sea."

"Right away, Captain Bergeron sir."

He took the cab to Victoria station, tipping the driver. Upon entering the station Bergeron purchased a first class return ticket to Brighton, then went into the gentlemen's lavatory.

Once he had changed his clothes, transforming the city gent into a country rambler, he deposited the suitcase containing his city clothes – but with nothing through which he might be identified – with the left luggage clerk under the name Walsh. Captain Bergeron RCHA had effectively disappeared.

Dudley Spring walked to Trafalgar Square, from where he took the underground railway to Paddington station and made his way to the ticket office. He had considered buying a first-class ticket, which would have provided the most comfortable ride, but decided that a university student – even a moderately wealthy one – might have preferred to conserve funds by travelling second class. The clerk took cardboard tickets from a pile, removed a second-class ticket to Plymouth and stamped it with the day's date. Then he handed it to Bergeron. "Next train in fifteen minutes, sir," said the clerk pointing towards the platforms.

Before boarding the train, Bergeron stood and gazed at the train from the platform. The brown and cream of the Great Western livery complemented each other well, though the locomotive itself, he thought, could do with a damned good cleaning. He wanted a forward-facing seat, next to a window and away from the sun. That would be the right-hand side – starboard he preferred to think of it as. Soon he found a suitable carriage and an empty seat that fit the bill and so he sat down on it. He wondered whether it had been necessary to make all those convoluted arrangements not to be noticed. He thought probably not, on balance, but his father had always insisted that if any job was worth doing, then it was worth doing well!

Doors were slammed shut and the engine issued forth sulphur-stained smoke and steam. Whistles sounded, paddles waved and at last the train – as slowly as possible – inched itself out of Paddington station.

As the train built up speed Bergeron watched from the window as the landscape changed from the city houses to suburbia. Then the factories appeared, the Horlicks works at Slough being particularly visible. Urbanisation quickly transformed into countryside as the express thundered on. The train did not stop before Reading. Soon after, comfort overcame him and Bergeron slept.

Upon waking he found himself looking at a sign proclaiming Taunton station. Bergeron took the Crossing guidebook from his sack. *Better make a start*, he thought. *I think I'm ready to begin finding out about Dartmoor.*

Inside the front cover of the book he wrote:

D. Spring
London, 1918

Then he set to reading. Crossing began with a description of the boundaries of Dartmoor and a little about its history, before proceeding to provide a series of 'hints' for the Dartmoor rambler. Bergeron would never have described himself as a rambler, but he went directly to that part of the book, feeling sure it would hold some helpful information for him.

> *He will probably have read of the dangers of Dartmoor, and may have formed the idea that it is a land of mists and bog. It certainly cannot be denied that the moor is often enveloped in a mist in the winter, but such will not be found frequently to be the case in the season usually chosen by the visitor to make acquaintance with it.*

A chance of mist then; he winced at the thought.

And it must also be confessed that bogs are by no means rare.

Mmm. He smiled as he remembered some of the lads comparing a waterlogged support trench as to a Dartmoor bog.

But to be overtaken by the former, though sometimes proving rather awkward, is never dangerous, while the latter are only so to the rider to hounds who may be a stranger to the district.

Cross was a huntsman. Perhaps he'd ride into a bog and be sucked into its swamp like sponginess before Bergeron confronted him. No, Cross would be no stranger to Dartmoor. Bergeron read on, skipping tracts of Crossing's text as he did so.

The fen, or "vain", as the moormen call it, and which covers much of the more remote parts of the forest, consists almost entirely of peat, on which bog-grasses grow, in certain spots to a great height... often this ground will be found seamed in every direction, the rain having worn channels in the peaty surface, and these gradually widening and deepening, the whole tract is broken up by innumerable hummocks... In a dry season one may indeed pass through the fissures, for although the peat is soft he will not sink very far into it. I have many times walked for a considerable distance through these channels, my head being occasionally two or three feet below the surface of the ground.

Good Lord! Deeper than a bloody trench, he thought. But then, perhaps William Crossing had not been a tall man; a bantam type maybe.

He put down the book as the train pulled into Exeter St David's station. Three elderly women joined his carriage and bade him a good afternoon to which he doffed his hat.

"Colder than 'as bin," said one of them, "but at least it's dry, that's the main thing."

"It's goin' to rain later," replied a second.

"Oh, don't say that, Dotty!"

"That's what's my Charlie told me," said Dotty. "Rain later, 'e says."

"Well, I don't think so," said the third woman. "I take a look to the sky over west every morning, always have done, and 'twas red this mornin'. So, I says the warm will return dreckly. That's what I says."

"We'll soon see," said Dotty, and the three set to discussing the past week's trials and tribulations with Bergeron listening in. Tales of the failure of Ben Halliwell's garlic crop and of Doris Marley's problems with her hens kept him amused whilst he gazed towards Exmouth out of the train windows, marvelling at the wide and muddy estuary of the River Exe.

Bergeron looked at the grey open sea a short while later as the express thundered westwards and ran along the coast. Then they altered direction once more and now the locomotive worked its way northward, inland. As the train slowed down he watched a small flotilla of fishing boats enter Teignmouth harbour.

The women disembarked at Teignmouth where a porter pulled a large, brown-painted, four-wheeled trolley loaded with holdalls and suitcases. These seemed to belong to the rather loud family which accompanied him across the platform. Thankfully they boarded the compartment behind Bergeron.

After Newton once again he had the carriage to himself. The sea was no longer visible. In its place gently rolling countryside reached out on both sides of the railway line, and this in turn gave way to views over Dartmoor. Bergeron picked up Crossing once again.

A mire is of totally different character from the fen; it is really a swamp and is usually to be found at the heads of streams. Should the rambler inadvertently walk into one, he must at once retrace his steps, and on no account seek to go forward. Tussocks of rushes often grow on the edges of the mires, and these will afford secure footholds.

Crikey, he thought, *sounds dangerous.*

Mists sometimes suddenly envelope the moor in an impenetrable shroud; I have known my surroundings to be entirely obscured, and objects twenty or thirty yards distant rendered invisible, where ten minutes before there was not a sign of what was coming, and the mist has continued for several days.

Honestly, this is too much, Mr Crossing. He put the book down.

At Totnes, an attractive young woman sat on a bench made from varnished wooden slats stretched between cast iron supports that sported the GWR insignia. The varnish on the wood peeled and lifted forming an archipelago of rugged islets in a light brown sea. The woman was hatless, her hair pinned up, and she wore a dark blue two-piece in the modern style that revealed her pretty ankles.

An elderly man dressed in a grey suit and bowler hat got into his carriage, noticed the book and started up a conversation.

"Off for a tramp, are you? Knew the old man, actually!" He pointed at the Dartmoor guide.

"Crossing?"

"Yes, only vaguely, friend of a friend you might say. Hopkins, Diptford." He offered a hand. "Call me Bernard, everyone does."

"Spring. Dudley Spring, London. I'm a student. Archaeology – that's why I've got the guidebook."

"Archaeology, hey? Plenty of that on the moor. Spring, you say? Where you from, Mr Spring?"

"From Sussex, actually."

"Strange accent, not from round here that's for sure. Sussex, you say?"

"Yes. Spent some time in North America before the war."

"Did you serve?"

"Yes."

"Regiment?"

Bloody hell! Was this an inquisition? "Sherwood Foresters," he answered, quickly thinking of the name of an unglamorous regiment.

"Officer?"

"Lieutenant."

"Good boy, good boy." Hopkins stood up again and made a salute. "Well done, son," he said. "Well done!" Then he slumped to his seat and stared in front of him for some time.

"Lost my only son in that bloody war," he said. "Sorry, do excuse me."

Bergeron remained silent.

"He was a sailor. Killed at Jutland," Hopkins finally announced.

"I'm so sorry, sir. Wrong place, wrong time. It happens."

"Call me Bernard! I haven't been knighted. Not yet. His officer wrote to me, said my boy would have felt nothing – knew nothing about it. But I think that might be what all officers write to grieving families," and he looked at Bergeron expectantly.

There was nothing to say. Bergeron thought back to his conversation with Mrs Wainwright. Hopkins was right – of course. That is just what any OC would write to a bereaved family; but it didn't make it untrue.

The train had steamed through a tunnel. Smoke-infused steam floated in through the partially opened windows. Now it slowed into South Brent station. Bergeron looked to his left at the cluster of grey houses that demarked the eastern side of the village. To the right, he knew there would be open fields stretching to Dartmoor, speckled with occasional houses and farms. *Somewhere up there is Lower Aish House*, he thought, *and inside, right now I suppose, sits Cross.*

He heard the station master bellowing, "South Brent, South Brent. Change here for Kingsbridge, platform one. All stations to Exeter at platform three."

"This is my stop. I change here for the Kingsbridge branch. Primrose Line they call it." Hopkins held something in his right hand, and pushed it at Bergeron. "Here, take my card. Perhaps you'd do me the honour of visiting one day."

"Thank you very much, erm, Bernard." It somehow didn't feel quite right addressing the elderly man by his Christian name.

"Yes, that would be lovely."

"And good luck with your investigations. You can tell Mrs Hopkins and me all about it."

As Hopkins and the other passengers got up to leave the train, Bergeron felt compelled to get off here and now. He wanted to go over to the house immediately and confront Cross. Of course, he must not. There was Hopkins and far too many other people around who would remember the young man who disembarked the London-Penzance train. A tall young man with a knapsack. And a Dartmoor guidebook. No, he would stay on the train until Bittaford, a couple of stops further on, as planned. Always stick to the plan, unless the situation demands otherwise.

He waved farewell to Hopkins and looked at the card:

> *Bernard Hopkins Esq.*
> *Diptford*
> *Family Baker and Purveyor of Fine Cakes*
> *and Continental Pastries since 1894*

So, he thought, *Hopkins was a baker.*

Once out of Bittaford station, Bergeron bought a few supplies at the village grocer shop. Then he walked hastily uphill, passing to the west of the asylum and then along a lane which took him past Blackadon Farm and onward to the moor beyond it.

He walked swiftly and headed generally north, following the sinuous Ludd Brook until it petered out. Then he took a compass bearing to Spurrel's Cross, upon reaching which he walked due west crossing the River Erme, which was not difficult following a dry period. He met the elderly row of stones that continued up to Green Hill, stopping only once at the small circle which marks the southerly end of the stones.

There, Bergeron looked back across the landscape he had passed over. In the middle of the circle, with his back to the row, he was directly facing the cairn called Hilson's House and marvelled at the ingenuity of those ancient people who laid the stone row, aligning it perfectly north-south without compasses to aid them. On reaching the source of the Erme he set up the bivouac, his shelter for the night. He lit a fire and dined on bread, bacon and sweet black tea.

Once he had finished eating, he collected enough dry heather and bracken to make a sort of bed. Not perfect, but it would have to do. Then he covered himself with Mr Porter's jacket.

As darkness fell the air became cold which made sleep difficult for him. Bergeron considered tomorrow. He planned to march onwards to Princetown. At the post office, he would introduce himself as the student Spring and pick up his kit. The trunk was heavy, he would need to make several trips, but it would take no more than a couple of days to get everything back here and make a proper camp.

BASE CAMP

"Fire, fire, fire," he commands. "Stop, stop." It is a female voice.
"Ne le faites pas. S'il vous plaît, arrêtez."

Bergeron was woken by the dream as usual. His clothes were dripping wet with sweat. He lay still and silent in his rough bed and listened to the songs of skylarks, though he could not see them.

There was a gentle breeze which he was confident would soon move the light mist that shrouded the moor. With little thought, he swung into action a well-drilled routine of getting a fire roaring and making tea. As an artillery captain attached to an infantry company Bergeron had been entitled to a servant, but had preferred to billet alongside his team and had maintained a policy of sharing tasks with them. Both the leaf tea and sugar went together into the pot once the water was steaming. This made a strong, sweet brew which Bergeron enjoyed without milk.

Without his pack, but with map and guidebook stuffed into the pockets of Mr Porter's tweed jacket and Soignon in his hand, Bergeron walked quickly. He followed the old monks' track from the source of the River Erme and over Great Gnats Head. Fording the River Plym presented no problem and soon he sighted the farmhouse by Nun's Cross. An old man was tending his few sheep in a pen close by the house.

"Good morning!" called Bergeron pleasantly.

The old man stopped whatever it was he had been doing and looked up at him with suspicion. "Mornin'," he replied. "You'm lost?"

"No. Not lost, but tell me, how far to Princetown?"

"An hour. Less if you'm quick."

The old man returned his attention to his sheep as Bergeron walked on. Running north from the farm there was a good track, built and used by tin miners, which led into Princetown. He decided to follow this all the way.

Bergeron walked into Princetown at midday and entered the first pub he came across: The Plume of Feathers. It was dull inside, almost dark after the full light of a full, midday sun. The overpowering smell of furniture polish filled the air. A woman buffed the tables nearest the door. He confidently walked up to the bar. "A pint of cider, please."

The barman started and looked at him oddly.

"Sorry, it's the sun," he said, rubbing his eyes. "Cider?"

As his eyes had not yet accustomed themselves to the dark, he must have opened them as wide as possible in an effort to see. As he approached the barman the poor fellow must have been shocked at his appearance; his glaring, wide eyes must have tainted him with a look of madness. *What an arrival*, he thought.

"Yes, sir, straight away. Will that be sweet or dry, sir?"

"I'm from London, I don't really know. What's best?"

"I suggest medium, then sir. Pint o' the best cider this side of Exeter coming up, sir."

The barman turned and filled a pint glass from a barrel kept behind the bar. The barrel had a wet towel thrown over it to keep the cider cool.

"There you be, sir. That'll be five p'nce, sir. Thank you, sir, much obliged," he said as Bergeron handed over a tanner.

"Keep the change," he said, and made his way to a seat in a corner. First he smelt, and then took a sip from, the glass, savouring the bittersweet brew. He had read that the west of England had a reputation for first class cider, though he had tasted little of it. This was good; he was impressed. Then he drew breath before taking a much longer drink of the golden liquid. When he placed the glass on the table it was half empty.

He shouted to the barman, "Excuse me. Where will I find the post office?"

"Post office, sir? Can't easily miss it, I shouldn't think. Go out the front door and turn right. Cross the road and down towards the prison, sir. On the right."

He finished the drink in two more satisfying swallows and left. Inside the post office was a very pretty girl of about seventeen or eighteen, and she was the only person to be seen.

"Can I speak to the postmaster, please?"

"He's not here right now. What was it you wanted? Maybe I can help."

"My name is Spring and I'm from London. I sent a trunk here. It ought to have arrived earlier this week. Can I collect it now?"

"I don't know about any trunk. I'll have a look out back. Just hang on there a minute."

The girl disappeared into the back room of the shop. Bergeron could hear her moving boxes and papers around. Eventually, she called out, "Found it! At least I think so."

She came back into the shop. "But I can't shift it on me tod, sir. You'll have to come through and help."

Bergeron went into the back room with the girl. It was dark and he could smell food cooking in the kitchen beyond. They took hold of an end of the trunk each and, with him pulling and the girl pushing it for all she was worth, they manoeuvred the trunk through to the shop front. In the daylight Bergeron now recognised it.

"That's it," he said. "Thanks ever so much for helping with it." He pushed a pound note into the girl's hand.

She looked up and Bergeron saw that her eyes were a pale green colour. The girl's face reddened.

"Oh no, sir. That's all right. It wasn't a problem, really."

"Look, do take it. I have to ask another favour of you, and so it would make me feel better if you did."

"What other favour?"

"I can't carry everything in the trunk at once. So, if I could leave it here, I'll take half today and come back later for the rest."

The girl looked at him a little apprehensively.

"It's my camp equipment," he continued. "Tent, blankets, that sort of thing. And my books. I'm a student you see. Archaeology. I'm staying on the moor for a few weeks, doing a research project. Dudley Spring."

He offered his hand, then swiftly pulled it back as he realised a real English gent would never dream of shaking hands with a common shop girl. She now looked even more embarrassed.

"Sorry. What's your name?" he asked.

"Martha," she said.

"Martha, look, I'll take what I need from the trunk and leave the remainder here. I promise to return in a day or two."

He filled the backpack that was in the trunk, cramming into it all that he could. Then with help from Martha, he pushed the trunk back into the room behind the shop front. Leaving Martha to her thoughts, he quickly departed the post office before she could object and went to the village stores where he bought some supplies of food. Knowing that in a small and isolated community such as this people were likely to gossip freely, Bergeron was careful to tell as many people as possible about himself and his work as the archaeology student, Spring.

He told the old woman in the stores about his project; the mapping and detailed observations that he would make of the Bronze Age burial cists and mounds on the southern moor. Then he sauntered over to a café and ordered high tea, repeating this story to anyone who would listen. Later he revisited the Plume of Feathers and regaled a group of men with tales of student life in London. He was enjoying himself.

The old boys told him the story of how the prison – originally built in a previous century to house American and French prisoners of war – was put to good use during the war.

"Yer, scores of they conchies were billeted there," said a local.

"Them worked hard, though, boy. I'll hand that to 'em," added his compatriot, and Bergeron chuckled at the very idea of two men – both at least in their sixties – addressing each other as 'boy'. It reminded him of his time with the West Country regiments.

At last, at about six o'clock, wishing them a good evening, he left. He had stayed too long and had drunk too much. Dusk was falling and soon it would be dark. As quickly as he could with the heavy backpack, Bergeron set out to retrace his steps of that morning back to the makeshift camp at the head of the River Erme.

He moved easily enough across the moor as his eyes adjusted in the falling light. His thoughts were eclectic: the war; Cross; Martha in the post office; Lizzie at the Nag; Ryan – where was he?

After an hour, he stopped and stood dead still. Not because of the heavy pack. His wandering mind hadn't noticed as a mist had descended over the moor. Bergeron couldn't see. Where was he?

What was it that Crossing had suggested if this happened? He couldn't remember. *Think man, think.*

All that the visitor needs to take with him on his rambles over the moor is a stout stick, a sandwich case, and – as before named – a pocket compass.

Good advice. Why the bloody hell didn't I bring a compass? It was coming back to him, slowly. Yes, that was it:

If a stranger be overtaken by…

A sweat suddenly came over him. Bergeron felt it rising from his stomach to his face; this was just like the war when he had lost contact with a raiding party and found himself totally lost in no man's land somewhere in front of the Bois des Buttes. *Don't panic! Keep calm, control, control. Come on, Crossing, come on, mist you mean…*

> *If a stranger be overtaken by mist he should, when not certain of his bearings, endeavour to find a stream, and having done so, follow it till he reaches the borders of the moor, or some road. Attempts to strike a straight course over the moor will assuredly fail; he will only wander in a circle.*

Well, that wouldn't help, his chosen campsite was on a high spot and following a stream as Crossing suggested would take him further away from it. But all the streams and rivers around here must come from that high spot, and if he could find any one of them, perhaps he could reverse Crossing's admirable logic and follow it uphill to his bivouac.

It was in the same instant that the tactics to get out of this mess came to him, that Bergeron spotted something strange. Where he was, he did not know. That, and how to find his camp, would have to wait. For of one thing Bergeron was now certain: in front of him about thirty yards away was the figure of a man.

He stood perfectly still looking at the stranger and counted off 180. The figure didn't move in those three minutes.

Bergeron crouched low. He silently loosened the straps on his pack and slipped it from his back. He remembered he had packed his knife. This reassured him. He reached in the rear pocket of the pack for the weapon and found it, thankfully, for this was by far the best knife he had ever owned. And he was ready to use it.

For another five full minutes – Bergeron counted the seconds – he crouched without moving a muscle, straining his eyes in the darkness so that he might see well. The figure did not move.

Could I be mistaken? he asked himself. *Could it be a cow or pony?* No, it was a tall figure; it had to be a person. A man. Perhaps it was the shepherd he had spoken to earlier.

He left the pack and slowly, without making a sound, he moved to the right, keeping the same distance between himself and this stranger. Bergeron assumed the man would be right handed, most people were. If he had a pistol the man could use it more easily to his left-hand side. Bergeron positioned himself on the stranger's right, which had an added advantage: if the stranger was armed and turned to shoot at Bergeron, the movement would open up the man's chest making him more vulnerable to a frontal attack with the knife.

The figure did not move, but stood bolt upright and stock still.

Silently, Bergeron began to close him down, cutting the distance between himself and the man to ten yards.

What do I do now? he thought. It would be folly to attack the man, after all he was doing no harm. Again he waited. Nothing.

Time to take the initiative, he thought. Bergeron stood up and shouted, "Good evening, sir! Are you lost on the moor tonight?"

No reply. Not a start or a movement.

Bergeron moved closer and thought he could make out an arm. No! Not an arm. By God, a stump! Thoughts ran quickly through his mind. Was the man deformed? Perhaps he was wounded in the war.

"Excuse my asking, sir. Do you need help?"

Still no reply as Bergeron now moved ever nearer, knife at the ready.

Silence and mist covered the moor. Then Bergeron chuckled and turned around to collect his backpack, no longer worried about making any noise.

Well, he thought, *at least now I know just where I am*. It was not a man at all, but the cross by Nun's Cross Farm. Taller than a man, and in the dark of a night made darker by the Dartmoor mist, looking like an upright figure stood stark still, with a stump of an arm on each side.

Using Nun's Cross as a fixed and known point, Bergeron made his way to the infant River Plym, and soon found the ford he had crossed that morning. Then he set off in more or less the correct direction and worked his way slowly back to camp. The mist had lifted a little, enough for him to make his way through filtered moonlight, and eventually he reached his bivouac and pitched the small tent.

Tonight, he had woollen blankets to warm him. He considered it had been a good day with much accomplished, though he was now very tired. Snuggled into blankets and under a canopy of canvas, Bergeron thought about the girl in the post office, but his thoughts soon turned to Sarah Wainwright. Then there was Lizzie – just as nice and more accessible. With these pleasant thoughts, he drifted into a deep sleep.

IF THE WEATHER HOLDS

Bergeron had been in his camp for three full days. The rabbits were plentiful – though he found he was sharing his catch with a vixen. He had only caught the briefest glimpses of her, but her evidence was clear to see in his robbed snares. *Still*, he thought, *more than enough for both of us.*

He had taken a rest day after his first visit to Princetown. He took the opportunity to check through his belongings, re-pitch the tent he had thrown up in darkness and take a closer look at some of those stones and cists.

On Thursday he had returned to the post office to collect the rest of his kit. The girl Martha wasn't there, which he had considered a pity. He spelled out to the postmaster that he would be around and about for most of the summer – depending upon the weather, how the work went and how funds lasted. Bergeron would call in weekly to collect any post. A pound note helped ease any objection the postmaster might have had. "Oh, and I'm expecting company. An Irishman might call in a few weeks' time and enquire of me by name. Please would you give him this." He handed over a large envelope which contained a letter for Ryan and a small brass compass.

Of course, he had again taken the opportunity of repeating his cover story to anyone and everyone – *Old Uncle Tom Cobley and all.* The ploy seemed to be working. He presented an informal and relaxed persona and felt almost a local when the barman at the Plume of Feathers called him Dudley.

Today was Friday. *That's enough of the preparations*, thought Bergeron. *It's time to engage in another piece of research, nothing to do with prehistory this time.* He had decided to track down Cross.

Bergeron set off early and walked east from the camp, fording the River Erme at a point close to the circular Iron Age enclosures of Erme Pound, just where the river bends to the south. Following the stream, he too swung south for some miles, before picking up the drovers' track from the moor to the village of Ivybridge. Farmers used this track to take their beasts onto the spring and summer pastures of the open moor. In late autumn the animals were brought down to lower fields. Once a year, the Dartmoor ponies were rounded up and driven along tracks such as this to be sold at the annual pony fairs. People from distant towns and villages would flock to these events.

The shade offered by the oak, ash and beech trees lining the track was welcome, for the sun was high in the sky now and its heat oppressive. Soon the track brought him into Ivybridge and he saw the immense viaduct that carried the railway track across the River Erme. He climbed the steep flight of steps on his right, following a signpost to the station. He did not have to wait long for a train into South Brent.

He decided to avoid the village centre; there was no need to be there and he was still a little worried about being recognised. As he walked quickly away from South Brent station and the church, Bergeron sighted the village cricket green. He slowed to consider the options. Cross had always been a keen sportsman and cricketer; it was likely that he would be here sometime. Perhaps he would be playing or umpiring; or, if he were not fit enough, then spectating. But he would surely be here.

This offered him opportunities to observe the major, but he ran the risk of being seen. He would also need a cover story that in no way linked him with Dudley Spring, who should be miles away measuring megaliths and stone rows.

Of course, he thought, it would be most natural for a casual by passer to pause a while to take in part of a game. If he carried his binoculars, he could pass off as a birdwatching enthusiast from Exeter or Plymouth out for a day's spotting. His field glasses would be equally as good for observing Cross as they were for looking at the dippers by the river, or the blue tits and jays in the trees and bushes. He needed to know when the next village cricket match would be.

Well, there was never a time like the present for pressing on, he thought, so he went in through an open gate and approached a middle-aged man who was rolling the square and hailed him, "Good afternoon."

The man halted his labours and looked around.

"What a fine afternoon it is for a game of cricket. Preparing the pitch, I see. Will it take spin following these weeks without rain?"

"Like as not 'twill," the groundsman replied as he turned towards Bergeron. He leant against the roller.

"And do you have a decent spinner who can take advantage of the conditions?"

"Indeed we do," he replied. "Tom Luscombe is as good a wrist spin bowler as any I've seen hereabouts, and I've seen some good 'uns I can tell 'ee."

"Ah, but do you also have a batsman who can hold up an end against any spinner the opposition might have?"

"Now that the major is back 'ere from abroad, we does, yer. And 'appen he'll do more than hold up an end – he can proper slog 'em, can the major!"

"And when would this game be, that you are preparing the pitch for?" asked Bergeron, as casually as he could manage.

"Third Sunday in April. We's a playin' Cornwood. We start at two o'clock prompt. Dreckly after church and Sunday lunch. That's if the weather holds, mind 'ee."

He'd got what he wanted and before the old man had finished talking Bergeron had turned away from him and was walking onwards. "Must be off, good day, sir," he said as he continued his journey. *So, Sunday it is*, he thought.

He wanted to gain a good look at Lower Aish House. He walked past the vicarage and on over Lydia Bridge. The gateway to the house was on the left, but Bergeron carried on past it. He walked instead along a lane that bent around to the left and ran parallel with the Aish Estate, but always at least two fields away from the house itself and the gardens. Making sure he wasn't spotted, Bergeron forced a way through the hedge and into the first field. He found a group of trees that offered him good cover and settled down. From this convenient hide he had a wonderful view of the Aish buildings and the bridge behind them. He took a pencil and his red covered notebook and proceeded to draw himself a map.

Bergeron sat there for over two hours. In that time he saw several shapes moving around the rooms – servants probably. Nobody left the house and there were no visitors.

Then at around about four o'clock, Bergeron saw a car drive over Lydia Bridge and turn into the driveway of Lower Aish House. It was a grey-coloured Lanchester Forty which he recognised at once as it was basically the same as the armoured cars he had seen all over Belgium and France. The Lanchester drove up to the front door and stopped. The engine was cut. A chauffer in uniform stepped out of the front and when he opened the rear door Bergeron watched as a well-dressed couple stepped from the car and into the house. It was Major and Mrs Malaby Cross.

Information gathered, but how was he to retrace his steps without passing the house, the cricket field and groundsman again? He decided to carry on along the lane to the Kingsbridge Road station and catch the first train west from there.

Unfortunately, this time he had a long wait for a train. Once on board, to confound any chance observers, he decided to stay on the train as far as Cornwood rather than alighting at

Ivybridge and retracing his steps of the morning. From there he had a long walk to camp to consider. If he went by the most direct route from Cornwood to the base camp he would probably be forced to cross bogland in darkness, so he decided to follow the river, keeping as much as possible to the higher land on its western bank. It was longer, but more certain. A mist had begun to descend over the moor with the setting of the sun, but by now he was much surer of himself and he soon located his camp. The whole expedition had taken him less than nine hours.

THE FIRST GAME OF THE SEASON

Unusually, South Brent cricket ground was in the garden of the vicarage and Reverend Ansty's gardener doubled as the groundsman.

Cross arrived at one thirty. He and Ansty looked out of the lounge over the ground.

"What a lovely sight, eh, Ansty?"

The land belonged to the church and was loaned to the parishioners. Ansty was proud of this form of public service. The vicarage conservatory doubled up as a pavilion in the summer. There was a small, portable scoreboard together with an area where the few spectators could sit on blankets placed over the grass.

"Good afternoon, ladies," said Ansty as he greeted the four or five women who gathered, either to watch or to gossip. "Grand afternoon, Mrs Wainwright, Miss Wainwright."

Sarah Wainwright was standing behind a young man in a wheelchair. "Good afternoon, Peter," said Ansty. "Are you going to keep score for us?"

"Yes, Sarah will help me."

The ground was bordered by the river on two other sides and by the road on the third. On the boundary wall, which ran between the road and the garden, Ansty spotted a tall man in a tweed jacket sitting. He seemed to be taking in the scene and waiting for the cricket match to begin.

Cross came out of the vicarage dressed from neck to toe in white and wearing the cap of King's College, Cambridge. *Bloody outrageous that he should be captain*, thought Ansty.

Cross walked onto the square alongside the Cornwood captain. He deftly flicked a coin into the air, caught it in the palm of the same right hand and banged it down onto the back of his left.

"Heads," called the other man.

Cross removed the hand covering the coin and both men looked down to see how it had fallen. "It's tails," said Cross. "Bad luck, old boy. You can field first."

Five minutes later Malaby Cross was preparing to bat. Aided by the umpire, he painstakingly aligned his bat with the middle stump. Then with his right foot he scraped in the earth a mark which corresponded with his middle stump. Like all good batsmen, the major needed to know exactly where his stumps were.

The game began when a giant of an opening bowler from Cornwood started his run in from the church end. The bowler sprinted in, jumped and let fly the first delivery which sped towards Cross. The bowler was fast, but the delivery was a little too wide to be dangerous. *Leave it, leave it 'till you've judged the pace of the wicket*, Cross told himself.

The second ball was straighter and Cross decided to forward defend.

The Cornwood bowler bounded in again. He was gaining pace, thought Cross, but the next delivery was slightly overpitched and too far outside the major's off stump to be a threat. Cross pushed forward and followed through, driving the ball through the unmanned mid-off position.

"Yes!" called Cross. "Two, come on, Pearse!"

The batsmen completed their runs and Cross again took up his guard. The next ball was similarly wide, but shorter. Cross took a step backwards and brought down his bat upon and across the ball, causing it to speed towards the boundary. Pearse began to run towards Cross's end, but Cross, knowing how sweetly he had struck the ball, was confident it would beat the fielder. He didn't move. That was six runs off the first four deliveries.

The Cornwood giant improved and the next two deliveries were of good line and length, bringing out textbook forward defensive shots from the major, who pinched a single off the last and so kept strike.

The first ball of the next over was a short loosener, and was pulled by Cross to square leg for four. Eleven off the first seven balls was a good start.

So it continued. After forty-five minutes the two had put on sixty runs, when Pearse, *a tidy player himself*, thought Cross, received an absolute brute of a spinning ball from an older fellow bowling slow left arm. He was caught at slip for fifteen. The fielding side, and the few villagers who had turned up to watch, clapped him off.

Ansty was next in and he limped up to the crease.

"He won't bother us much," sniped the Cornwood captain to his fellow slip fielder, who smiled.

The Reverend Ansty knew very well what they were sniggering about. Both men had noticed the vicar's pronounced limp. But Ansty was an Oxford cricket blue and no mean batsman, though he did say so himself, being particularly effective against spin.

He limped up to Cross. "No quick singles I'm afraid, Major," he said.

I might not be able to run very well, he thought, *but I won't need to.* There were five balls of the over left for Ansty to face. He defended the first two, watching carefully how the ball turned off the track – from off to leg. The next delivery was on his legs and he swept it to the boundary for four. The following ball was tossed up and Ansty drove it high over the head of the fielder at long on. The umpire signalled six runs. The last ball of the over he drove into a gap between two fielders. It was an easy single – possibly two runs. "No!" shouted Ansty.

The batsman did not change ends once during the remainder of the South Brent innings. Cross had quickly realised the vicar could not run, and so he adopted a similar strategy; anything he could not put away for four or six was either left alone, or they simply did not run.

As though spurred on by Ansty's inability, the two of them set about demolishing the Cornwood bowling attack and a clinical accumulation of runs commenced. At half past four, with Cross on 110 and Ansty on 48, the latter was bowled out and South Brent declared at 177 for two. All the players made their way to the conservatory pavilion. The spectators inside the garden went in with them, Sarah Wainwright pushing the wheelchair.

At this point the tall man on the wall, who had stayed to watch all the South Brent innings, decided to leave. Anybody taking an interest in him would have observed him making his way through the village, stopping by at the church, then following the lane to Wrangaton and the Kingsbridge Road station, from where he took a train.

Nobody saw him; or if they did, they took no notice because nobody took any interest in a loan rambler, or ornithologist perhaps, out for a nice day in the late summer sunshine.

Doncha Ryan Departs the Emerald Isle

"You did well, Donny boy. Good lad!"

It was the day after the Bantry ambush. Ryan had walked most of the way to Clonakilty where he met Tom Deans in Mrs Deasey's tearoom. The room was light and airy and looked out over the main street. Orla Deasey, Mrs Deasey's youngest and, thought Ryan, most attractive daughter came over to the table at which the two men sat.

"What'll yous be wanting?" asked Orla.

"Now what will you have to eat? It's my treat," offered Deans.

"Thanks, Tom. Are you serving high tea yet, Miss Deasey?"

"Sure."

"Fish and chips, please," he told the waitress.

"I'll have a fish too, but not the chips," said Deans, "and a pot of tea."

Orla Deasey turned to go.

"I'll have peas and plenty of bread and butter, please," added Ryan.

"Will that be brown bread, white bread or pan bread?" asked Orla.

"Brown soda. Oh, and ask your mammy if she has any boxty."

"You hungry then, Doncha?"

"Aye. My dad told me 'eat well when you can, Doncha – for you never know what's around the corner, son'."

Orla Deasey turned around to go off to the kitchen. Ryan noticed that she had a good arse and long legs.

"So, Doncha. Tell me all about it."

"Nothing much to tell, Tom. In war, surprise is everything. And this is a war. The guns and ammunition are safe, not a shot was fired. No casualties on either side, but a lot of embarrassment on theirs. Have I earned my leave?" asked Ryan.

"Aye, 'course you have, Doncha."

Deans looked at Ryan and laughed. "You daft bugger, 'course you have. Make your way to Glandore tomorrow. Then get your arse down to the harbour and ask for Skipper Paddy Malone. When you find him say *Freeman* sent you. That's the code word, Free-man. Get it?"

"Who thought of that, Michael bloody Collins?"

"And here's the gun."

Deans took his own revolver, a Webley, from his inside pocket and handed it to Ryan. "It's loaded, by the way, and here are six more rounds. You never know," he grinned. "Oh, and Doncha, if possible I would like it back one day."

"Sure, Tom."

"Here." Deans passed him a note.

Ryan looked at the paper. It had a name, McGuire, and an address in London written on it.

"To get back," said Deans "your first option is the same way you got there. Negotiate that with Malone. If you're in trouble, get to London and look up Sam McGuire. Not unless you have to, mind."

Ryan took the note, revolver and the six bullets. "Thank you, Tom," he said. "Thank you very much."

"Don't mention it, Don. Just come back safe and sound. There's more work to be done here. Things are about to get nasty!"

THREE DAYS IN LONDON

Monday

Bergeron didn't want to stay at the Russell Hotel again. He didn't like the place and Rottingdean was well within the distance for a day trip to the capital; staying over may cause suspicion. In any case, he had a much better idea.

He walked from Paddington to Covent Garden and entered the Nag. Lizzie caught his eye immediately and she was at his usual table in the rear corner almost before him.

"Nice to see you, Mr Bergeron! Are you growing a beard?"

"Yes, thought I'd give it a try. What do you think?"

"Suits you! Now, what can I get you?"

"Whisky, please, Lizzie. And my name's Marc. Call me Marc."

She came back with the whisky and some water.

"Sit down for a minute, Lizzie, will you? I have something to ask."

"Can't. Not allowed. But I'm finishing in half an hour. Meet you in the White Lion if you like?"

"Righto. See you there."

He left and wandered around the market for a while; it was late afternoon and the place was rapidly emptying.

The White Lion was on the opposite side of James Street to the Nag. Both pubs looked very similar to each other, as the whole area had been modelled on an Italian piazza by some arty-farty Victorian architect. Bergeron walked into the

Lion, bought himself a double scotch and sat down. The place smelled of stale beer.

Lizzie walked in and found him immediately in the small bar.

"Get you a drink?" he asked her.

"Blob, please."

"Blob?"

"White wine and hot water."

"Not a particularly summery drink, is it?"

"Nice though!"

He bought Lizzie the drink, and another whisky for himself.

"What did you want to ask?" she said. Directness was Lizzie's way.

"I need somewhere to stay, just for a couple of nights. It's rather complicated, so I don't..."

"You can stay with me. It's nothing special, just rooms over by Soho. But you're welcome to stay for as long as you like, Marc."

"Thanks. You sure it'll be all right?"

"Sure."

"That's settled then."

They drank up, left the pub and walked west along Long Acre before turning right onto the Charing Cross Road towards Lizzie's rooms. Neither of them spoke, but after a while she pushed her left arm into the gap between Bergeron's right side and his own arm. Once into the building it was up two flights of stairs and through one of three doors on the landing.

"As I say, not much to look at, is it? But it's clean and homely, like."

"It's fine, just fine, Lizzie. I need to wash a few things, travelling light as you can see."

"I'll do it for you," she said.

Bergeron handed over his pack which contained some dirty clothes.

"Undress!" she said. "I might as well wash the lot while I'm doing it."

Bergeron turned away from her and took off his boots and socks, then removed his shirt.

Lizzie looked at his back and, noticing the scars, she winced. "Oh my, do they hurt?"

"Not now, but they did, yes."

He dropped his trousers and took off his pants. She moved forward and put her hands on Bergeron's shoulders, gently massaging with her fingers and thumbs. "You are a strong boy!" she said. Then she lightly kissed the scars on his back. "Kiss them better for you."

As he turned around to face her, he saw that Lizzie had already removed her blouse. Now the tops of her breasts were fully visible and her nipples pushed through the flimsy fabric of the bodice she was still wearing. She looked nothing like Sarah Wainwright, he thought. Lizzie's shape was fuller – a woman not a girl. And Lizzie was altogether... how could he put it? Less urgent; more desirable.

Lizzie looked him in the eye. Her gaze then drifted down, and it fell upon his chest, his waist and lower still. After a few seconds of this, Lizzie looked him in the face again, blushing. They both smiled.

He slowly removed her bodice. Not being able to help himself, Bergeron gazed at Lizzie's breasts and the sensation he felt between his legs confirmed that they were having an effect.

They moved towards the bed. Lizzie, now fully undressed, pulled back the blankets, pushed him onto the bed and climbed on top of him. He traced the index finger of his right hand around her belly button, then up to her breast, her left breast. Softly, gently he squeezed it.

"That is so lovely," she said. "Do it some more. Please, Marc." She saw him looking at her. "It's rude to stare," she said and she smiled at him again.

Eventually, both spent, Lizzie moved off him and nestled into his embrace. She asked, "You didn't need to stay here, did you, Marc? You could have stayed anywhere. You've got money, I can see that."

"I don't like spending it," he lied.

"That the only reason?"

"And I've been staying in hotels way too long."

"Truth?"

"All right. I wanted to stay with you. I've always had an eye for you, couldn't you tell?"

"'Course I could tell. Wasn't sure you were going to get around to asking though." She laughed; it was contagious. They made love again.

★

Tuesday

All through the morning Bergeron stayed in Lizzie's rooms. He was tired; she hadn't allowed him much rest. At ten o'clock she went off to the shops, came back with food and drink which she prepared. They ate, drank and then had more sex. Of course, they both knew it could not last: he had the nagging thought of returning to the West Country, whilst Lizzie already had experience of falling in love with young men who then disappeared – whisked away to face danger.

In the afternoon, Bergeron went back to the offices of Anderson & Finn, reported to the receptionist and was soon taken through to Gerry's room.

"Please wait here, sir," said the receptionist, an elderly man wearing a dark suit. "Mr Finn shouldn't be long. Can I fetch you a cup of tea?"

"Yes please. That would be nice."

Bergeron sat and waited for a few minutes when Gerry Finn walked into the room.

"Well, hello, Captain Bergeron." Gerry greeted him with a smile and a long, firm left handshake. "How are you?"

"Fine, Gerry, thank you. How's life been treating you?"

"Can't complain, can't complain. Business is looking up and the old man's made me a partner as promised."

"And Mrs Finn? How is the fair lady? What does she do with you so busy?"

"Good, good. Surprised you'd think she's a stay-at-home wife! She's very well indeed, thanks, old boy. Working at Anderson's New Hospital. And how are things with you?"

"As usual, Gerry. Up and down. Still considering what to do. Need some advice, actually."

"That's what I'm here for."

"You're here to take my money, Gerry, and well you know it!"

"Ouch! That stung! Now, now don't be a nasty captain. You know I always give preferential rates to former comrades-in-arms."

Finn took an envelope from his desk and thrust it at Bergeron. "Letter for you – from Ireland."

Bergeron took the envelope. He opened it with Gerry Finn looking on expectantly. His eyes ran quickly along the few lines scrawled on the paper it contained, immediately taking in the contents. Then he put the envelope into his jacket pocket.

"Only joking, Gerry. Any other post? You're my only contact with mail from the outside world, you know."

"Sorry, nothing, old man."

"I need advice on my will, Gerry."

"Ah yes, thinking of popping off, are you?"

"You never know what's 'round the corner."

"So, you walk under a tram and it all goes to some old auntie in Brighton. Simple."

"Old Aunt Maude is in Rottingdean, actually. And that's the point. She is old. But now that both my parents have gone – well, who else do I have that I might leave it to? No one, Gerry. There are no other family members left. I am simply the last of the Bergerons," he laughed.

"Last of the Bergerons," affirmed Finn. "Fenimore Cooper could have written a bloody book about you then, never mind the Mohicans! What advice do you want, exactly?"

"Just tell me, what are my options, Gerry?"

Gerry Finn sat back and thought for a while. "Best advice I can give you is to marry and have a few baby boy Bergerons, if you get my drift."

"Not an option just now, Gerry. You know me. No trouble attracting them, but keeping them? Something always seems to turn up. There was a girl back home in Canada. I thought… but we ceased writing some time ago, and I expect she's gone and married elsewhere by now."

"Friends?"

"Just one. From the war. But I don't think he particularly needs it."

"You religious?"

"No."

"Charity, then. I can look into it and come up with the likeliest list for you if you want me to."

"Is that the best you can do, Gerry?"

"I'm a solicitor, Marc, not a bloody magician. How much are we talking about, anyway?"

"I received all the profits from the sale of Father's business in 1916. It's well invested. Pays me an annual salary which varies according to stock prices. Last year it was around £2,000. I spend a tiny fraction of it. You know me – simple tastes. And anyway, up to this year I wasn't even spending all of my army pay. So, it's been rolling up since then."

"What are you plans, Marc?"

"Not too sure. I have some business here in England that might take me up to autumn. After that? Back to Canada, I suppose. Nothing to keep me here. Mother had friends in Clifton. I promised I would visit them to explain exactly what happened. Then? Back to my old regiment I suppose – the good old Royal Canadian Horse Artillery."

"Clifton?"

"It's a small place in Ontario. Mother didn't want to stay on in Quebec once Father had died."

"Here's my advice. Leave it for now, you look healthy enough. I will consider options on the charity side of things. Call in in a week or so and I will have a list for you. In the meantime, Marc, find a wife!"

"Thanks, Gerry. I'll think about that suggestion. Did you find out anything about those French children?"

"Debreux has been trying for us, but nothing to show yet, old man."

★

Wednesday

Alan Toynbee collected together the pencils and papers from his desk and placed them neatly into a drawer. Then he took a duster and cleaned the blackboard; nothing worse than coming into a classroom in the morning to find yesterday's geography all over the board, he thought.

He had a report to write for the headmaster on Chester, a strange boy with blonde hair and no friends. Once that job was done the rest of the day was his own.

★

In the morning, Bergeron went to the letter that Gerry Finn had handed him. It was from Ryan and he read it again:

Ballynacarriga

Monday

Dear Boss,

No problems. I will be with you by end of next month, but I don't have a date yet. Will bring the goodies as you requisitioned. Where will I find you?

Ryan had never been a good writer. Indeed, his lack of education exposed the inadequacies of the British system, thought Bergeron, for he knew Ryan to be a highly intelligent man. *That doesn't matter*, thought Bergeron. *It isn't for his literary style that I want him along.* Bergeron quickly penned his reply:

Don,

Just report to the post office in Princetown, Dartmoor. Ask there for Dudley Spring.

The postmaster will have instructions for you.

M.B.

He would post it later. It was time to say goodbye to Lizzie. He had spent far too long in her arms already, and he knew that if he left it much longer the temptation to abandon revenge and stay might prove too enticing to resist. It was now or perhaps never.

"Do you really have to go?" she asked.

"I'm so sorry, but yes I have to," he said. "It's my aunt, you see, she can't manage on her own anymore. I'd intended getting a train back to Brighton around midday, and it's well past that now."

He looked at Lizzie and her sad, watery eyes. He moved towards her and took her in his arms, kissing her deeply on the lips.

"Look, Liz," he said, "I promise I'll be back soon, but I really just can't say when it will be," and with that he kissed her again and was on his way.

Lizzie watched from her window as Bergeron walked towards the Tottenham Court Road. He had intended to hail a cab to take him to Paddington, but his thoughts were miles away, firmly focused on the days ahead. So much was he elsewhere in his mind that he didn't at first realise his name was being called.

"Bergeron! I say, Bergeron!" Eventually, he stopped and turned. A man in civilian clothes, his own age or similar, had crossed the road and was bounding towards him.

"It is Bergeron? Marc Bergeron, Royal Canadian Horse Artillery, isn't it?"

He tried to look blank in order to gain some thinking time, though Bergeron had recognised Toynbee at once.

"Toynbee. Lieutenant, well, was. 7th East Kents. You were attached to my company for a while."

Bergeron smiled. "Steady the Buffs!" he said and he held out his hand.

"Steady the Buffs," Toynbee repeated, and both men laughed. They shook hands vigorously.

"Toynbee! Well, what a bloody surprise!"

"Fancy meeting you here! Time for a drink, old boy?"

"In a bit of rush Toynbee. Why not walk along with me?"

"Yes, why not. Keeping busy, are you?"

"Sort of, yes. Staying on the south coast with my aunt. Needed to do a few jobs in town, that's all."

Bugger, he thought. *Where to lead the bloody fool? Not towards Paddington.* The Russell was obvious so Bergeron led Toynbee in that general direction. They turned right at the museum.

As they walked on, the hotel came into view, and Bergeron decided to grab the bull by its horns.

"Perhaps I do fancy a drink, as a matter of fact. The Friend at Hand is as good a boozer as any." He waved them down a side street.

They sat at a table and ordered whiskies.

Toynbee took a sip, and spoke first.

"Do you keep in touch with many of the others?"

"No, not really. Just one: ex-Ox and Bucks officer, Finn. Met him in hospital, don't suppose you knew him."

"No. I remember Tull, do you?" asked Toynbee.

"Tull, yes. Officer in the Middlesex Regiment. Walter, wasn't it?"

"That's him," said Toynbee. "Good footballer, good man."

"I didn't know he played football."

"You are joking, Bergeron!"

"No. Not at all. Canadian, remember. Wrong size ball anyway."

"Tull had been a professional. Tottenham Hotspur and Nottingham Forest, I think."

"No!"

"I'm not pulling your leg, one of the first black professional footballers."

"Really? I had no idea. Well, he was a bloody good infantry officer, that's for certain. What became of him?"

"Lost. Body never found."

"Bastard war!" said Bergeron. "Do you keep in touch with anyone?"

"Bernard Cripps from the regiment, he's the only one. Oh, and Julian Feltham, but I knew him before the war. He's a doctor now. You've met Feltham – he was asking about you. Problem?"

"Dreams. Bad dreams, that's all."

"And Feltham could help?"

"No. Bloody useless!"

"Come on, old man, tell me the whole story, won't you. How did you end up with our lot?"

Of course Toynbee knows, thought Bergeron, *but he just loves reminiscing.*

"Picked you out of a great big bag of lovely options, of course. Wanted to serve with the best!"

"Really? Foo-Foo, that's what Toddy called you!"

"Yes – and I bloody hated it."

"Ruddy good job you were there though, Bergeron! Without you… Well, you know better than I, when we were attacked at Vendeuil, well, like as not we'd all have bought it."

"Oh, don't exaggerate, Toynbee!"

"I'm not exaggerating. You were a hero, Bergeron. At least, you must admit, it was a good enough display to get you your gong."

"Yes, the gong – as you call it. Well, the way I see it is that they wanted a few heroes. Easiest time to get a medal is when things are going badly for the army you know. That's the way it works. There's no place for cowards in war, Toynbee, that's for sure. In my opinion, there's no place for heroes either."

"If you say so. Anyway, right after that show you left us, didn't you? Moved to a battalion of the Devonshire Regiment – or was it the Duke of Cornwall's Light Infantry? Something like that, I heard."

"Well, yes and no, as a matter of fact, Toynbee. You see, once I left you I was posted again, to Staff this time. Well, I had a very jolly time there, playing around at HQ at Montreuil-sur-Mer, and that lasted a couple of months, till Jimmy, the chief linguist there, took a bit of notice."

"Jimmy?"

"Jimmy Marshall-Cornwall."

"Never heard of him," said Toynbee.

"No reason why you should. Anyway, Jimmy cottoned on that our hero could speak a few languages himself. I'm not bad at languages you see, even if I say so myself."

"Just out with the bloody tale, Bergeron!"

"Once the German attack had been held, he thought that my knowledge of French and German might be put to better use. So, he had me *smoothing* the lines of communication between our lot and the French. Don't know about smoothing, manufacturing a balls-up more like. Picking up some useful bits of info along the way. So I was moved to another British infantry outfit, this time to one on the Allied right flank, shoulder to shoulder with the French. Not much to do, in all honesty."

Bergeron took another sip of whisky.

"But what you picked up was wrong in a sense, Alan. I was with the Devonshire Regiment for a while, 2nd Battalion. Never with the Duke of Cornwall's though. After my spell with the Devons, I was posted to the South Devon Light Infantry."

Toynbee almost choked on his scotch.

"The South Devon LI, was it? Which battalion?"

"3rd," replied Bergeron.

"I had no idea. Bloody hell, I remember them. You must have come across Howard Wadham, then?"

He took another, longer sip of the whisky. *Why didn't I just let him think it was the bloody DCLI?*

"Want another, Toynbee?"

"Go on, then – yes! Cross and Wadham – what reputations they had. Did you ever meet them?"

"Yes and no," he lied. "Heard of them both, sure. Who didn't? Never met them though. Two more Johnny Walkers and some water, here! I was mostly working at battalion HQ. Never got down to company level, you see."

He paused to think then carried on.

"You know what it's like. Even in wartime a battalion is an extended family, Toynbee. Companies and platoons, it's smaller, nuclear elements. Attached odds and sods like me are seen at best as the awkward in-laws. Anyway, Alan, that's answered your question, hasn't it? So, what have you been up to since? Still writing, are you?"

"Still trying to, yes."

Toynbee began fidgeting. He tried each of his pockets in turn, searching for something. "Decommissioned at the end of '18. The army didn't need so many subalterns, and anyway, I never intended staying on. I'm no soldier – not like you. I'm teaching now, as a matter of fact, just back for the new term."

"Teaching what?"

"History."

"Will you teach them about the war?"

"Not yet – but one day, yes I suppose so."

"Good school?"

"Nice one. A prep school in Bloomsbury – just finished for the day as a matter of fact. I say – we could take in a show? What do you think?"

"Sorry, Alan – can't. Really sorry! As I said, off tomorrow. Need to pack."

"No, no. No need to apologise. I understand. What are you doing now anyway, Bergeron? Funny to see you here. No plans of returning to the home country?"

"One day, perhaps, yes. Not ready yet. Things to do, you see. I've taken a break from soldiering, but I aim to return to it – and to Canada, eventually. It's just that I'm not sure when, that's all."

"Here it is!" announced Toynbee. "I knew I had it somewhere." He passed a piece of paper to Bergeron; it was clearly a sheet of lined paper torn from an exercise book, on which was a handwritten sonnet. Bergeron read it out loud.

"She shall not know.

I'll show no sign of terror
Whilst I lie with her in bed.
She'd simply shudder at the horror
Of my lingering fears and dread.

I'll stay awake tonight
To silence guilty utterings,
And she'll know not my fright.
Argh! – damned sleep. My mutterings

Must be most alarming.
My love awakens. I sweat from fear.
'What have they done, my darling?'
She touches me. Holds me near.

However intimate we may become, through our flesh and in our heads,
She can never know the darkness through which her soldier treads."

"I say, Alan, this isn't bad at all."

"Mmm. Do you really think so? I don't know, still work to be done. Some of the rhymes, and that line ending '*through our flesh and in our heads*', I don't much care for. Wanted to use thoughts, you see. Not heads."

"Do you suffer dreams, Alan?"

"No. No, never. I know some chaps do, though. I just, well, just made it up really."

"Look, Toynbee, I have to be off. Have you finished?"

"Yes, suppose so." Toynbee took his glass and drank up. The two men shook hands.

"Look, Bergeron, take my card, and any time you're in town, or if you need a hand at all, just look me up." Toynbee handed him a card with contact details.

"Thanks, I, erm, I don't have one."

"Not a problem, Marc. But promise to keep in touch."

"Yes, I will. I promise."

Toynbee walked south, towards his flat, but after taking just a few paces he turned and shouted.

"Northampton!"

"What?" asked Bergeron.

"Not Nottingham, Northampton."

Bergeron looked puzzled.

"Walter Tull's club was Northampton Town. I think."

He walked as far as the hotel entrance, turned to check that Toynbee was no longer in sight, then continued north towards Euston Road. Soon Bergeron was once again on an express train from Paddington bound for the west country.

A Letter from England

Clifton, Ontario

Mrs McKenzie sat in her favourite chair reading the *Daily Enterprise*. It was cold for the time of year and the old lady was wrapped in a woollen cardigan and had a lightweight woollen blanket around her shoulders. It was tartan, green and yellow tartan. Anne worried that her mother might be going down with the flu.

The elder McKenzie let the paper fall from her grasp. "Anne," she said, "tell me, was it worth it?"

"Mother?" replied Anne McKenzie.

"Well, the war ended almost two years ago. I'm so relieved, of course, but I wonder was it worth all those poor boys' lives."

Anne sighed. Always the same question. "Yes," she said.

"Yes? Do you really think so?"

"I mean, no. No, it probably wasn't worth it, but what does it matter now?"

Anne knew that it mattered to her mother, just as it mattered to any mother who had lost a son at war in a far-off land. Mothers wanted to know their sons had not died in vain. "I'm sorry, Mummy," she offered, weakly.

Mush began barking. She was out in the garden and had spotted somebody slowing down near the McKenzies' gate.

Jim Alexander, one of three Clifton postmen, was used to dogs. He was good with them. In his line of work, he needed to be. Jim offered the back of his hand to the large Malamute; he found that it always helped to let a dog have a good old smell of him. Dogs relied much more on their nose than their eyes to tell the difference between friend and foe, somebody once told him.

Anne and her mother turned towards the window to see what the dog was barking at.

"Look," said Anne's mother. "Is that the postman coming along to deliver at our house? Excitement indeed!"

It was unusual for post to be delivered to the McKenzies these days and so the dog had possibly overreacted. Mush was loud rather than fierce, however, and was now fussing around the postman, tail wagging furiously.

Jim sauntered up to the front door of the McKenzie house and posted a single item through the letterbox. Then he walked slowly back along the garden pathway, giving Mush a farewell tickle under the chin.

Anne walked quickly to the door and picked up an envelope. She gazed at it in her hand. It was a white, foolscap envelope and the postage stamp told her it was from England. She brought the franking mark closer to her eyes and read the postmark, dated two weeks earlier. The most unusual thing about the envelope, however, was that it was addressed to Anne herself.

"It's for me, Mother. From London, England. What on earth can it be?"

"Well, open it, girl. Open it."

Anderson & Finn
Solicitors at Law
Lincoln's Inn Fields
London

11 May 1920

Dear Miss McKenzie,

I am writing in my capacity as the solicitor representing Captain Marc Bergeron, RCHA.

My office is Captain Bergeron's postal address and an amount of unopened correspondence, seemingly written by yourself to the captain, has recently come into my possession. It seems there has been some confusion and lack of expediency within the military.

I am now able to reply on the captain's behalf as, thankfully, you had written your address on the reverse side of some of the envelopes. By the handwriting I see that all the letters were written by yourself. It is quite clear that these letters have remained undelivered – and unopened – for some time.

I would like to take this opportunity of informing you that Captain Bergeron is perfectly fit and healthy. He is away from London at the moment and I am unsure of when he will return.

You have my assurance, Miss McKenzie, that as soon as he does return from his business I will deliver the aforementioned correspondence to Captain Bergeron at the first opportunity.

Yours sincerely,
Gerald Finn, Esq. (Partner)

Tears rolled silently down Anne's cheeks.

"What is it, dear? Do please tell me?"

She turned to her mother and smiled. "He's alive, Mother. Marc is alive! He never received my letters!"

Back to Dartmoor

From his vantage point on Eastern White Barrow Marc Bergeron saw a lone figure briskly walking along a line that led from the farm at Nun's Cross to his own makeshift camp. He took the field glasses from his knapsack to check. Sure enough it was the Irishman, Doncha Ryan. He looked just the same as Bergeron remembered him. *God*, he thought, *is he really so small? Let's have a little fun!* He immediately dived down to take cover.

As instructed in the note left at the post office, Ryan made himself comfortable. Whilst he was making a brew, Bergeron circled behind him and crept up on him. Ryan was sitting outside the small tent sipping his tea, staring into thin air and singing, as usual. *He's daydreaming*, thought Bergeron.

"Stand to, Bombardier!" shouted Bergeron in what he considered to be a reasonable imitation of a British army sergeant's voice.

At first Ryan didn't move a muscle. Then he rose and turned slowly towards the command. A big grin broke out on his face.

"You ought to have posted sentries out on that hill," said Bergeron, pointing to Green Hill behind him.

"No need. Heard you a-rustling through the bracken, boss," he said. "Pretty certain it was you, but had this ready – just in case." He looked down to the Mauser which was in his right hand, most of it covered by his jacket. Don Ryan, reliability personified.

"Good to see you, Doncha. Good to have you here."

"And it's bloody good to see you, boss!" he replied, standing to his unimpressive full height. "The beard suits you."

"Do you think so?" Bergeron brushed his left hand against the bristles. "My mother would have said it makes me look dirty, but I can't afford to be recognised."

"Tea?" asked Ryan.

"Yes please. How was the journey, Don?"

"Good enough. Fishing boat from Glandore. That's near Skibbereen," he added, seeing that Bergeron was vacant at the place name.

"A skipper called Malone, a tough-looking old man. The sail to England took a day and a night. Bloody seasick the whole time. That small boat was pitching and rolling along, so it was. The voyage was bearable. Just. Once on dry land I was fine. Malone decided to drop me near a place called Lynmouth rather than in Wales. He said it was more secure. The authorities might try to track a boat from Ireland to Wales, but never to North Devon. Anyway, meant I could walk to Princetown across Exmoor and Dartmoor, with the advantage that nobody would see me approach."

"You walked it then?"

"Aye, I did."

"How far is it?"

"Getting on for eighty miles, I should think. Took me two days to get north of Princetown. Did the remainder just now."

"Still fit then?"

"Aye."

"That's good. There'll be more walking to come. So, you got to Princetown. What then?"

"Went directly to the post office to enquire about Dudley Spring. Nice-looking young thing gave me a package."

"That'll be Martha."

Ryan went into his pocket and dug out a compass and a

letter, and gave them to Bergeron who pocketed the compass. Then he reread what he had written just a few days before.

You made it, Don. Thank the Lord!

My camp is on the moor, to the south east of Princetown.

Do not attempt this journey except in good visibility.

There's a path behind the pub that heads south east towards a distinctive hill. Follow it to a stone cross near a small farm.

Then use the compass.

First go south east from the farm to a ford on the river. There's another track which first goes south, then east towards a clay pit. You will see the spoil heap clearly in front of you. My camp is by a brook between the Broad Rock and the clay pit – there are no other camps around about. If I'm not there do make yourself at home.

I am assuming you have room in your pack. Buy some supplies, include a bottle of whisky.

"So, I just followed your instructions, boss. Easy, like."

"Did you get the whisky in Princetown?"

"No," Ryan replied. "They had none in the stores." Then he smiled again. "But I've brought you some of the real stuff from Ireland."

"Let's have some with the tea then. Good old Thunder and Lightning." They sat down to talk and plan. This was likely to be a long night, thought Bergeron.

"How's things back home, Don?"

"Bastard police and soldiers!"

"I meant the family?"

"Not so good, you know."

"Tell me."

"It doesn't matter, boss."

"Go on."

"Well, you'll remember that Padraig – he was my elder brother – was killed on the Somme in '16 near Ginchy – with the Fusiliers. Well, if that weren't enough for my mammy, Eoghan – he's my younger brother – he was... well, he was killed in a farming accident back in August last year. Careless near a threshing machine. Young idiot."

"I'm sorry, Doncha. Really sorry."

"It's not so much me, boss. It's my mammy. It's all too much for the poor old girl to take."

"How does she cope?"

"She doesn't cope. Just sits. My sisters can't think of what to do with her at all. But then that can't be helped, and us talking about it won't do a deal to help. So how are things with you, boss?"

"A darn sight better now I've got something to do and you're here to help."

"What have you been up to? Have you found Cross?"

"Oh yes, not just found him, I've been stalking him. I've made a few trips to South Brent. Bastard Cross is there all right. I've spent a lot of my time watching. I know his every move. Let me tell you, Don, I made a good stalker."

"Good work, boss. Did you manage to speak to May or Jeffries?"

"Yes, both. May told me he saw Wainwright's body with a gunshot to the back of his head. I'm sure that's so because I've seen his tunic – there's hardly a spot of blood on it."

"You did what?"

"I traced Wainwright's mother. Saw his jacket and found his diary, but wait. Lieutenant Jeffries is convinced Cross went up the line just before Billy Wainwright was killed and came back soon after. None of the others saw any Germans. Your suspicions seem correct, Doncha. What's more, Cross definitely covered it up. I read what he wrote to Mrs Wainwright. Tosh!"

"Bastard."

"Wainwright's diary had the name of the medical officer

who attended the firing squad: Captain Feltham. Only he didn't attend at all. He turned up two days later and forged some paperwork. Feltham did examine the body though. Cause of death was a single pistol shot to the head."

"Cross! The murdering bastard," said Ryan. "But why?"

"Oh, I'll tell you why. I found out from Trant," said Bergeron.

As they sat and drank Bergeron related to Ryan just what Eber Trant had told him in Mrs Trant's kitchen.

I thought Eber would know something. Bastard Cross!" said Ryan. "Where's he now?"

"Home. I had a close look at him. Found out Cross would be playing cricket."

"You went to watch him play cricket?"

"Let me tell you the pains I went to. I wanted to make sure that I was seen coming from the Plymouth direction, the west – rather than from here. So, I walked down the River Plym. I'll show you on the map, here."

Bergeron pointed out the route for Ryan to see. "Then I caught an eastbound train at Cornwood. Once at South Brent I made my way straight to the cricket field. The players were on parade just as I arrived, so I found myself a nice seat on a wall and there he was."

Bergeron fell silent, recalling that moment. For the first time in almost two years he had cast eyes on one of the two men he hated and had sworn vengeance upon.

"Major bloody Cross. I daren't get too close, but had a good view from the wall – so I just sat there and watched. People saw me, of course they did, but there was absolutely nothing unusual about somebody watching a game of cricket. My position was mid-wicket..."

"Boss, I'm Irish, remember. I have no bloody idea where that is. Surprised you do."

"Oh, I didn't know. I love cricket. Played a bit myself. My

mother's side of the family, you see. French Huguenots – lived in England for generations. Anyway, it doesn't matter. Mid-wicket gave me a splendid view of Cross's face whenever he took strike at the village end. Good view of his backside, of course, whenever the batsmen changed ends."

"And has it changed much, the bastard's arse?"

They both laughed.

"Actually, he's not altered at all – well, not that he should have. Flat forehead and sharp, pointed nose, the bushy black moustache and slightly prominent chin. He looks almost *aristocratic,* you know. Watching him there, I was fascinated by his calm and purposeful dominance of the entire proceedings."

"Calm and purposeful, was he? Well, he won't be calm when he sees you! He'll think it's the end of his season, so he will!"

"After forty-five minutes or so the other opening batsman was caught out. Then I had the shock of my life! Who should be walking out to bat next?"

"General Haig? How should I know? Go on, tell me."

"None other than Richard Ansty."

"Ansty! What the hell is he doing here?"

"I had no idea that he had returned to South Brent, but I'll come to that later. Anyway, he's here and we'll just have to cope with that. I carried on watching – couldn't take my eyes off them. Clearly, they got along with each other reasonably well, judging by their chatting to each other between overs, and sometimes after Cross had cracked another ball to the boundary. But then, Ansty always did have that ability to get on with just about everyone."

Ryan lit another Woodbine. "Want one, boss?"

"No, Don. You must stop calling me boss, and no references to Bergeron whenever we can be heard. I'm Dudley from now on. Is that clear? Dudley Spring."

"Yes, Dudley. Perfectly clear, Dudley. By the way, Dudley,

who am I?" Ryan collapsed laughing; the whisky was beginning to have an effect.

"Not too sure yet," Bergeron responded at last. "No. Listen, it gets worse, Don. There were some people watching, women mostly, but a young fellow in a wheelchair was with them. It was Roebuck!"

"Lieutenant Roebuck? Jeez! In a wheelchair, you say? Then, with injuries like his, I'm not really surprised."

"Bloody hell, Don. You're missing the point."

"I am? Must be the grog."

"The point is, Don, they're all here!"

"All?"

"Let me finish. I was rattled by all of this, as you can imagine. The cricketers went in for tea and a horrible, worrying thought struck me. South Brent would be fielding next. What if either Cross or Ansty should be sent to field on the boundary near to where I stood? I'd be recognised at once, Don."

"I'm not so sure, boss. They wouldn't be expecting you, for one, and that beard."

"Anyway, I decided to leave straight away while the players were taking tea. I didn't go back the way I'd come, but decided to walk back to the camp, and that road took me past the church. When I saw Ansty I supposed that either he was living with his father – which didn't seem likely – or that his old man must have popped off and Ansty came back to take over the parish."

"That makes it a bit iffy," said Ryan, looking worried for once. "I've nothing against Mr Ansty. Better officer than most, erm, present company accepted, boss!"

"You mean *excepted*. Sure enough, I read on the sign at the church door that Ansty's father died in 1918."

"We'll need to make sure he doesn't get involved, boss. We'll have to be extra careful."

"We'll need to be more than careful!" said Bergeron.

"They're all here! I should have bloody well thought of it before. The 3rd South Devons were based on the South Hams Rifles – a pre-war Territorial outfit. We both knew that. They all came from the same bloody place, and they're all back here now. This makes things much more difficult for us. There are potentially scores of men who might recognise me; hence me growing this beard and using various names in my detective work. Maybe some would recognise you too. Perhaps we should call it off for now. Wait for another opportunity. Wait till he moves away for some reason."

"Can't, boss. No way. Got to get back in two weeks' time. Maximum. But calm down, think about it. Nobody is going to recognise me. After all, I only really mixed with the flaggies. So I can go anywhere."

Bergeron considered this. "Yes, I suppose you're right, but your accent might give you away."

"I'll keep my gob shut! You? Well, Cross, Mr Ansty and Mr Roebuck would probably recognise you, so you'll have to keep out of their way – like you did at the cricket. The men? I don't think so, especially now you've grown the beard. I don't think any of them would recognise you, boss."

"Well, I suppose it doesn't change that much. You're right. We'd have to be careful anyway. It's no different. Don, if by chance Ansty does recognise either of us, then leave him to me. Got it?"

"Boss… I mean, yes, Dudley."

They ate some of the food Ryan had brought from Princetown. Talk of the problems they might face subsided as whisky was drunk. Bergeron's attention switched to more practical matters.

"You've still got the Mauser, then."

"Aye. Wouldn't go anywhere dangerous without the old broom handle by my side," Ryan grinned.

"And the hat."

"Aye, that too."

"I've still got my knife," said Bergeron, pulling the knife from the leather sheath worn at the back of his belt and handing it to Ryan.

"Ah, and isn't she a beauty? Well, the two of us could open a museum between us, so we could," he joked.

"Have you brought anything else?" asked Bergeron.

"Yes," said Ryan and began to delve into his pack. He handed Bergeron the British army service revolver.

"Mind out, Dudley, it's loaded. And here's another half dozen rounds."

"What's happening in Ireland, Don? It sounds pretty grim from what I read in the newspapers."

"Well, that's the English papers for you."

"Come on, then. Tell me your side."

"It's war now. Breen and Tracey, acting on their own, killed two police in Tipperary. Real bastards, so they are. Glad they're on my side! Police are getting rough, real rough. But the funny thing is this: every time they go into a place and burn it, or beat up someone, or worse, we get more support from the people. Then, a little later, we ambush a convoy, or raid their barracks, or shoot a Peeler. They retaliate, by taking it out on the people – reprisals. And so it goes on. It's hard sometimes, believe me, knowing that because we've raided a barracks the police are going to take it out on some innocent poor bugger. But that's how it is. Anyway, Tom Barry has a plan to stop that. He's about to send a message to the senior British officer in Cork to say that for every house of a Catholic set afire, the boys will burn down the home of a known Loyalist. That'll curb them."

"Maybe, Don. Maybe."

"Perhaps," said Ryan, "when we've finished this business with the major, you should come back with me. The boys could teach you a thing or two and I don't doubt you'd come in handy."

"No, Don. It's your fight, not mine. After this, I'll be back to Canada. Back into the artillery. Figured I might make a career out of soldiering. Since my parents died, the business looks after itself. I pay the managers well and it leaves me with too much spare for me to worry about money. So, I might as well just do what I enjoy, and what I'm good at. Soldiering. Anyhow, let's not go there yet. We need to talk about the major. Do you want to know my plan?"

"Plan? Got a plan, have you?" Ryan asked jokingly. "Go on then, but not before we've had another whisky."

Ryan poured them both generous tots of neat whisky into the cups that were still warm from the tea.

Eventually he asked, "So what's this plan of yours, boss?"

"We'll need to switch camps – it's too far from here. We leave the tent empty and go down to South Brent by day, across the moor. Set up a bivouac on the edge of the moor overlooking the village. We will need to watch the place all day to make sure he is in and there are no visitors – the fewer people there the better. We wait until nightfall. Then we go up to the house and we simply knock at the door. A servant will answer and we storm in. You keep the servants and Mrs Cross quiet in a room by waving your gun at them and pretending to be a mad Irishman."

"Not hard, boss."

"Meanwhile, I find the major, tell him why he is about to be executed and shoot him in the head. As I said in my letter, we'll only need one bullet."

"What if the servants get uppity?"

"Doncha Ryan, you're not going to shoot any of the servants, are you? Nor Mrs Cross. It's him we want dead. You'll just have to be convincing!"

"Right-oh."

"Then we quickly leave before they gather themselves and back up onto the moor as quick as we can, making sure we're not spotted."

"I've got a better plan than that. We make sure we *are* spotted!"

"What?"

"We make sure we are spotted, going in the opposite direction. South. Then we wheel around back onto the moor. It will take us longer, but when the police make enquiries, which they will the next day, some helpful folk will say they saw two men with Irish accents heading south. It will throw them off track completely. Can you find a route?"

"Good thinking, Don. Yes. The police will swamp the whole of the South Hams. Yes, I can find us a usable route. Where's that map?"

"Sure," Ryan said modestly, "we do it all the time in Ireland. But I don't care for your idea of doing it inside the house. Too many people about. Doesn't he go out?"

"Every morning he walks through the fields behind the house. He stops by a gate on the upper field, looks at his cattle. Most days, but not every day, he brings a dog with him. It would mean doing it in daylight, of course."

"Would we be disturbed, or seen?" asked Ryan.

"Don't expect so. He gets up early. So far I've never seen anyone else about."

"I think we should go for that," said Ryan.

"What if he has the dog? Would kick up a fuss that dog."

"Then we play it by ear," said Ryan. "Dog and we come back another morning. No dog and he gets the bullet."

"Let me think about it then. Let me have the revolver, I want to try it out."

"No need. Use my Mauser, it works fine."

"I think I'd rather kill him with an English gun and an English bullet, Don, if you don't mind."

"Mind me asking why?"

"Not at all. I just think Tozer and Billy Wainwright would have preferred it that way."

They stared at their whiskies. Bergeron was first to break the silence.

"Look at this, Doncha," he said pointing with his right arm towards a movement on the bracken up wind of the camp. There a vixen poked out her nose and sniffed the air.

"She'll not come any closer now that you're here. Doesn't know your smell yet. I've been feeding her."

"You always did like dogs, boss. Remember Poilu?"

They both smiled.

"Boss, are you sure we're doing the right thing, here?"

"It's black and white, Don. Life for a life and all that. Cross is responsible, and he's going to be punished. Now, if you're not up for it, all very well. Nobody's ordering you."

"When then?" asked Ryan.

"We'll do it your way, in daylight, away from the house. We rest tomorrow, move out the following day and bivouac as the original plan. Strike first thing the following morning, in the fields as Cross surveys his land and his livestock."

★

The next day the two of them had tidied around their camp and quickly carried out an equipment check. They left at 1400. Bergeron led the Irishman down from the moor, along the pathways he now knew so well. Talking as they walked, the two made good time into South Brent, arriving in the village well before dark.

"Right, Don, into pubs and beef up our cover story. People around here remember strangers, especially those with accents. I'll pop into the woods and choose a good spot for a bivvy. Then I'll hang around here. Just stand on the bridge once you're back."

"Fine, boss."

Ryan went first to the pub by the crossroads, the Anchor.

From its looks, he thought it may have been some sort of coaching house in its day. He told the barman there that he was an Irish traveller looking for work. Was there anything? Then he moved into town and repeated the story in the Packhorse and the Royal Oak. At ten thirty, having drunk surprisingly little, he left the Oak and re-joined Bergeron by the bridge. They walked from there along the Drovers' Road to the moor's edge and bedded down for the night.

★

Bergeron had chosen a good spot for the ambush, a point where the path crossed a hedge by way of a wooden stile. There was a good long view each way, but with heavy cover on each side of the stile.

Unless he decided to alter the course of his morning walk, which Bergeron deemed unlikely, Cross would come from the north east. Cross wouldn't see him hidden behind the hedge. Meanwhile, Ryan was positioned in another hedge running at right angles to the first, from where he had an even better panorama and could see if anyone approached.

They took up their positions. Ryan removed the Mauser from its holster. The old-fashioned pistol was manufactured in such a way that its wooden holster doubled as a detachable shoulder stock which could be fitted to the pistol's handle. This effectively converted the pistol into what looked like a sawn-off rifle or carbine. Ryan hardly ever used the stock, but today he decided that he would. If he needed to use the gun, which he doubted, he didn't want to miss. He attached the stock and waited.

Ryan saw him first. The major was alone as they had hoped. No dog. The job was on.

★

Bergeron pointed the Webley at Cross's chest.

"Do you still think I'm being unreasonable, Major Cross?" he asked.

Cross remained silent.

"Let's talk about Billy Wainwright."

"Nothing to say. It was so very sad about young Billy. Killed in an enemy raid, that's the official account, Bergeron. That's what was reported to the regiment and to his mother and that's exactly what happened."

"Exactly what happened, is it?" said Bergeron. "Is it? Really? You see, that's not what Lieutenant Jeffries thinks."

"You've spoken to Jeffries?"

"To Jeffries, to Sergeant May, to Bombardier Ryan – spoken to all of them."

"Sergeant May? Who the bloody hell…"

"Exactly! Who the bloody hell is Sergeant May? You don't know May, do you? That's what struck me when I read your letter to Mrs Wainwright."

Cross looked shocked.

"Oh, surprised, are you? You didn't know I'd seen that, did you? I had tea with her the other day, as it happens."

"You what?"

"Yes, met Billy's mother, his sister…"

"That floosy? She's been shagging anything in trousers since Peter Roebuck had his balls blown off!"

"Now, now. No need to go casting aspersions, major. The Wainwrights told me everything. Mrs Wainwright showed me the letter you sent her. Very good of you, that, by the way. Very noble, I must say. 'If it is any consolation to you, Mrs Wainwright, I would have you know that your son was killed instantly. I am sure he did not feel a thing.' No. No, he didn't, did he? That's because you shot him in the back of the head, isn't it?"

Cross said nothing.

"It was a very comforting letter you wrote to Billy's mother, Major. Though you went a bit too far when you wrote that you'd spoken to the men. When did you ever speak to the men, Major? 'Who the bloody hell is Sergeant May?' You don't know because you never speak to the men. That's what convinced me you were covering something up."

"It was a German raid. That's exactly what happened, Bergeron." Cross's voice was getting louder.

"No it isn't. Billy Wainwright died from a single bullet through his head, the back of his head. You shot him then made a mistake with that letter. I can see why you'd want to try to make it easy on Mrs Wainwright, but why on earth did you write that you had spoken to Wainwright's men? The letter is evidence that you were covering up."

Cross fidgeted again and Bergeron waved the Webley.

"Now, let's turn our attention onto CSM Tozer, shall we?"

"Wadham was to blame in that sordid affair over Tozer, not me."

"You wanted Tozer dead for your own reasons, didn't you, Cross?"

"I don't know what on earth you are talking about, Bergeron."

"Yes, you do! Tozer was your bastard half-brother, wasn't he? Eber Trant told me everything. Maids have ears and brains, Cross, and Trant's sister has worked in your family home for so, so long."

The sky still retained a red tint of early morning sunlight. Cross looked up at it and shrugged.

"Keep still and listen. Your mother never forgave your father for shagging Eileen Tozer, did she? But Father was otherwise disposed. His will made it clear that everything was to be left to old Mrs Cross. But if she died first it would be split, with a third of the Cross estate going to Eileen Tozer or her heirs – and there was only one: your half-brother, CSM Tozer."

Cross was staggered. How did Bergeron know all of this?

"You weren't worried, because everyone thought Old Man Cross would pop off before your mother. That's not the way it worked out, though, is it? When your mother died during the war, you came back and argued with your father about the will – you wanted it changed but he wouldn't budge. Nancy Trant heard everything, Cross. So you went back to France and gave Wadham free rein to persecute Tozer and eventually kill him. Billy kicked up a fuss, so you killed him too. Now you have to accept responsibility."

"Captain Bergeron, even if I should accept responsibility, what gives you the right to come here enforcing it, eh? Tell me that. Just because you have that bloody gun in your hand. I doubt you've the stomach to use it. Not in cold blood. That's murder, you know?"

Bergeron paused. He lowered the pistol so that its barrel pointed towards the ground.

"Will you admit it?"

"Yes! Yes, I shot Wainwright!" Cross shouted. "Yes, I bloody well egged on Wadham and covered up for him after! Come on then, Bergeron, shoot me if you're going to."

"Calm down, major. You'll wake the neighbours."

For what seemed like hours to Cross, Bergeron simply stood there gazing at him.

"I'm not going to shoot you, major. I'll give you a choice."

Bergeron transferred the Webley into his left hand, holding it by the barrel.

"Tozer died because you wanted all the blasted money. You had Wadham put him on that charge, kill him and fake a firing squad. That led to Billy Wainwright's murder. So, option one is that I hand you this revolver and walk away. As soon as I'm out of sight you use it on yourself."

With that, Bergeron offered the pistol to Cross.

"If I don't?"

"If you don't, and remember it's your choice, then I'll go straight to Gee-Gee, I'll inform the regiment and my solicitor. I'll tell them everything."

"What makes you think anyone will believe you?"

"Others know you killed Wainwright. Lieutenant Jeffries knows, Bombardier Ryan knows. Oh, and 'who the bloody hell is Sergeant May' knows too. They'll all talk. I have the letter, and I have Billy Wainwright's tunic – there's no evidence of a shot through the heart."

Bergeron looked at Cross and shook his head slowly from side to side.

"Everything will come out. It will be dirty, major. Not nice for Mrs Tozer or Mrs Wainwright. Not nice for Gee-Gee, and certainly not nice at all for Mrs Malaby-Cross. So, it's up to you. Do as I suggest, now. Everyone will believe it was the stress of the war and you'll be remembered as an honourable soldier. I won't do anything to contradict that memory."

Cross looked long and hard at Bergeron. Suddenly he seemed to decide.

"Come on, give me the bloody revolver."

"Good. I'm pleased you made that choice." Bergeron removed five bullets from the pistol. "Here, just do it."

He handed Cross the Webley and slowly turned his back to the major. With measured footsteps Bergeron began to stride away.

Cross examined the revolver. He was well used to weapons – handguns and shotguns. He carefully checked that the chamber containing the single bullet was in the firing position. He paused for what seemed like a long time and looked at the Webley, as though considering his next step.

Then Major Cross held the pistol at arm's length pointing towards Bergeron. The fingers of his right hand gripped the handle and now he clasped his left hand around his right, firming his grip. He took careful aim as the tall, young Canadian artillery officer walked away from him.

Cross paused again. He knew what he must do. To achieve a kill with a single bullet wasn't a particularly easy task, but he must. He must, he simply could not afford to miss. Cross knew he should begin high and bring the pistol down slowly until the barrel pointed directly at the centre of Bergeron's back.

Exhaling, Major Cross slowly squeezed the trigger.

The single shot rang out sharply across the fields. Wood pigeons and collared doves exploded from their perches and soared high into the red sky over Dartmoor.

★

The Reverend Ansty started. *That was a gunshot*, he thought.

He rose from the table and looked out from the vicarage towards the moor. The shot sounded as though it had originated from the fields between Major Cross's place and the hamlet of Aish.

He gazed out of the window and listened for more shots. Nothing. *That's strange*, thought Ansty. *We usually get folk shooting pigeons at weekends; and the sound, not really like a shotgun, was it? In fact, it sounded more like a pistol. Must be somebody after wood pigeons though*, he thought, *couldn't be anything else.*

★

Many other villagers had heard a single gunshot from the direction of Aish and, like the Reverend Ansty, they had wondered just what it was. It was more than a year since the Armistice and the end of the fighting. The fields around South Brent had witnessed little of the wartime activities, but now an ex-army officer fell to the ground and lay in the South Devon soil – dead.

THE ROAD TO ENNISKEAN

"By God!" exclaimed Ryan. "Am I glad that's all over."

Bergeron and Ryan had run noisily through South Brent village centre. Then they had taken the lane to Avonwick where they ran past the village school and into the post office. Ryan had waved his gun at the postmaster and demanded £20, but the plucky old man refused, and so off they went towards Diptford.

Once having established this clear route to the south, the pair swung to the west and began to backtrack. Being much more careful now, travelling through the fields and making sure they were not seen, they skirted around the villages of Ugborough and Bittaford and out onto Dartmoor. Now they could slow down and make their way back to camp for a night's sleep.

Next morning, they quickly dismantled camp and between them carried everything to the main Plymouth to Tavistock road. A bus took them to Yelverton station and now they were sitting comfortably bound for Waterloo on the Southern Railway route. So sparsely populated was that train that they had a carriage to themselves for most of the journey.

★

"Are you all right, boss?"
"Yes, why?"

"Just wondering, that's all. Can I ask something?"

"Ask away."

"Well, are you sure we did the right thing?"

"I'm sure of nothing. Cross was right, wasn't he, Don? As he said, it all happened in war. He was far, far from perfect – but which of us is? I did some awful things too. Some nights I still wake up sweating – been dreaming about that farmhouse near Vimy, you know. Those kids. Maybe Cross was just... that's why I couldn't shoot when it came to it. That's why I gave Cross the revolver and told him he had to finish it himself."

"Aye, and he turned the bloody gun on you!"

"Lucky for me you're still as handy with the Mauser. Thanks, Don."

"Anyway, I'm glad it turned out the way it did, boss. Means I've got less explaining to do."

"What do you mean?"

"Well, suppose Cross had topped himself with the Webley. Then, I suppose, you'd have had to leave the revolver beside him to make everyone think it was a suicide. Yes?"

"Yes, that's what I'd thought."

"Well, that there Webley isn't ours to leave, you see. It belongs to Tom Deans, Commandant of the West Cork Brigade, and I promised Tom I'd give it back to him if I possibly could."

"That takes the biscuit, Ryan! That's just like you! Kill a man one day and worry about being accused of petty theft the next."

"It's like this, boss, as I see it friends are friends, but enemies are bastards!"

Bergeron smiled.

"And there's plenty of both across the water. Are you sure you won't be coming to Ireland with me? There's a cracking fight going on and we can do with men like you."

"No! Certainly not, Don. It's not my fight. I'm neither

Loyalist nor Republican. I'm just a Canadian far from home. More than that, now this is done I think I'm ready to say a few goodbyes and go home."

Bergeron gazed through the window of the carriage. "As I said, it's far from black and white, Don. Anyway, Wadham has run to earth. If I knew where he was I'd stay on just to get him, but he's disappeared and that's that. It's all done, Don."

"Now that's where you're wrong, boss."

"What do you mean?"

"It's far from all done. You see, the bastard Wadham hasn't disappeared at all. In fact, I know exactly where Captain Wadham – Major Wadham now, as a matter of fact – is. He's in Dublin Castle trying to make trouble for the Volunteers. Raising some new kind of force – counter-terror squads, so I believe they're being called. That's what my sources tell me. Anyway, whatever they're called, they mean trouble. More especially if Wadham has much to do with it."

"You bastard, Ryan! You bloody knew this all along, didn't you? Why the hell didn't you tell me before?"

"Oh, I meant to. Matter of fact, I found out just as Postman Casey brought me that letter. But I just didn't get chance to talk to you about it, boss. We've been busy, you know!"

Bergeron looked hard at the Irishman. "Bastards! Both of you. Well, it looks like I will be going to the Emerald Isle after all."

"True enough, boss, you'll soon be on the road to Enniskean."

WHAT IS LOVE?

Ryan was gone. Bergeron had arranged for his luggage to be sent to Aunt Maude's in Rottingdean, then went straight to Lizzie's place. She wasn't at home, so, using the key she had given him, he let himself in. After he had washed, shaved and dressed in clothes he left there, Bergeron walked over to Lincoln's Inn Fields to Gerry Finn's office.

"Good to see you, Marc."

"Any news from this Debreux in Arras, Gerry?"

"Yes, actually," said Finn. "Better sit down."

Bergeron sat in the comfortable, high-backed lounge chair at the end of Gerry's desk. It reminded him of something his mother would have liked.

Gerry Finn pulled open a drawer of his desk and took out a piece of paper which he handed to Bergeron.

"Thanks, Gerry. Much appreciated. I can deal with it from now on."

"There's more," and Gerry Finn handed Bergeron a dispatch case full of letters.

"You'd better read these, old man," he said.

★

Dear Marc,

I have written to you many times since receiving my last response from you. I know you may not read what I now have to say, my dear, and I do not expect your reply. I simply want to tell you why I write.

Why do I write? To begin, you should know that I have always written. I recall when at school the delight I felt when a teacher – Mr Rowland, it was – set me to compose an essay about a sandwich. I can still remember the feeling of excitement as the character I at that moment invented began to develop a persona of her own. At first it was a little bit like a child dressing a doll, but then I realised that writing gave me control – I could make a character do anything I wished. On paper a figment of my imagination becomes an avatar through which I may explore worlds of my choice or my invention.

Since then I have written regularly. I have written short stories, struggled with poetry (which I do not like so much) and am trying to complete a novella. And, of course, I write to you, my dear.

Writing has become part of me. These days writing defines me; perhaps it always has done so. Let me give you an example. When people ask me, "What do you do, Anne?" I reply – "I am a writer." Do you see? Writing has changed from something I might do – a practice – into something which I am; it has become a part of my identity.

Now I will reveal something amazing. I have written to you about my sense of control when inventing, describing and developing my characters in my stories, but this ceased some time ago. Now, the characters I imagine describe and develop autonomously. They define themselves but through my pen. If I have written 500 words and go back over them, why, I am surprised by what I read! They have taken over control of themselves. Can you imagine that?

Sometimes, I must tell you this, Marc, when I am busy writing I feel as though I am simply flowing along. It's difficult to explain, but it is as though the world around me and even time itself are suspended by my writing. Allow me to clarify that statement: I mean by my practice of writing, not the text I produce. Oh, I feel sure that sometime in the future a clever philosopher – or psychologist – will develop a theory about this and take the academic world by storm! You may deduct from the previous sentence that I have been delving into the writings of Mr Jung. I obtained recently an English language translation (by Beatrice

Hinkle) of his Wandlungen und Symbole der Libido *and it is most interesting. Yes, I know YOU would have read it in German.*

Finally, I write because my writings are my stories. That doesn't read quite right. What I mean is my writings constitute my story. They will remain once I depart this world. The world, the human world, of course, is made of stories.

Now, don't you think for one moment that because I write stories they are not true. They are true because they are authentic. My stories come from within me – the author – or from my characters; and even then, I remain the author.

With that I must stop. I do not know if you will read this letter, but if you do then know what is true. I love you, Marc Bergeron.

Forever your Anne.

PS I just looked up authentic in my thesaurus and this is what it says: true, reliable, dependable, faithful, trustworthy, accurate, genuine and realistic. That's good enough for me! AM x

A deafening silence pervaded the office. Finn considered Bergeron, who was ashen faced as he read Anne McKenzie's letter.

"She loves you, does she?"

"What is love, Gerry?"

"Love's a funny old thing, you know, Bergeron."

"You think?"

"Have my doubts about its existence, you see."

"Going to tell me, Gerry?"

"Well, it's easy really. You see, some things exist in a tangible sense. For example, let's take a tree. Oh sure, people may call the tree different things in different languages. And, of course, there are many different species of tree. There may even be arguments about the borderlines between a tree and a bush. But, at the end of the day, unless – that is – we get ourselves side-tracked by questions like 'can anything exist outside of human perception of it?' you know the score. If a tree falls to earth in a forest and nobody is there to see or hear it, did it fall? Better not go there, I think. The tree is there. Agreed?"

Bergeron looked somewhat bemused. "With you so far, Gerry," he said.

"Now, there are other things that don't exist in anything like the same way. Those things that people think up simply to help them manage their social comings and goings. Let me think… monarchy, republicanism, democracy – they all make good examples. These things clearly don't exist in the tangible way the tree exists. Agree? In other words, they don't exist apart from human beings, people, us. Still with me, old boy?"

"Yes. Well, I think so. Did you study philosophy, Gerry?"

"Yes, I did. A bit. Politics and Philosophy as a matter of fact, Cambridge. Studied under Bertrand Russell and a young PhD student of his: Wittgenstein. Damned clever bloke. He asked me to read the draft of a book he's working on – Wittgenstein that is. Anyway, I'm thinking of going back to do a doctorate at some stage."

"You want to be a doctor? No, Gerry. Look, I saw you when some of those boys came in, you were. You were…"

"Not that sort of doctor, you chump! Doctor of Philosophy. Ontology. The study of the nature of existence – been thinking about it a good deal."

Bergeron took a sip of tea. "I had noticed your books. Go on."

"Well, where was I? Oh, yes. Now, and this is where it gets a tad tricky, there are some things which most people assume exist in the first sense…"

"Like the tree?"

"Good boy, well done there! But in fact, they only exist in the second sense. For example, learning, or thinking…"

Bergeron quickly took another sip of his tea to avoid having to say anything.

"These are 'things' – well, no, they're not, actually – that we think about, and talk about so often, we elevate them to a higher form of existence. The Greeks would have called it 'reification' – making a thing of that which is not a thing. With me?"

"No."

"Now, for me, love is one of these. A reification. Love cannot possibly exist apart from humanity. This, in two ways. First, without two humans, there cannot be love."

"Wrong," said Bergeron.

"Pray, tell me."

"I love Mush."

"Mush?"

"My dog."

"Good. Good example, Marc. I'm very happy to accept that. But you can't have love without at least one human."

"Hold on, Gerry. Hold on. Now you're telling me Mush's dad didn't love Mush's mum?"

"Hey. You're really quite clever, aren't you?"

Bergeron looked blank; he said nothing.

"Well, that brings me onto my theory of the second way in which love cannot exist apart from humanity. Let me think. Now, Mush's dad might have loved Mush's mum – as you put it – or Mush's mum might have loved Mush and the rest of the litter, but only if a human had been around to observe and, what's more, tell the world that she (or he) did so. Because love – like monarchy, republicanism, independence, learning, thinking and all those other blasted reifications – is a human conceptualisation. So, as I see it, Marc, love is more like democracy than it is a tree, if you see what I mean."

"Probably not. Does it matter, Gerry?"

"Well, it might mean that two people agree that they're

in love – with each other. However, at the same time they might have very different conceptualisations of what it's all about. Could be awkward, might lead to misunderstandings – problems. What do you think?"

"I think you're too bloody clever, Gerry. I also think I've been here too long and that it's time for me to go back home. Canada."

"Will you end up marrying Anne?"

Bergeron said nothing. Then he swept the letters into the small case he had brought and rose to his feet. "Thanks, Gerry. Thank you for all you've done for me. I really do appreciate it."

Finn got up and they shook hands – Bergeron's right hand, Gerry Finn's left.

Bergeron walked towards the door and turned the polished brass handle before looking back at his friend.

"Gerry," he said, "if I do marry Anne, would you to be my best man?"

"Delighted, old boy. Delighted."

★

"Do you love her? This Anne, do you?"

"Love. Who knows what love is, Lizzie? Do you? My mother once told me that I would know love when I met it. For me, love may never be defined or explained."

"Oh, why do you never give a straight answer?"

"There isn't one, Liz."

She looked at him, dumbfounded. He noticed that her face was reddened and she was sniffling. He was sorry the news was affecting her this way.

"It's easy to like somebody," he continued. "Easy to find somebody... attractive. But love... I don't pretend to understand it."

"Then you don't love her. If your mother said you'd know it, and you don't, you can't. Do you like her?"

"Yes, of course."

"Find her attractive?"

"Ye-es."

"And me?"

"Both."

Lizzie looked away, turning her head to the window. The day had steadily darkened and now heavy rain pummelled the street. It was one of those thunderstorms that are rare in Spring, but haunt late summer in southern England.

"What about you, Lizzie?" he asked. "What do you know of love?"

She wiped an embryonic tear from her left eye, hoping Bergeron hadn't noticed.

"Alf Singleton was the only man I ever loved. He was killed in 1916. Man, did I say? No, Alf was still only a boy – by the time he died he wasn't old enough to walk into the Nag's Head and order himself a drink! He was snatched from me… and now you."

She turned to look Bergeron in the face. "No. I'm not saying I love you, Marc. Too soon. I think it may have – would have – happened though. Given time."

She rose.

"I'm sorry, Lizzie. I really thought she'd gone away. Found somebody else – oh, I don't know exactly what I thought. I was sure, absolutely convinced, she was no longer mine. I want you to know," he stood up too, "I wasn't 'leading you on' or anything like that, Liz. I wouldn't do that to you."

"I know. What will you do now?"

"I've some business to deal with. In Ireland. Then I'll return to Canada; meet Anne. Then – who knows? What about you? What will you do?"

"Me? What can I do, Marc? Not go gallivanting all over

267

the bloody world like you! Sorry. I'll work here. Maybe meet a nice man. Marry. Kids – too many of them. Bring them up – proper as I can. Come back here after, more work. Become old and worn out before my time, like my mam and my granny. Then die. What did you expect?"

She thought she saw a tear in Bergeron's eye – but, no. "I'm really very sorry," he said.

"Don't be. It's not your fault. Come here."

Lizzie put her arms around him. *For the last time?* she wondered. She pulled him to her breast and kissed him. Once. On the lips. Then she turned and walked out of the Nag's Head leaving Bergeron standing there alone.

EPILOGUE, 1921

Sarah Wainwright struggled to push the wheelchair further to the front of the crowd that had gathered to observe the ceremony. Scores of people crowded the square and many, she noticed, were wearing their Sunday best outfits. She saw schoolchildren and their teachers, relieved of classes, congregate by the bridge.

"Are you comfortable there, Peter?" asked Sarah.

"No, I can't see very well here. Could you just get me up on the pavement, please?"

Sarah tried, but the wheelchair and Peter were too heavy. Two men in sailor's uniforms came over.

"Let me help you there, Miss?" asked one of them.

"Oh, yes please," she answered.

Peter Roebuck noticed how the sailors looked lecherously at Sarah. *Why? Oh, why did it – did I – have to end up this way? In this bloody chair?*

In other circumstances, he thought, *he and Sarah might have married and had children.*

Peter Roebuck was lost in his thoughts as Francis Bingham Mildmay – Conservative Member of Parliament for the Totnes constituency, dressed in the uniform of a major of the 10th Battalion, East Kent Regiment – walked up and prepared to pull the cord that held the Union Flag in place, draped over the new village peace memorial.

As the flag was lifted away, Peter and Sarah looked at the long list of names carefully chiselled into the granite.

"Such a lot of sailors," observed Sarah.

"Only to be expected in a place like this, being close to the sea."

Peter gazed at the names. Amongst them he noticed many names of men from his own battalion: Carpenter R Private 3rd SDLI died 1915; Grimes F Sergeant 3rd SDLI died 1916; Tetley A Private 3rd SDLI died 1915.

And there were others he had served alongside: Trevelyan W Corporal 3rd SDLI died 1918; Tozer Sidney MM CSM 3rd SDLI killed in action 1918; Wainwright William Cecil Lieutenant 3rd SDLI killed in action 1918.

There followed a one-minute silence, during which a rifleman in full dress uniform sounded the Last Post. Following the Reveille, the crowd raised a cheer to their glorious dead, and there were shouts of "God save the King". Sarah and Peter remained silent.

The crowd gave way and in twos and threes people moved away. The two sailors went into the pub.

Sarah Wainwright had brought a small bunch of red roses to place on the memorial close to her twin brother's name. Peter watched as she walked over to the memorial and turned to face him.

"Peter, what is a CSM?" she shouted.

"It's a Company Sergeant Major," he replied.

★

Serge Fagonet sat in his small dining room, in his small, overcrowded house in Clermont Ferrand and read the letter again, then he turned to his wife. *"Marie-Pierre, est cela une blague?"*

"Non! It's not a joke! God has answered my prayers. Soon they will be off our hands," she replied. "The boy will get a good education and later he can repay us for our kindness."

"But the girl, it says she too is to be educated."

"Why not?" asked the wife.

"What's the use of a woman being educated?"

"I say again, why not? Just because you never went to school, you idiot! Young Eugene will go to school and his sister too. Later, she will also pay us back."

"Tell me again who has provided this fortune?" asked the husband.

"It is not clear. The letter is from a lawyer called Debreux. He says he represents a Canadian soldier. An artillery officer. In my opinion that speaks for itself – it's got to be the bastard that shelled the Ramuel's farm. He's trying to salve his conscience."

HISTORICAL NOTES

There never was a South Hams Light Infantry, but Bergeron and Ryan needed an anonymous regiment to which they could be attached, and in which dastardly deeds could be done.

As I had always intended the post-war action to take place in the South Hams, the idea of a local regiment appealed to me and so there is some similarity to historical fact. The South Devonshire Regiment, created in 1741, was amalgamated into the Duke of Cornwall's Light Infantry in 1881. Later, four Territorial battalions of the Devonshire Regiment (the 4th, 5th, 6th and 7th) were formed from pre-Haldane rifle volunteer units. The 5th Devons were formed in 1908 from a merging of the 2nd (Plymouth) Battalion and the Haytor Volunteer Rifles. This battalion recruited volunteers from Plymouth and South Devon, including the South Hams. Until 1908 this battalion wore the green number one dress tunics of the Rifles, but reluctantly converted to red following the Haldane Reforms. I don't know if they referred to their soldiers as riflemen, but I like to think so.

There was no conscription in Ireland until 1918, Between 1914 and 1918 many Irishmen volunteered to fight in the British army. The reasons for joining up that Don Ryan gives Tom Deans are almost exactly those related by the IRA leader, Tom Barry[1].

The photogrtaph on the deducation page is of Martin John

---

1   Barry, T. (1981) *Guerrilla Days in Ireland,* Cork: Mercier Press

Damerell, and is how I imagine Eber Trant. Damerell was from Woodlands, then a village near Ivybridge. He volunteered in 1915 and was killed in action (probably by British machine gun fire) on 6 September 1916. He was seventeen years old. As well as the photo of him, his family still has the postcard sent to them by the Government showing his grave marked by a wooden cross in Delville Wood Cemetery, France. Martin John Damerell is also commemorated on the Ivybridge war memorial, as are all the men Eber Trant sings about in his rendition of 'Widecombe Fair'.

My account of the battle of the Bois des Buttes is based on Aggett (1995).[2] The young commanding officer of 2 Devons, Captain (Acting Lieutenant Colonel) Anderson-Morshead died at the Bois des Buttes, as did most of his battalion. He has no known grave. The Croix de Guerre avec Palme was presented to the battalion on 5 December 1918 in honour of its ferocious rear-guard action at the Bois des Buttes, 27 May. Marc Bergeron played no part in the battle, but there were British gunners fighting the Germans that day. 5 (Gibraltar) Battery was deployed in support of the French south of the River Aisne. The Croix de Guerre was also awarded to the battery following their actions on 27 May.

Today, all battalions of the Rifles (1 Rifles being the descendent unit of the Devonshire Regiment) together with the officers and men of 5 (Gibraltar) Battery (now part of 19 Royal Artillery) wear the ribbon of the Croix de Guerre.

Most of my tale of the 7th Royal East Kent Regiment near Vendeuil in March 1918 is accurately based on accounts in Macdonald (1999)[3]. Captain Fine was based in the old fort, with Lieutenant Colonel Ransome's battalion HQ to the rear. There was no RCHA officer anywhere near as far as I know –

2   Aggett, W. J. P. (1995) *The Bloody Eleventh: History of the Devonshire Regiment, Vol. III 1915 – 1969*, Dorchester: Devon and Dorset Regiment.
3   Macdonald, L. (1999) *To the Last Man, Spring 1918*. London: Penguin Books.

and there were certainly no reports or suspicions of discontent, let alone mutiny, amongst the British units fighting in that area – but I simply could not resist having Bergeron call out "steady the Buffs!"

By coincidence, the local MP Francis Bingham Mildmay was an officer in the Buffs. Mildmay had served in the 2nd Boer War with the Queen's Own West Kent Yeomanry, which was later dismounted to become the 10th (Royal East Kent and West Kent Yeomanry) Battalion, East Kent Regiment, in February 1917.

The action in Devon takes place in a triangle between Cornwood, Diptford and South Brent, and on Dartmoor to the north, mostly in actual places. It is possible to follow the instructions that Bergeron left for Ryan at the Princetown post office and reach the area of the moor where I imagined their camp to be. Ryan shot Major Cross by a hedge in a field to the south of the lane which now runs between Lydia Bridge in South Brent and Aish.

You can read more about South Devon during the war years, and the actions of the Devonshire Regiment in the First World War in my book *South Devon in the Great War*[4].

---

4   Rea, T. (2016) *South Devon in the Great War*. Barnsley: Pen and Sword.